To Jennifer

Breathing Space

Sylvia May

Sylvia May

TURQUOISE MORNING PRESS

Turquoise Morning, LLC
P.O. Box 43958
Louisville, KY 40253-0958

BREATHING SPACE
Copyright © 2014, Sylvia May
Trade Paperback ISBN: 978-1-62237-369-7

Editor, Amie Denman
Cover Art Design by Calliope-Design.com
Stock art by thinkstockphotos.com

Digital Release, November 2014
Trade Paperback Release, December 2014

Keywords: Women's fiction, literary fiction, contemporary, reinvention, island story, women, novel, female

To my sisters:
We'd be friends even if we weren't related.

BREATHING SPACE

Sometimes walking away from your life is the only way to find yourself.

Lydia's vacation on Hyde Island turns into a journey of self-discovery. The island so entices her that she decides to stay, forsaking her family and obligations in Toronto. Her new life on the lush green island is peopled with a hippy scientist, a dashing southern gentleman, a slimy boss, and an undocumented Mexican hotel maid with a sad history. As Lydia makes one questionable choice after another, she soon begins to understand why she so easily succumbed to Hyde Island's lure.

Chapter One

I am in a pocket of time that has nothing to do with my life. My feet slap the damp sand; my hair blows awry. Inhaling the moist salty air, I move in rhythm with the surf. The crimson-clouded sky, its magnificence stopping me in my stride when I started out this morning, is now varying shades of blue and magenta. The deserted beach brightens in the rising sun. It goes on forever and I am conquering it. All I hear is the sound of my progress, waves hitting the shore, seagulls calling.

In ways more complex than distance, I am far from home and each step takes me farther. I revel in my temporary release from there, where demands dictate, expectations overshadow, responsibilities pull, and where simply living tightens my chest. Here on Hyde Island I can breathe. This calm is what I want. This freedom is what I need. If only I could stay here always.

"Lydia, wait." Words fly to me in the wind.

I turn. My sister Tilly is running toward me, her T-shirt flapping and heavy breasts bouncing. She waves something. When she reaches me she leans over, hands on her knees, panting. "Why didn't you wake me? If I'd known you were going for a walk, I'd have come with you."

"Sorry. I wanted to be alone for a while." What I wanted was to have time away from Tilly. I love her, but even at the best of times, her domineering personality can be overwhelming. After a week together, I have been rendered almost voiceless.

"Oh." Tilly straightens. Her cheeks are flushed and her brown eyes glisten. Perspiration plasters the curly tendrils escaping from her ponytail. "Okay."

I instantly feel remorse for my thoughts. "I didn't mean we can't walk together. Let's go." I link my arm with hers and hug the soft flesh of her upper arm, feeling her sticky sweat.

"Actually." She pulls her arm free. "I came looking for you because Dan phoned. I told him you'd call right back." She holds out the cell phone. "You left it on the counter."

"Was it something urgent?"

She shakes her head. "I don't think so. He just misses you."

I stick the phone in the pocket of my shorts.

Tilly touches my arm. "Lydia, you haven't talked to him all week. What's going on?"

"Nothing. I've been immersed in my painting. No brain space for Dan." What I don't say is that this hiatus from my husband has revealed to me some truths about my life with him. Truths I'm not ready to face and, in all honesty, wish had not surfaced in my consciousness. Fingers of anxiety begin to clutch at me, squeezing away the serenity I'd achieved. My earlier calmness recedes with the outgoing tide. My chest tightens. I spin around. "Come on, let's walk."

We stride without talking for a while, pushing against the wind. Small puddles left by the early morning's tide dot the beach, and we weave ourselves around them. I slow my pace so Tilly can keep up. I sense she has something she wants to say but don't encourage her. I'm trying to regain my mood, my solitary space in time.

Her voice prods at the peace I crave. "I think Dan called so early because he figured he'd be able to catch you before class."

"He'll see me soon. Today's our last day here." I stop and stare at the horizon. "Isn't this the most amazing place?

8

I mean, look." I sweep my arm, encompassing the sun reflecting on the water, now a shimmering ball peeking from behind clouds, the sand spanning miles of beach, the tide-wall of rocks. Green scrub and yellow grasses cover the dunes. Behind them, the branches from the Live Oak giants swoop over the embankment. "It's unreal. It has nothing to do with our lives back in Toronto, and for a little while I just want to experience being *here*. Not there." I walk again, trying to shake Dan away from our conversation.

Tilly steps quickly to catch up. "But you can't ignore your husband just because you're on a holiday."

"I'm not ignoring him. I'm taking a break from him."

"Okay." She exhales in resignation.

We walk on, not saying anything for a while. Then she says brightly, "Final class today. Your painting has really improved. I knew it would. Do you think you'll finish your triptych in time for the exhibit tonight?"

We've come to Georgia, to this little piece of paradise, to take an "Abstract in Acrylics" class at the Hyde Island Art School. It's the first such workshop I've ever attended, although Tilly has dragged me to a few art classes over the years. My sister, who is considerably more creative than me, painted three spectacular canvases this week. I am a reluctant artist, insecure about my abilities and still uncertain if this pursuit will become a passion. Over the past four days, I've produced two paintings I've scraped off and obliterated and have almost completed a somewhat better three-paneled one.

"I think I'll finish it in time. Are you going to start something new today?" I step over a puddle.

"I don't know. I think I'm abstracted out. Maybe I'll just help set up the exhibit today. And we should start packing and cleaning the cottage. We need to get away early tomorrow."

"You know what, Tilly? I don't want to go back." As soon as I say it, I realize the idea has been poking around my subconscious most of the week.

"Me neither. I can't believe school starts in eleven

days. I woke up thinking about lesson plans. We've had a great week, though, haven't we?"

"Yes." I swallow, hesitant to elaborate on the notion that is germinating in my mind.

"I love this island." She turns her head toward me. Two tiny suns are reflected in her eyes, and they bounce as she walks. "Wouldn't it be cool if we had a little art studio here—and a gallery? We could build a house with two wings, one for you and one for me, with a common living room and kitchen. We could paint all day, and people would come from all over the world to buy our paintings." She smiles at the horizon.

Impatient with her make-believe, I yank her back to reality. "Tilly, I'm not talking fantasy. I really don't want to go home."

"Holidays are always too short."

"No." My mouth suddenly feels dry. "I mean I'm not going back." As I say the words, something loosens inside of me, like a sash untying itself.

She stops mid-stride and gapes at me. "What?"

I exhale loudly. A sliver of doubt edges into my thoughts.

"That's crazy." Tilly walks over to a group of rocks and plants herself on a large flat one. "Come sit."

The rock beside her is on a slant, and I shift around to get comfortable, tightening my muscles to stay erect. The wind has calmed, and the sun is higher in the sky, heating the air and stoking the humidity. My shirt sticks to me, and I blow hair out of my eyes.

Tilly puts her arm around my shoulders, making me even hotter. "I knew something was going on. Did you and Dan have a fight?"

"No, it's just that…" What is it exactly? I sidle out from under her arm and pace in short steps. Little sanderlings run along the shore, their legs moving so fast it's difficult to distinguish their tiny feet. I want to run with them.

This week my time at the easel was a journey of

introspection. As I attempted to translate the shapes, shadows and colors of the island into some kind of abstract interpretation, my mind opened up to new possibilities where my current existence receded into the background. The ideas that blasted through my brain were vague, but the realization that my life needs to change was not. Now, here on the beach with Tilly, I am suddenly enlightened as to how I can bring about this change. Combing fingers through my hair, I attempt to articulate what I'm feeling. "This week has taken me out of myself. It's like my life back home doesn't exist, and—"

"Vacations are always like that. That's why people take them."

"But this is different." I sweep aside my doubts, heeding instead the inner voice that first brought the notion to the surface. "I like the idea that my life in Toronto doesn't exist. I feel like I'm finished with it, ready for something new."

"Finished with it? What on earth does that mean?" Her eyebrows knot in confusion. "Everybody wants to escape sometimes. I dream about it too. But we don't actually do it. We can't just erase our lives and start new ones."

"Why not? People move away all the time. Leave their families. Divorce."

"Is that what you want to do? Divorce Dan? After twenty-seven years?" Alarm leaps into her eyes. "Lydia, I know he can be a pain, but he loves you."

Queasiness clenches my insides and I sit back down. "No. It's just…I just want to stay here for a while."

"You mean like Shirley Valentine from that movie?" Her tone is laced with incredulity.

I picture myself sitting alone at a table, wearing a sun hat, holding a glass of wine. Or on a shrimp boat, trying to look sexy as I help with the nets. I laugh half-heartedly. "And serve eggs and chips to tourists? Definitely not. Besides, we haven't seen too many hunky fishermen around here have we?"

Tilly chuckles, sounding relieved. "Nope. None better

looking than Dan anyway."

I stare at her. "The spirit of her story appeals to me, though. She simply wanted to live her own life on her own terms. That's what I want too."

She sobers. "But you can do that in Toronto. You don't need to cast everything aside for that. You have a good life, Lydia."

I shake my head.

"I think you need to call Dan." She gestures toward my pocket that holds the phone. "When you hear his voice, you'll feel grounded again. I'm sure when you talk to him, you'll be eager to go back home."

"You don't understand. Dan is part of what I want to leave behind." I push my shoe into the hard sand. "Our marriage is empty. Dan just isn't involved in it. He hasn't been for a long time."

"You've told me that before, but I don't get what the heck you mean by that. He's a great husband. A hard worker. A good father. You don't appreciate what you've got."

"Tilly, you see a different Dan than I do. You always have. How many times in the past have I tried to talk to you about this? You just don't hear me."

"I hear you complain about a good life. Lots of women would give anything to have what you do."

I exhale loudly. "Marriage is about more than working at a business and staying in at night. Dan is an emotional void. He lives in his own world and barely acknowledges me. He's not there for me."

"He's always there for you. For the family."

"Only materially." I bite my lip. "Dan does a good job of showing people that he's a good guy. But at home, when he's not on, he withdraws inside himself, and I get nothing out of him. He makes me feel invisible in my own home."

"I'm sure that's not true."

I glare at my sister. "You don't get it. There's no point in discussing this with you. You invariably take his side. I finally see a way to make my life better, and I'm going to start by staying here on Hyde Island. This island calls to me. It has an effect on my psyche that I need to try to understand, and I can only do that by staying here."

She gazes at me a minute, then tries a different approach. "Okay, let's say I leave you here. Where will you live? Agnes wants the cottage back today. And what about money? You think Dan's just going to say, 'Great, I'll support you while you desert me?' What will you do?"

Her questions jumble my thoughts and create noise in my head. "I don't know, Tilly. I haven't thought about all that."

"Well, you'd better think about all that." She talks fast. Complications tumble. "You have a husband and daughter. A house. A store. Responsibilities. And what about me? Am I supposed to show up without you on Sunday, tell Dan you've decided to start a new life? Tell Carly her mother's abandoned her?"

I interrupt her with a snort. "I wouldn't be abandoning Carly. She's an adult on her own, living her own life." The echo of my words gives me pause. "She doesn't need parents anymore. She barely includes us as it is." My statement reflects the most recent encounter with my daughter a month ago, when I saw her leaving the family planning clinic as I passed by. She became flustered when I called her name and faced me with pale cheeks and despondent eyes. My maternal antennae quivered. I felt an overwhelming need to mother her, but she was determined to give me only the barest details in response to my questions and not share any of what she had been through. "I'm an independent woman," she declared. "I don't run to Mommy every time I have a problem. Please leave me alone." She made me swear not to tell anyone I'd seen her there, especially Tilly and her father. I haven't heard from her since, even though I've left phone messages and sent emails.

I stare at the horizon. "My staying away won't trouble her at all."

"Oh, Lydia, you know she's just establishing her

independence. She still needs you."

"Right. She needs me." My throat tightens. "You've always been a better mother for her than me."

"Don't start in with that again." Her words shoot out like bullets. "I'm only her aunt."

Despite her defensiveness, there is a flicker of pride in her eyes. I have no desire to rehash this thorny subject, knowing what the inevitable conclusion will be: Tilly is a saint and I am inadequate. "Never mind. The point is I'm not going back."

She frowns. "But what about work? Dan can't manage the store on his own."

"He can manage it fine without me. He cares more for that store than he ever did for me."

"That's not true. I know he adores you. You're like his other half."

"Hardly." But I barely whisper this.

She sighs and stares at the horizon, squinting in the bright new sun. "Well, what about me? I need you too."

I'm suddenly very tired. "Why do we always have to live our lives for other people? I want to live for me for a change."

She turns to me, shaking her head. We continue to spar back and forth. I don't want to listen to her anymore. Finally I tell her, "I'm not asking your permission, Tilly."

"Look." She stands up and steps right in front of me, pointing her finger like a mother scolding her child. I'm briefly transported back to when we were motherless children, our father too busy for us, and Tilly taking charge. With a feeble smile she says, "I'm older than you so I can tell you what to do." She delivers this line in jest all the time and usually we end up laughing.

Not now, though. I stare at her and raise my eyebrows. She pulls in her finger and touches my arm. "Lydie, you can't seriously be thinking of doing this."

I break eye contact, shifting my gaze to the shimmering water.

She takes her arm back. "You'd hurt the people you

14

love. You'd regret it too, once the novelty wears off."

I find myself nodding, feeling chastened. "Maybe." Tilly has a point. I can't just run away from my life because of a random idea that popped into my head. My petty complaints and selfish desires don't justify such rash behavior. Do they?

"Come on," Tilly says gently. "Let's go back and have some coffee and breakfast. You need to get to class and finish your triptych. You'll feel better when that's done." The hair bristles on the back of my neck. She never stops adopting a mothering role in our relationship. Even though I'm a forty-six-year-old woman, she can still make me feel like a chastised child.

"Go ahead. I'll be there soon." Despite my hesitation a few minutes ago, the resolve for my idea grows stronger.

"I know you'll do the right thing." Tilly gives me a little hug. Her tone tells me she thinks she's chased this foolhardy idea out of my head.

In the glare of the sun I shield my eyes and watch her plod slowly across the sand, becoming smaller the farther she gets. At the wooden steps that arch over the dunes, she turns and waves at me. I wave back.

Last Sunday, immediately after we arrived on the island, we explored the beach. Even though the tide was rising, we walked along the incoming surf. The water rose above our ankles and we ran to the stairs. Our escape route, we called it.

In the distance, Tilly climbs the steps and disappears behind the dunes. I sit back on Tilly's straight flat rock and begin to devise my own escape route.

Chapter Two

I follow Tilly outside, carrying a box filled with kitchen things we brought with us and didn't use. It is still dark because Tilly wanted to get an early start on our long drive. The air is silent and clear.

Excited and edgy because of what I'm about to do, I recall our thrill at arriving after two days in the car. We were delighted by the lush greenness of the island and the wonderful little house stocked with everything we needed, and full of enthusiasm about our coming week. I'd hoped to recharge my soul and expected the painting and my time with Tilly to rekindle my zest for life. To quell the apathy that had drained my spirit.

All that did occur, but not in the way I expected. My zest for life has been rekindled, but for a new life here on this island. And the apathy has morphed into—I don't know—something akin to anticipation. The possibilities seem endless if I just keep moving forward.

Still, I'm conflicted by trepidation. All day yesterday and throughout my sleepless night, I've second-guessed myself, knowing my decision is unconscionable, but always arriving at the conclusion that I have to embark on this journey.

I put the box in the trunk of the car between Tilly's suitcase and painted canvases, spreading it all to fill the space she left for my things. When I slam the trunk shut she looks at me surprised, her face shadowed in the dim light of the lamppost.

"Your stuff is still in the house. Why'd you close it?" Tilly's voice is slightly panicked.

"I'm not coming with you." I step away, clenching my fists to keep my hands from shaking. "I'm staying here."

Her head jerks back. "Staying where?"

I spread out my arms. "Here."

"In this house?" she screeches.

"No, of course not." I glance around in the darkness. "Somewhere on the island."

"But I thought..." She shakes her head, calms her voice. "After our talk on the beach, you didn't say anything more about staying. I figured you'd given up on the idea." She exhales loudly.

"I hadn't. In fact, I'm even more convinced that I should do this. I didn't want to upset you so I didn't say any more about it." I wrap my arms around her. "I'm sorry, Till."

"Oh, Lydia." She pulls out of my embrace and locks eyes with me. We stand like that for a minute, the streetlight spotting us, actors in a play who don't know their lines.

She touches my arm. "Let's go inside and have a coffee. We don't need to leave right away. Let's talk about this."

"No." I shake my head. "I don't want to talk about it. I've already decided. Please just go." I am eager to be released from her judgment and cajoling, not wanting to risk that she'll cut through my thin veneer of resolve.

"So you've decided to leave your family just like that? You're staying here without giving a thought to them? And I'm supposed to drive all the way back to Toronto alone? You'd abandon me to driving twenty hours in the car by myself?"

I bite my lip and nod.

"You can't...what am I supposed to do? What are you...?" She stops, inhales, swallows. "What am I supposed to tell Dan and Carly when I arrive in Toronto without you?"

Until this very moment, I wasn't completely certain I could go through with it, but Tilly's protests propel me forward. I hold out two envelopes I'd stuck into the pocket of my jeans. "Give them these. You don't have to tell them anything."

"No." She puts her hands behind her back. "I will not help you with this. I'm not driving away without you."

"You know you'll go home no matter what I do. I am staying here." I wave the letters. "Please give these to Carly and Dan so they'll have some kind of explanation."

She expels a loud breath and takes the envelopes as if they are poisonous fruit. "I can't believe…" She wipes her hand across her eyes. "You can't do this."

"But I am doing this," I say in a gentler tone.

"You can't think this is permanent. You just need a few more days. I could try to delay…."

I close my eyes and shake my head. When I open them, she is staring at the letters, turning them over in her hands. "At least call me every day?"

"Email me if you need to." I don't tell her I've considered throwing my cell phone into the ocean. I fold my arms across my chest. "You'd better get going. It's a long drive."

Abruptly, Tilly drops the letters and grabs my shoulders. "Lydia. Snap out of this. What you're doing is crazy. I'm not leaving without you." Her fingers dig into my skin as she shakes me.

"Let go, Tilly." I pull her hands off and push her away.

She glares and stoops to pick up the letters. "What is with you?"

"Stop trying to change my mind. I'm going to do this. I need to." Tears prick my eyes and I don't want her to see this. I blink and quickly say, "Please leave."

As I reach out my arm to steer her toward the car, she veers away, opens the passenger door and tosses the envelopes on the seat. She slams the door shut. "I can't go." Her hands are at her hips, elbows jutting out. "I won't."

"Yes, you will. I want you to."

She looks so upset, so disappointed, I almost relent. Hold firm, I tell myself.

She brushes past me to the driver's side. "I hope you know what you're doing." She sounds more angry than

18

resigned.

"I do." I touch her arm. "This has nothing to do with you, Tilly. You know that, right? You're a great sister."

She shakes her head. "Whatever." She looks at me, her eyes pleading and glistening with tears. "Will you come home in a few weeks? Or sooner, maybe?"

I shrug. She opens the car door and then whirls back to me. "Please, Lydia. Don't do this."

I hug her. "I love you, big sister." Gently I prod her to the car.

She climbs into her seat and rolls down the window. "I can't believe this." She turns the ignition and the car roars into life. "Are you sure?" Her voice is small, imploring.

I don't dare give voice to the tendrils of doubt that are infiltrating my psyche. "Bye, Tilly. Drive safe."

"Lydia."

I back up into the shadows and raise my hand in a wave. She stares ahead for a moment and then looks behind her as she backs out of the driveway.

I watch the red taillights disappear. Uncertainty tightens my spine. Stretching my back, I gaze at the sky. In the direction of the beach, a sliver of dark orange glows, not yet enough to bleed into the black above me. The longer I stare the more stars I see. The moon is missing a piece of its side, making it not quite a circle, and as I watch, a ghostly cloud floats across it.

Inside, the house seems too bright. I lean on the door behind me, my hands flat in the small of my back, nausea taking hold of my gut. I inhale deeply. My suitcase and art supply box sit in the hall. The panels of my triptych lean on the wall behind them. I must find a place for these things. And myself. I want to be where no one can bother me.

I shake my head. Why am I thinking like this? I don't understand myself.

In the kitchen I pick up my travel mug of coffee. Tilly's mug is sitting on the counter staring at me, and I feel a pang of regret that she left without taking it with her. I shake it off. Family concerns aren't part of my life right now.

I pull out my sketchpad and open it to the first clean page. On the white paper are indentations of the words I'd written to Dan and to Carly all jumbled together. I wonder what might show up if I rubbed a pencil lead over it. Would my *sorry* to Carly darken? Or my *it's not about you* explanation to Dan?

I don't color the pencil across the page. Instead I write down the list that has been buzzing in my head all night.

House—realtor—rent?

Money—bank, bond—DON'T use credit card!

Job—?

Vehicle—bike—Electric cart?

I stick the pencil behind my ear and think about how I need money to make this work. If only I had my own bank account. Why was I so stupid not to keep my own money? Five years ago, when my dad died, Tilly and I shared his assets. Dan and I used my half to pay off our mortgage and invest in a business. He left the transporting industry, and I left my job as a bank teller to open a sporting goods store. Sporting goods! Not that I know anything about athletic shoes or skates or bikes or hockey gear, but I have always been good with numbers, organized and efficient. So I run the office and Dan runs the store. The store of his dreams.

Not all the money went into the business. We put some aside for Carly, if she ever decides to stop living the wild single life and settle down, a nest egg for a house. Thirty thousand dollars in bonds. I wonder if I can cash a bit of it in without Dan knowing, to help me start my new life.

I am shocked by this thought. What kind of person am I, to think about stealing from my daughter's future? Still, it is my money. And I will pay it back eventually.

I need a job. What can I do on an island that is anonymous enough to make it hard for Dan to find me?

The ludicrousness of that question propels me against the back of my chair. This is a small island. Why would I think I could hide? Tilly and Dan both know I'm here, so they can find me any time they want. Really I should leave this place, go somewhere that neither of them would expect.

But I can't. Not yet. Hyde Island was what convinced me to stay. Hyde Island has some kind of pull, some kind of hold on me, and until I figure out what it is about this place that allows me to breathe, I simply can't leave.

I'll have to be diligent. Keep my wits about me and stay aware of anyone looking for me. I'll find a job where I blend in and become invisible. Becoming invisible should be easy for me, considering I feel that way in my own home most of the time.

Perhaps I could work at one of the hotels. Or maybe in the kitchen at one of the restaurants. I'd have to become familiar with grits and figure out how to cook catfish. Learning about southern cuisine would be fun.

I glance around the room and ponder where I might live. The owner of this house, Agnes, was emphatic we be gone by nine this morning, so I must get out of here soon.

I tear the list off the pad and stick it in my pocket along with the pencil. It's still too early to apply for jobs or even go to the bank, but I'm impatient to start things moving. I can't just sit in the house and ruminate until the rest of the world wakes up. After locking the door behind me, I take the rickety bike out of the carport and wheel it down the driveway.

The sun is rising, coloring the sky and washing the darkness away with blush. I pedal furiously under the Live Oak giants along roads toward the beach, squinting in the brightness of the morning sky, hoping to spot a place I might be able to call home.

Chapter Three

Disappearing is not an easy task. There is always some kind of trail, people you encounter, footprints left somewhere. I guess the only way to really disappear is to die, but even then there are complications. Someone has to deal with your body, put your ashes somewhere, make decisions for you, about you. Remember you.

I ponder this as I sip my iced latte in Coffee HydeOut, tired, sweaty and hot from my bike ride around the island. I found a few *For Rent* signs and noted their addresses. When I'd exhausted the neighborhoods, I rode on trails, through the brush, under the trees, along the swamps, hoping I wouldn't bump into an alligator or ride over a turtle. I cycled until the sun was high in the sky and the heat drenched my skin in sweat. I rode like I was being chased.

Why? Why am I running away from my life? It isn't such a horrible life. I've managed to endure it all these years, even found moments of joy. True, my marriage is hollow. Dan is a workaholic who barely acknowledges my existence, and he's an emotional void. I discovered that about him shortly after we married, but by then it was too late. Still, we live comfortably; we have a nice house, want for nothing.

Want for nothing? Pshaw. I want for something. A husband, who notices me, validates me, who is keen to spend time with me. For years, I've tried to engage him with special dinners, dates to movies and bowling alleys. I've endured live hockey games, cheering along with Dan whenever his precious Leafs scored a goal, hoping that might help rekindle our bond. But still he sits most evenings in his recliner with the television remote in his hand, flipping from hockey game to golf to who knows what, drinking scotch and falling asleep. He won't concede anything is wrong with our relationship, claims he's happy, claims *we're* happy, and has refused to go to counselling with me.

But something is wrong. Happy couples don't live like this. We hardly eat meals together because he comes home late from the store. Our conversations are one-sided. If I want to tell him something, I have to repeat it several times to get a response out of him. We barely touch each other, don't connect anymore. Most nights I go to bed alone and Dan seems oblivious even to my kiss when I say goodnight. I've stopped kissing him.

There is no feeling of loneliness stronger than being in a marriage where your husband does not see you.

I guess that is what I'm running away from. Being a nobody in my own life. Here on Hyde Island, where people don't know me, I can redefine who I am and become someone. I feel it in the air I breathe as it floods my lungs with hope. Something about this place pulls me out of myself and fills me with an expectation I will find something I didn't realize I was missing. This rash move to stay is more about me running to this than away from Dan.

I drink some coffee, reassured by my justification. But my inner voice won't leave me alone. There is more to my life than my marriage, it says. Tilly, for one. Carly, for another.

Carly. I still sting from her parting words a month ago. "Leave me alone." Staying here on Hyde Island will certainly fulfil that request. Did she really mean it? She was emotional when she said it, having just followed through on a difficult decision. Yet all these weeks after, she has stayed silent with me, not responded to any of my overtures. She has shut me out and won't let me in. I can't force myself into her life no matter how hard I try.

I know I caught her off-guard, know she hadn't intended to tell me about her pregnancy or the abortion. Poor Carly, going through all that alone. Her choice to do that, but still.

Tears sting the corners of my eyes. I pull away from

those thoughts. They dredge up other long-ago memories I'd rather not revisit. Instead I focus on why I'm proud of her. She'll be twenty-seven in a few weeks and already she's a successful business analyst, living on her own, supporting herself. She runs marathons, volunteers as a Big Sister, is beautiful, happy, independent.

I have to admit that even before I bumped into her at the clinic I barely heard from her. Most of our conversations were phone calls instigated by me. And her "hello" was always so—I don't know—like "what do you want now, Mom?" I guess I should appreciate her self-sufficiency, take some credit for it even, but it feels like all those years of nurturing our relationship are suddenly meaningless. Poof, gone like a puff of smoke.

I sit back. Nothing about my old life makes me want to return to it. My daughter has no time for me. My sister, who does everything better than me, has expectations that are impossible to follow. I don't like the store or my job in the store. Every day I wake up to go to work, feeling as if I'm stuck on a train from which I can't disembark. I see Dan thriving in the business, fulfilling his dream, and always I feel like I'm left behind. Like I've lost me. Lost what I'm all about. I don't even know what my dream is anymore.

Still, I know there are many people in the world who would envy my fortunate life.

Could I be losing my mind? It isn't normal to just up and leave your life. To want to disappear. Is it? Something is wrong with me.

That notion doesn't deter me. Lydia Burgess is going to vanish and be reborn as someone new. Someone happier. What I told Tilly is true. I don't want to go back.

I wonder where Tilly is right now, if she's stopping for coffee or gas. How will she explain to Dan about leaving me behind? And Dan, will he quiz her and give her the third degree? I wonder if he'll get angry, yell at Tilly. Probably not. I can't picture his reaction. He's so wrapped up in himself that I don't have any insight on his thoughts.

Maybe he'll be relieved. I just don't know. I can imagine, though, how awkward it will be for Tilly, and a sudden flush of guilt engulfs me.

I drain my cup and toss it into the trash. Back outside I walk to the bank. Across from Coffee HydeOut, it's located in the strip mall that is pretty much the whole commercial area of Hyde Island, not counting the two hotels and a few restaurants. There's a grocer, pharmacy, bank, post office, gift shop, liquor store, a clothing boutique, and two realtor's offices. As a strip mall, it belies its appearance, with its tiled roof and attractive brick façade. It looks more like a fancy shopping resort. In the parking lot are little islands with palm trees.

The ATM lets me take out only three hundred dollars. How on earth can I start a new life with just three hundred dollars? The bank manager tells me I'll have to come back with my passport since our bank account is in Canada. Disappointed, I step outside, scan the storefronts of the plaza, and find the realtor whose signs dot the island. The door jangles as I open it. A thin, angular woman with big blonde hair sits at the desk.

"Mornin'. Can I help y'all?" Her southern drawl charms me immediately. I wonder if I can learn to speak southern.

"Yes." I pull the piece of paper out of my pocket. "Is Rip Satcher in?"

"No, he doesn't come in 'til eleven."

I look at the nameplate on her desk. "Lonny Sue, I'm interested in renting a place on the island and would like to make an appointment to view these." I hand her the paper, realizing as I do so that I've used the back of my list for the addresses. "I need to have that back," I add as she takes the paper.

"No problem. I'll just jot these down and have Rip call you. Do y'all have a number where he can reach you?"

I give her the number of my cell phone, feeling my pockets for it, not finding it. I must have left it at the house. I watch her write the number down, wondering how she can manage with her incredibly long polished nails. Then I remember that if I'm to disappear, I don't want to leave a trail. "Is it okay to pay the rent in cash?"

She looks at me quizzically. "It's a bit unusual, but I suppose you can do that." She must be suspicious of me. Only criminals pay in cash, right? "Can I have your name? So Rip knows who to ask for?"

"I'm Lydia Bur…" Horrified at almost blurting out my real name, I fake a sneeze. What a dope I am. I should have thought this through before I started. "Sorry. Allergies." I sniff and try again, distorting the portion of my name I'd already spoken and tacking on my maiden name. "Li-dee-bra…Lideebra Anne Cooper." Honestly. Lideebra?

"I beg your pardon?"

My face is hot. I say with conviction, "Lideebra Anne Cooper. Just Anne Cooper is fine."

She writes it down and hands me back my list.

"Thanks. I guess I'll hear from Rip soon." What kind of a name is Rip anyway? No better than Lideebra.

I practically run out the door and grab the bike. I ride away fast, hoping Lonny Sue forgets my blunder and will only remember my name is Anne Cooper. I hope I can remember.

There is a car in the driveway when I arrive at the cottage. My stomach flips, thinking at first it's Tilly, come back to try to change my mind. Then I realize it's a Jetta, not a Civic, and it's black, not navy. Agnes, our friend who owns the house, is coming out the front door, and I remember she was due to arrive around nine this morning.

She must wonder what my things are still doing there. We told her we'd be gone early. Now I have to come up with a story, one that will allow me to remain anonymous here. I mean, she knows me as Lydia Burgess and I've become Anne Cooper. Lideebra Anne Cooper.

"Hi, Agnes." I stop beside the car, the tires skidding a little as I brake and lay the bike on the grass. She takes two grocery bags out of her trunk. "Need some help?"

"Oh, you are still here. Thanks." She hands me four

bulging Piggly Wiggly bags. "I saw you'd left a lot of stuff behind. Where's your car?"

"It's Tilly's and she has it." Agnes walks ahead of me toward the house. The handles of the plastic bags dig into my fingers. "I've decided to stay on the island a bit longer."

Agnes stops and stares at me through her purple-rimmed glasses. Her gray eyes, remarkably the same color as her spiky short hair, show dismay. "But I can't have you here. I've got a…" She pushes her glasses up. Her cheeks flush pink. "A friend coming to stay with me."

"A friend?" Happy to take the focus off me, I ask in a singsong voice, "Perhaps a gentleman friend?"

"Well." She tosses her head and continues toward the house. She's amazingly spry for a woman of seventy-eight. "It doesn't matter who. The point is you can't stay here."

"No worries. I've arranged other accommodations. You won't see or hear from me." I wink at her as she holds the door open. "So you and your friend will have all the privacy you need."

"Oh, stop."

I plunk the bags on the kitchen counter. "But I might need your help moving my stuff. Since I don't have a car here. I was wondering if I could borrow yours."

"What about Tilly?"

"She's gone. Had to get home. School starts in a couple of weeks, and she's got to get her classroom ready."

"But how will you get back to Toronto?"

"Oh, my husband's coming to get me in a few weeks." I'm surprised at how easily the lie crosses my lips. I'm not even blushing.

"All right, you can use my car if you don't take too long."

"Thanks, Agnes. It'll be no more than an hour, and will probably be later this afternoon, if that's okay. My place won't be ready until then." What if I don't get a place today? I have no idea what I'll do if I don't hear from Rip soon. What if I get a place, but can't move into it right away? Panic rises, but then I think, hotel. Of course. I can check into one of the hotels until I find something. Hopefully, they'll accept cash. I take a deep, relieving breath and start to help unload groceries. Ritz crackers. A hunk of cheddar. A can of olives.

"By the way, I love your triptych." Agnes takes two wine bottles out of her bag. "The way you blended the reds and the yellows. And a great sense of light that emerges through the three parts. Did you enjoy the class?"

I first met Agnes at a painting class in Toronto a few years ago, introduced by Tilly, and she and Tilly meet up every so often at other art workshops. Although Agnes is really Tilly's friend, she clicked with me more than with my sister. She was the one who encouraged us to come to Hyde Island for the abstract art course.

"Yeah, it was good. I learned a lot about working with acrylics. But Agnes." I spread my arms. "This island is amazing. Such a beautiful spot. I never want to leave."

She looks at me over her glasses, as if she's suddenly figured out exactly why I'm still here. "I know what you mean. It's a little piece of paradise."

I'm about to gush some more about the beach, the Live Oaks, the Spanish moss, when the opening notes of *Für Elise*, digitalized, invade the kitchen. Thank God, there is my cell phone on the counter beside Agnes. She hands it to me. Stupidly, I flip it open without checking the call display, thinking it's Rip. Hoping.

"Lydia, what the heck is going on?" It's Dan. And he sounds angry. Well, not angry exactly. Indignant and perplexed is more like it, making me wonder what crisis has hit the store today.

"Dan. Hi." I turn away from Agnes, hunching myself around the phone as best as I can. "What's up?" Why, oh why did I answer the phone?

"Tilly called me from somewhere on the I-95. She said you're not with her and you were staying on—"

"She called you?" Darn Tilly. Dan wasn't supposed to know until at least tomorrow. I shift my eyes to look at Agnes, wondering if she can hear his voice. It's pretty loud.

She's casually putting things in cupboards, humming quietly, pretending she's not listening. I walk outside, closing the door behind me. "Calm down, Dan."

"How can I calm down? Here I'm expecting you home sometime tomorrow and—"

"Dan, listen." I push the words out of my mouth, which has suddenly become very dry. "I'm not coming home." There. I said it. Now he knows. I cringe in expectation of his reaction, wanting only to end this call.

"What the hell does that mean? Of course you're coming home. Tilly said she'd turn around wherever she was and get you. She said—"

"I wrote you a note that explains it all. Tilly will give it to you when she gets there tomorrow. I can't go into it right now." I gaze at the huge eucalyptus tree in Agnes's yard. The scent of it makes me dizzy.

"A note? You owe me more than a note, Lydia." His voice is shaking. Is he crying? If he's crying, I can't do this anymore. I hear him exhale. "Look, I don't understand what's going on with you these days. But if you need more time away, you've got it. Just let me know how long—"

I hate myself for doing it, but I push the red button on the phone, cutting him off. Then I turn it off and snap it closed. Wiping a tear from my cheek, I slide down and crouch, leaning back on the eucalyptus.

I am a horrible person. How can I treat Dan like this? Surely he deserves better.

Yet I've started on this road and something inside of me propels me forward and I can't stop. I don't want to stop.

Staring at the bike lying on the grass, I am struck by an urge to ride again, to have the air brush my face and fill my lungs, pedaling so fast I run out of breath. I find myself picking it up.

The wheels squeak as I frantically pump the pedal. Over and over again, the bike seems to shriek, *What are you doing? What are you doing?*

I shout aloud. "Leave me alone."

My shortcomings keep pursuing me, pounding in my head. I've run away from Dan, hurt Tilly, discarded my daughter, abandoned my responsibilities. And I've left Agnes without a word.

Still I keep on, along the road, and then turn onto the trail that runs through the protected wetlands. The marshes, with wooden boardwalks crossing them, are busy with buzzing bugs, croaking frogs, and tall grasses waving in the breeze. A musty, damp scent penetrates my nostrils. I am the only human here. I ride, bumping on the wooden slats, as if hunted by my own impulses. My butt bounces uncomfortably on the seat, but I don't care. I deserve the pain.

When I finally reach the other side and am again on the road, I stop, panting. It's too hot to be working so hard. Sweat runs down the sides of my face and my shirt sticks to my back. A drop of perspiration trickles between my breasts. I feel no relief from my self-condemnation. In fact, the deserted, muggy swamplands I've just been through are a perfect metaphor for my emotional state.

Wiping my hand across my forehead, I look around and swat at mosquitoes. Ahead are trees and shade, respite from the blaring sun and suffocating heat, where I can refresh and strengthen my resolve. I walk my bike along the road toward them.

In the distance my eye catches something white through the yellow and green foliage. I lay the bike down and venture into the grass wading through it under the shade of the enormous trees. I climb a slight incline. Off toward the horizon, I can see the dunes by the beach. A hundred yards farther I find myself in a clearing with sand and gravel on the ground, and a small white camper in the middle of it. To one side, a weedy fire pit is surrounded by three wooden stumps, and tied between two trees is a raggedy clothesline. A garden patch has been sectioned off with rocks, but it has only scrub growing in it. Off to the other side, I see a pathway leading to the road I could have used if I'd gone a bit farther.

Does someone live in this little hideaway? It seems deserted. I make my way to the door and am about to knock when I see the best part. In the window is a hand-written sign that says *For Rent*. With a phone number.

My heart starts beating fast. This is kismet. Why else would I have found this place if it isn't meant to be my home? I pull the phone out of my pocket and turn it on.

Chapter Four

I walk up the driveway of a charming little red brick bungalow with yellow shutters. Its garden is weedy and the grass patchy, but the front yard has an amazing cluster of Live Oaks grown bent by the wind. An eerie yet magnificent troupe of dancers, they'd upstage any flowers.

As I knock on the door, I finger the pile of bills in my pocket. Nine hundred dollars for the first two months' rent. It took some doing getting that out of the bank, with all the hassles of my Canadian account not being in the Hyde Island bank and their regulations requiring my passport. But eventually I got my money. I took three thousand total from our checking account. Dan will be livid when he finds out, but it'll probably be ages before he does. I'm the one in charge of our banking.

The door opening startles me away from thoughts about Dan. A tall, thin man with a grizzly gray beard and his hair tied back in a ponytail peers at me through a pair of John Lennon glasses. "Hello." He's wearing shorts and a bright tie-dyed T-shirt. Have I arrived at the sixties?

"Hi, I'm Anne Cooper." It feels good to be using my maiden name. I stick my hand out. Do old hippies shake hands? "I called you earlier about the camper?"

"Oh, yeah." He grabs my hand with a firm grip and shakes it up and down. "I'm Bill Alpaca. Nice to meet ya. Come on in and we'll talk business."

The door opens right into the living room. I'm not sure what I expected to see inside the house, but it doesn't look like a hippy abode at all. No peace signs, beaded curtains or hookah pipes. There's a worn but very cushy looking gray couch facing a big flat-screen TV mounted on the wall. Newspapers are scattered on the coffee table. Chairs with green cushions and interestingly carved wooden armrests sit at right angles to the couch. On a side table stands a lamp shaped like a lighthouse. An open roll-top desk in the corner is crammed with papers and books. Shelves line one wall, filled with more books. And turtles. In fact, turtles are all over the room. Clay turtles on the desk shelf. Stained glass turtles hang in a window. Carved wooden turtles wedged among the books. And a collection of empty—at least I hope they're empty—turtle shells fill a small cabinet with glass doors.

"I've got papers for you to sign in the kitchen." He leads the way through a little hall. At the end of it, we walk through a multicolored beaded curtain, the strings rattling as they fall back in place. Ah, here's the hippy touch.

I smell fried onions and my stomach grumbles. The counter and stove are clean, so I'm guessing the onions were eaten for breakfast or an early lunch. On the table are printed pages that look like a contract, a pen and a key on top of them. For a minute I hesitate. What if he asks for identification? Should I revert to my real name? Make up some excuse about being confused?

He pulls out a chair and motions me to sit down. "So you want to rent open-ended, huh? Not sure how long you plan on staying?" He sounds like he's truly interested, his voice low and gentle. I notice, as he sits down, that his eyes are very blue.

"No. I recently discovered this island and decided I want to get to know it for a while. Just not sure how long that will take." I take out the wad of money to try to get the conversation off me. "I have two months' rent here, in cash." I pat the pile straight as if it were a deck of cards and push it over to him.

He looks at the bills, then up at me, then at the bills again. "And you're here by yourself? No family?" I see him looking pointedly at my left hand. Shoot. My wedding ring. I should have taken it off. Quickly I cover it with my right hand.

"Nope, this is just some me time. Trying to find myself." I force a chuckle. "You can understand that kind of thing, right?"

"I'm not trying to pry." He shakes his head slightly as if denying an accusation I didn't make. "I respect your privacy, Ms. Cooper."

"Anne, please."

"Anne. As long as you pay the rent and take good care of the place. That's all that concerns me." He picks up the money and starts counting it. When he finishes, he looks directly at me through his glasses. "And if you're looking for a place to be away from things with lots of quiet, you found it."

I nod. "That's what I want. To be away from things."

He stares at me again, for what seems like a long time. I shift in my seat. He pushes the paper and pen over to me. "Here's a rental agreement I need you to sign. Standard stuff. I need one month's notice before you leave. And this second month's rent is a security against damage that'll go to last month's rent if everything's okay. So your next payment will be..." He looks up at the calendar on the wall. The August page has a picture of a baby turtle making a road of tracks on the sand. "September fifteenth, a month from today. If you're still here then."

I look over the contract. I expected it to be the generic kind of thing you'd buy at Office Depot, but it looks like he typed it up himself. Four hundred basic rent, fifty to cover electricity and water. At the bottom is a place for me to sign and another line for him to sign. I turn to the second page. It's a copy of the first. I swallow and pick up the pen. Here goes.

Instinctively I start my signature with a flourish of an "L" for Lydia and instantly I freeze. Damn. Now I have to use Lideebra. I was hoping to drop that name and just go by Anne Cooper. I sign both copies, date them, and pass them to him. He takes the pen and looks at the page.

"Lideebra, huh? Don't think I've ever heard that name before."

"Oh, you know, great-great-grandmother. I only use it for official stuff. I just go by Anne, really." Afraid he'll ask for my driver's license or something I change the subject. "You seem to like turtles."

"As a matter of fact, it's the turtles that brought me to this island." He signs the agreements and passes one copy to me, then leans back in his chair. "I'm a turtle biologist."

"Really?" Imagine studying only turtles. Can they be that interesting?

"Yup. Twenty years ago I came here to observe them hatching and I ended up staying." He looks pointedly at me, pushing his glasses up. "Lots of people end up doing that. Staying, I mean."

"Uh huh?"

"I lived in that camper by myself at first." He nods. "Rented it, like you, then ended up buying it. I'm glad you're going to be using it for a while. It's been empty for years. Not too many people want to stay there nowadays. They rent houses or the villas down by the beach. Or drive their own campers down and stay in the campground."

"You mean no one's been in it for years?" It occurs to me I should have had a look inside before signing the agreement. I envision mouse droppings in the corners, cushions chewed, lots of spiders, and involuntarily I shudder.

"Don't worry. I check it out and clean it regularly. And stay in it myself every so often." He shrugs. "I've been thinking I should just sell the thing. But I can't bring myself to do that, you know? It's where my Vera and I first started out."

I learn that when Bill Alpaca was studying the turtles that come to the island to lay their eggs in the dunes, he met his wife, Vera, a turtle biologist herself. They lived together in the camper and moved to this house after they were married. Bill has lived here alone since Vera died three years ago.

"Of cancer." He looks so sad I want to give him a hug. "It was a very difficult time."

Abruptly he pushes his chair back. "You must want to get yourself moved in. If there are any problems with the place, let me know." He hands me the key.

I follow him to the door. "Thanks Mr. Alpaca, er, Bill." Remembering we're on a first name basis. "I'll call if I need anything. I still have your phone number."

"And listen, Anne." He leans in, his hand on the open door. "I know what it is to want to get away from things. So if you need any advice in that department, you know where to find me."

I ponder those words as I walk down the driveway, feeling his eyes on my back. I get on the bike and pedal away. It seems I have an ally in this escape plan of mine.

****

I lean back against the hard couch cushion and wrap my hands around the wine glass as I admire my new home. Outside the night is black. The blue gingham curtains that I've closed to shut out the darkness flutter weakly in the gentle breeze. They are dusty and have tiny dark spots at the hems, so washing them has been added to my to-do list. I've cleaned the place quite thoroughly, but even as I did that, I accumulated a catalogue of tasks to complete at another time.

The built-in lamps cast a cozy glow around this efficient little abode. I've cooked my first meal, a fried egg and tomato sandwich, in the compact kitchen. It may be small but is very workable, with a two-burner stove and mini-microwave. It's stocked with dishes, pots, utensils, and a frying pan. The half-fridge reminds me of the bar fridge we bought for Carly when she moved to university, a memory that briefly causes me to tremble. She was so full of anticipation at finally being on her own, not unlike what I'm experiencing here. I had a tough time letting her go, almost resenting her excitement at moving into a future that didn't include me. I was losing my baby, the one element in my life that made everything else bearable.

And now I've discarded her just like that.

I suck in a deep breath. No, I correct myself. She discarded me ages ago, starting with that move to the dorm. Of course we were proud of the way she embraced her independence so enthusiastically. Wouldn't any parent be? Still, she left us behind, barely giving us a thought. She left me. With Dan and emptiness. And a month ago, she cut the final tie with scissors so sharp, it sliced through my heart.

I shift my mind away from all that, choosing instead to focus on my new life. I stare at the blue and green plaid cushioned bench by the built-in table where I ate my supper. The whole thing folds down into a bed, I believe. I've been in a camper that had a similar table setup, but I haven't tried it here. Since no overnight guests are expected, I don't have to figure it out. The built-in couch on which I'm lounging also has blue and green plaid cushions. It's not the most comfortable, but it will do. On the opposite wall is a storage cupboard with a long shelf on which I've displayed my triptych.

The two doors at one end of the camper are so narrow, it seems this camper is made for very thin people. One door opens into the tiniest bathroom I've ever seen, other than in an airplane. It was rather grungy when I moved in; the toilet was filthy and the shower had black spots of mold in the corners. What else can you expect when a man owns it? I spent a good hour scrubbing it, using half a bottle of bleach. The other door opens to a bedroom with a bed that is surprisingly comfortable, lamps built into the wall on each side, and lots of cupboards. I've unpacked my clothes, stored my painting gear, and made up the bed with a new set of sheets that I bought. Blue and yellow striped.

I can't believe I've done it, settled on the island in my own place. Decision made yesterday and here I am. My new home. Even though I didn't choose the decor, even though I have very few things of my own here, even though it's a little dated and shabby, it is already starting to feel like mine. Only mine.

The move went fairly smoothly after I left Bill's place with the key. Agnes, bless her heart, let me use her car for most of the afternoon. I was able to move my stuff in one trip, and then drove across the bridge to Brenville so I could shop at the Piggly Wiggly for groceries and Target for everything else.

Agnes was quite inquisitive when I returned her vehicle, though.

"Where have you moved your things to?" she asked when I handed her the keys.

"Oh, I found a cute little place. On, um." I raised my eyes to the sky. "I forget the name of the street."

"Is it a ranch? A semi? A townhouse? One of those condos?"

I didn't want to answer. If I told her it was a camper, she'd find it. I nodded vaguely. "Hey, Agnes." I pointed to her bike leaning against the garage wall. "Do you use your bike much?"

Appearing startled at my abrupt change of subject, she stared at me and then looked at the bike. "That old thing? No. My knees can't take it anymore." She chuckled. "Nor can my rear on that hard saddle."

"Can I buy it from you?"

Just then a white BMW turned onto her street and headed our way. Agnes got all flustered. "Oh, there's my friend. You have to go now."

"What about the bike?"

"Sure, sure. It's yours for twenty dollars." She prodded me toward the bicycle. I wanted to get a look at the person in the car so I took my time digging out the money.

"Never mind. Just take it," she almost hissed. "Go."

She was so ruffled, I decided to give her a break. I zipped down one side of the driveway on my new wheels, just as the car drove up the other. I managed to catch a glimpse of a silver-haired man in the driver seat.

Now, thanks to Agnes, I have my own transport to get around the island. Brenville is quite a distance to ride, and although I may cycle there some time, the little grocer in the plaza has essentials. For the time being, I've stocked up pretty well.

I wonder if I'm doing the right thing by not letting

Agnes know where I'm living. She is a friend to me, here where I know very few people. Still, it's the way I want it for the time being, until I figure out my future. To keep a low profile, not let too many people find out where I'm living. Just in case Dan comes looking for me. I don't want to face him until I'm ready. Until I can do it on my own terms.

If ever.

I suddenly get fidgety and can't seem to sit still. I pace around the room, a difficult task in such a cramped space. I waver between exhilaration and dread, overwhelmed by what I have done. Just like that, I've abandoned my family, my life, my home. What kind of person does that?

The island.

Those words pop into my head. Yes, that's it. I have been bewitched by the island. Some force in this green humid place is pulling at me, challenging me to examine my life and make it better. Hyde Island has a power I do not understand, and I have succumbed to it.

I flop back on the couch and gulp some wine, coughing after swallowing too quickly. I wipe the sweat off my forehead and stare at the triptych, suddenly recognizing I painted my decision into it: the swirl of dark colors in the first panel, the light that is almost not there in the second but grows to a luminous burst in the third panel when I finally thought, *yes*. My subconscious knew before I did that I would do this.

The cell phone ringing startles me. That darn *Für Elise* ringtone. I swear I'm going to change it. I just stare at the phone lying on the counter beside the tiny sink, which is where I threw it. I'd turned it off after hanging up on Dan and then again after calling Bill Alpaca, and didn't think any more about it. But after unpacking and settling in, I realized I hadn't canceled the realtor, so I used it to call Rip Satcher's office. When I turned it on, the voice mail light was flashing, but I ignored it and just made the call. Lonny Sue remembered me, although her stumbling over my name so flustered me that I must have forgotten to turn the phone off when I was done.

The ringing stops. No little ding-ding to announce that the caller left a message. The message box is probably full. I'm sure there are lots from Dan or maybe Tilly. Probably not Carly, since Dan wouldn't want to upset her until he figures things out. I should check, I know, but find it easy to resist doing so.

I keep thinking about throwing the phone in the ocean. Cut all my ties with my past. For reasons I don't want to examine, I'm unable to do it.

I recognize it would not be difficult for Dan to find me if he wants to. He knows where Tilly and I went, where Tilly left me. He could trace the bank where I withdrew the money. It was stupid of me to settle here on Hyde Island. I should have gone somewhere completely different.

Yet something about this island put the idea in my head, something about here made me do this. I have to stay until I find out what that is. Until I figure out why.

Setting down the glass, I jump off the couch and pick up the phone. Then I change my mind and put it back down and open the door. Outside, the humidity smacks me in the face. Darkness surrounds me like shawl. It's a little eerie. I seem very far from civilization. No street lights nearby. No lit houses.

I walk away from the camper, finding comfort in the glow shining through the curtained windows as I look back at it. Moving farther into the bush, I slap my legs at the biting mosquitoes. Once I'm in the tall grass I can no longer see the camper, and I stop and raise my arms in entreaty, to whom I don't know. "I'm home." I shout. "I'm me. I can be whatever I want."

A rustling to my left makes me jolt, and as I run back to the camper, I wonder what kind of wild animals live on Hyde Island.

Chapter Five

Several years ago a friend of mine lost her husband to cancer. Maggie was devastated of course, and we rallied around her, boosting her up in the midst of her grief. After things settled down and she no longer cried every time she thought about him, she sold her house, claiming it was too hard to move forward in a place filled with memories. Not knowing exactly what she was going to do next or where she wanted to be, she rented a sweet little apartment on Avenue Road a few blocks from our house. I helped her settle in, painted walls with her, hung curtains. Every Tuesday evening I'd cook dinner with her and we'd watch chick flicks. I'd often drop in for tea or wine after work. Always, when I sat in her bright little living room trying to take Maggie out of her sadness, I felt envy.

Not envious of her loss or her grief. No. What I coveted was that place of her own. Her future to fill with whatever she desired. The opportunity to live life on her own terms, without having to consider anyone else.

"You're too good a friend to her," Dan would say in a resentful tone as I yet again walked out the door with a bottle of Pinot Noir in my hands. Little did he know, indeed I barely admitted it to myself at the time, that, in part, I went to Maggie's to soak up that sense of freedom and independence.

Maggie's apartment invades my thoughts, as I lie in bed unable to sleep. She eventually took a job with a company that has her traveling all over the world, and she bought a log cabin in the Kawarthas for the few months of the year that she's actually home. Did she regret leaving her little freedom nest? I secretly wanted to take it over when she gave it up, but how could I? Leave Dan? Leave our marriage?

Yet now I've done just that.

This camper is not at all like Maggie's freedom nest. The humidity in here is stifling, coating a sheen of sweat all over my skin. I've kicked the sheets to the end of the bed because it's so hot. From tossing and turning on the thin foam mattress, my lower back twinges. The cicadas are making a ruckus outside and a faint mustiness permeates the air in the room.

What the heck have I done?

I jump out of bed and head for the bathroom. The face that stares at me from the mirror looks tired, hair askew and fuzzy from the humidity. But the hazel eyes are at peace.

I've heard that drinking hot tea in hot weather makes you cool, so in the kitchen I plug in the kettle. My to-list sits on the counter and I take up the pen and add *get a fan*. When I return the pen to the counter it nudges my cell phone. I stare at it, then take a deep breath and pick it up. I press one for my mailbox. The first message blares into my ear.

"Lydia, it's Dan. Why'd you hang up? What's going on with you? We need to talk."

I press seven to delete it. The next one is Tilly.

"Lydia, the drive is very boring without you. I can't stop thinking about what you're doing. Are you sure about this? I'll turn around right now and come back for you if you say..." A loud sigh comes through the speaker. "Anyway, I love you."

I bite my lip as I delete her message and listen to the next one.

"Sorry Lydie, I meant to tell you I called Dan and told him. I know you didn't want me to do that. But I think that maybe something's wrong with you."

Delete.

"Lydia, it's Dan. Please, hon, talk to me. At least tell me what you think I've done."

Delete. I swallow the lump that's wedged in my throat.

"What are you thinking? Are you leaving me for

good?"

Delete.

"Lydia, pick up your damn phone."

Delete.

"Hi Mom." My chest suddenly tightens. "Sorry I've been out of touch since I saw you last. It's just that I…well, never mind. That's all in the past. I wanted to tell you that I secured a lucrative contract for my company and they put me in line for a promotion. Isn't that awesome? By the way, let me tell Daddy. Oh, and I got your message about your painting week. Hi to Aunt Tilly."

Oh Carly, just when my heart allowed me to yield to your desire to be left alone, just when I've taken action so I can do that, you change the rules.

I snap my phone shut. There are still five unheard messages, but I don't want to listen anymore.

What will Carly think when she finds out what I'm doing? When she reads my note? Will she hate me? Feel abandoned? Will she understand? Staring at the phone in my hand, I'm tempted to call her, to explain.

But how would I do that?

The kettle sputters, steam billowing from its spout. I unplug it and take a mug out of the cupboard.

****

Closing the bank's webpage, I stare at the screen. I've just transferred three thousand dollars from our investment account to our checking to cover up my earlier withdrawal. Of course, I'll pay it all back when I can, since I don't want to be indebted to what I've left. This is me, on my own. Nevertheless, I am assailed by guilt. So I check out the store's business accounts to make sure things are okay. I normally wouldn't do this stuff on a public WiFi, but what other choice do I have? Anyway, the store seems to be managing all right financially, so I shake away the guilt and put it out of my head. I push Dan out as well.

I am in the business center of the Live Oak Inn, where last week Tilly and I had dinner at the restaurant in order to sample their famous, not-to-be-missed shrimp and grits.

We were charmed by the ambience of the place, especially the hotel, a sprawling one-story building with hallways of rooms branching out like arms across the grounds and along the waterfront. After our fabulous meal, we wandered around admiring the lobby, the library, the gardens and the beach. On our self-directed tour we discovered this business center, complete with free Internet access, just off the lobby. We visited here twice more, coming in through the back door, acting like we were paying guests and accessing the Internet with our laptops. Tilly needed to check her email, since school starts in a couple of weeks. I read my emails but answered none of them, because I just wanted to be away for the week. Instead I checked the news online and kept up with my scrabble game.

So here I sit again, stealing the Internet with my laptop. My hand briefly hovers over the track pad, ready to click on my mailbox. I stop myself. If I'm going to continue on this path, there can be no contact with anyone from home. Still on edge from the phone messages, I don't want to know what they have to say.

Instead I pull up my résumé and begin to fudge it for Anne Cooper. Somehow, this feels illegal, or at the very least, unethical, but I forge ahead. How else can I get a job? I just hope they won't check too closely. I'll be truthful about my qualifications, just change the details.

Since I don't know what kind of job I'll be applying for, or even what kind of jobs might be available on the island, I'm uncertain how to focus it. As a Canadian in the United States without a work permit, I'm probably not even allowed to work here. I sit back, stumped as to how to handle this.

Voices intrude on my rumination.

"Did you know Silvana and Rosita were deported? Now we're short two cleaners again." My ears perk up. The chair is angled to give me a good view of the hotel's front desk, where two people stand having a conversation. Curious, I strain to listen while I type gibberish, trying not to appear as if I'm eavesdropping.

A young woman wearing the hotel uniform, a jade green suit with a short tight skirt, is leaning her elbows on the counter. Her hair is pulled up with a clip, blond curls tumbling over the top of her head like silken froth. On the other side of the desk is an attractive young clerk, whose lean body, mocha skin and cleft chin make me think tall, dark, and handsome. He's wearing the male version of the green hotel uniform.

The woman, who looks to be around Carly's age, shakes her head. "Yeah. The last time that happened with Maria and Isabel, I was cleaning rooms for weeks."

"Me too. And man, some of those bathrooms were disgusting." Tall-dark-and-handsome shudders.

Silken-froth crosses her arms over her chest. "Floyd better not ask us to do it again. I'll just say no if he does."

"But you don't want to lose your job. When I balked last time, he threatened to fire me and give me a bad intern evaluation."

"I know. But Augusta can't do the place with just the part-timers."

Tall-dark-and-handsome starts shuffling papers. "Well, let's keep our fingers crossed that Floyd can find some more Mexican 'cousins' who want to work in the States."

"Why don't they hire legal workers for those positions? I mean, we go through this all the time."

I cannot believe my ears. Every time I'm perplexed as to my next step, a solution materializes. First the camper. Then the bike. Now a job? I close my laptop and saunter over to the desk.

"Excuse me."

They both stand up straight, putting official expressions on their faces. Silken-froth pulls at her skirt and lifts the end of the counter, scurrying to the other side to stand beside the clerk.

"Yes, ma'am," says Tall-dark-and-handsome, whose shiny gold nametag indicates his name is Nathan. "How can we help you?"

"I didn't mean to overhear, but do I understand

correctly that the hotel might be looking to hire cleaning staff?" My cheeks flush slightly. Here I am a qualified bookkeeper, a business owner and administrator, asking about a cleaning job.

Silken-froth and Nathan exchange glances. I peek at Silken-froth's name badge. Steffi. She looks at me. "We did just lose two of our cleaners. Are you looking for a job for your kids? Because it isn't really a seasonal thing."

"Well, no, for me."

Her eyebrows rise. "Really? Are you...ooph!" Nathan has elbowed her, cutting off her question. He smiles.

"You know it's cleaning the hotel rooms, right? Hotel maid stuff?"

"Yes, I do. I need a job and I am certainly capable of doing that."

"But aren't you staying here as a guest?" Incredulity peppers Steffi's question.

"Well, no." My throat becomes dry and I cough. "I'm not actually staying here. I was, uh, using the Internet." I shrug. "I know I shouldn't be doing that."

Nathan chuckles. "Oh, don't worry. We won't tell on you. We have a few regulars on the island who do that all the time and we let them. One old lady brings us cookies when she comes to check her emails." He leans closer. "We just don't let the manager know."

"Right." This is a good sign. Unscrupulousness among the staff might mean that this could be a good place to hide out, so to speak.

Steffi becomes all business. "So, have you got much housekeeping experience?"

"Well, no." I think about all the years I've cleaned my house. And the store. We've always done it ourselves, to save money. "I haven't worked in hotels before. But I have a good background in cleaning."

"We do have some openings, and I'm sure the manager will be posting the positions soon. In fact..." She looks at the door behind her. "I'll see if he's available." She hurries off.

Nathan picks up the papers he was shuffling earlier and taps them into a neat pile. "I hope you get the job. It'll be nice to have a maid here who can speak English. The housekeeping supervisor, Augusta, is from Georgia, but most of the other maids we've had are from Mexico and they only speak Spanish." He looks up. "Do you speak Spanish?"

"No." Could that be a problem? "I do speak French, though."

"Really?"

Steffi appears through the door. "Mr. Hill, our manager, said he'd see you now. Come on back." She lifts the end of the counter so I can walk through.

"It doesn't matter that I don't have my résumé?"

"Résumé!" Steffi and Nathan say this in unison, both with an amused expression on their faces. I notice that Steffi has an endearing dimple in her left cheek when she smiles. Nathan clears his throat. "I don't think Floyd cares about a résumé for the maid job."

"Oh. Okay."

I follow Steffi through the door into a hallway. Sunlight pours onto the green speckled carpet from a window at the end. A photocopy machine, file cabinet, and water cooler stand in a row along one wall. Three doors punctuate the opposite wall. Steffi knocks on the last one, and then opens it enough to stick her head in.

"Mr. Hill, here's..." she pulls back and whispers, "What's your name?"

"Anne. Anne Cooper." Way to go, me. I get it right the first time. And manage to drop that stupid Lideebra.

Steffi's head disappears behind the door again. "Anne Cooper. About the maid job?"

A disembodied voice, low, with a southern accent, says, "Show her in."

Steffi pushes the door all the way open and stands back. As I walk past her into the office, she whispers, "Good luck." A quiver of nervousness almost stops me, but I keep going.

Behind a massive desk, a man looks up from a magazine in his hands. *Ma-guy-zine.* I can only imagine what type of articles that contains. He's partially bald, with a comb-over, thin strands of brown hair stroked across the top of his head. As if that would fool anyone. The top two buttons of his light green shirt are undone and his jade-colored tie hangs around his neck like a slackened noose. His shirt sleeves are rolled up to the elbow, and his jacket, which of course is jade green, is flung over the arm of his chair.

He drops the magazine and stands with a surprised look on his face. Across his belly, his shirt is stretched so tight I'm surprised the buttons haven't popped. Blood rushes to his face as he leans toward me.

"Hello. I'm Floyd Hill, the day manager here at Live Oak Inn." He reaches his hand out for me to shake while his eyes appraise me. "Are you are here for the maid job?"

Do I not look the part? I'm sure he doesn't mean to be rude, but the way he emphasizes "you" makes the maid job seem like an insult. I refuse to take it that way. The world needs cleaners. Imagine spending the night in a hotel room that hadn't been cleaned. Right that minute, I decide that being a maid is an honorable profession and I square my shoulders as I take his hand. It's soft and pudgy. And sweaty. I give it one shake and let go.

"Yes I am. You know what they say. Cleanliness is next to godliness." Geez, how cheesy can I be?

He chuckles half-heartedly. "Right." Indicating the chair facing his desk, he plops into his own. "Please sit down."

I do and twine my hands together on my lap. It's been a long time since I've interviewed for a job, and I wonder what's coming next. My first impression of this Floyd is not a positive one, but he does have the power here. And I need a job. My mind is racing with ideas about how to handle this.

"I have to say, Anne. It is Anne, right?" At my nod he continues. "You aren't the, uh, usual type of applicant we have for these positions."

"You mean not Mexican?"

His round cheeks flush pink. "We like to help out those tryin' to make a new life for themselves, so yes, we do tend to hire non-Americans for the jobs that don't require, uh, specialized skills."

His hedging gives me confidence. I give him my most indulgent, professional, inviting smile. "Okay, Floyd. Can I call you Floyd?" I stop myself from covering my mouth, not knowing how that came out of it. This is a job interview, for God's sake.

Floyd narrows his eyes and a suspicious look flashes across his face. He sits back, folding his arms across his chest. Maybe he thinks I'm from Immigration or something. I lean forward. "I'm going to be honest with you. I'm Canadian and I want to live on Hyde Island for a while. The thing is, I don't have any money and I need a job." He raises his eyebrows, but says nothing. "Now, I figure you don't necessarily worry about things like work permits, so I'm hoping you can overlook the fact that I don't have one. What do you think?"

He puffs his cheeks and blows out a gust of air. "Wow. Not what I expected. But yeah, sure. Can y'all clean? Are y'all willin' to follow orders, not insist on doin' things your way?"

I feel elated. He's going to offer me the job. I nod vigorously and say, "Sure. Yes. I can follow orders. And I've been cleaning all my life, so that's not a problem." I sit back and try to tone it down, try not to seem too eager. Calm down. Be professional.

"Okay then. I can offer you five dollars an hour, any tips you share fifty-fifty with the management." Meaning him of course. My confidence sags, even as outrage starts to blossom in my gut. Can I manage on five dollars an hour? I quickly do the math. Five times, say, thirty-five hours a week? A hundred and seventy-five. Times four weeks is seven hundred a month. With my rent taking four fifty, that leaves only two fifty for food and everything else.

Plus half tips. That's not much. Maybe I'd somehow try to pocket more of the tips.

"Isn't minimum wage around seven dollars an hour?"

"Anne, Anne. Because you're not a legal worker, I put myself at risk. I have to protect the hotel against loss, you know? So I can only pay you five. It's what I pay all of my maids. Take it or leave it." He raises his hands in the air.

Slick as snot, my grandmother would've called him. I'm deflated. "Okay, I'll take it." At least my first month's rent is paid for. This is better than nothing, and I'll keep looking.

"Good. You'll work the nine-to-three shift. Six days a week. Clean all the rooms on your roster, but finish everythin' in the six hours. If it takes you longer we don't pay for the extra time. Take breaks only if you get the work done. Got it?"

I nod. I do not like this man and I hate that he's calling all the shots.

"Your supervisor is Augusta Lewis. Basically she's your boss. You and I." He waves his finger back and forth a few times, directing it first at my chest then his. "We won't have any need for contact."

"Okay." Thank goodness. If I had to deal with him every day, I might punch him.

"Now, fill in this form." He reaches into a desk drawer and pulls out a document. Smiling, showing his shiny white teeth as he hands it to me, he says. "Your name, address, contact info. The usual. Make up what you have to, includin' a social security number." He frowns. "Is Anne, what is it?" He raises his eyes to the ceiling as if searching his memory. "Cooper. Is Anne Cooper your real name?"

My new name is sort of mine. Anne's my middle name, Cooper my maiden name. "Close enough." I suddenly don't want to tell him anything more about me.

"You're not in any kind of trouble or anythin', are you? We're not going to have problems with crazy-ass husbands or boyfriends? Or Canadian Mounties?"

My cheeks grow hot. "No, of course not."

"Good. You can sit at the desk in the business center just off the lobby to fill in the form, and when you're done give it to Steffi. She'll take you to meet Augusta."

At the mention of the business center, I feel a slight panic. My laptop!

"Okay." I clutch the paper tightly and stand, eager to get out of this office. "When do I start?"

"Today. Augusta will show you the ropes, give you your uniform. Which will cost you fifty dollars, by the way. We'll dock your first pay."

"What?"

He smiles and shrugs but says nothing. What a jerk.

"Okay." I walk to the door and open it and then look back at him. "Uh, thanks. Nice to meet you, Floyd." I'm such a liar.

"Mr. Hill." He grins. "Since you work for me. And, by the way, your pay period doesn't start until tomorrow, since today you'll just be in training."

Bastard.

I practically run down the hall to the check-in counter, where Nathan stands leaning against it, a newspaper propped against the computer screen. My eyes dart to the desk at the business centre. Oh God, my laptop is gone.

"Hey, how'd it go?" Nathan folds the paper.

"Fine. Did you see anyone in the business center?" My voice shakes and I'm struggling not to cry. For reasons I can't explain, I don't want to lose this link to Lydia Burgess.

"No worries. I have your laptop right here."

"Oh, thank you." I exhale a huge relieving sigh as I take it from him. "You have no idea. Thank you." *I* have no idea. How can the loss of this connection to my past life upset me so much? Didn't I want to leave it all behind?

"No problem. So did you get the job?"

"I did. I start as soon as I fill this in." I wave the form. "Steffi's supposed to take me to Augusta Lewis when I'm done and then I start."

"You get along okay with Floyd?"

I hesitate. If I badmouth the boss to the wrong person

it might get back to him. I don't want to be fired. I need this job. At least until I find something better. "Sure. He's okay."

"That's a first. The guy's an asshole." Ah, youth. Spouting off about the boss when he doesn't even know me. I raise my eyebrows and he shakes his head. "Please don't tell him I said so. But we all think it. Luckily you won't be dealing with him too much. And Augusta's great. You'll like her."

"Really? I'm glad." I lower my voice. "Because I think Floyd's a bit of a jerk too."

"Yeah, he takes advantage of people, you know? Especially powerless people like illegals. And interns like me." He shrugs. "At least you don't have to worry about that, being an American citizen."

"Right." Let him believe what he wants. I'm not going to tell anybody anything until I know exactly whom to trust.

Chapter Six

I enter Room 40 and slide open the patio door to bring the outside in. Pointing my face toward the ocean, I breathe in the hot mugginess. No breeze today, but ocean air is better than the stagnant sleep smell hanging in the room.

I do this in all the units before I start cleaning. People stink. At least the stale air they leave behind does. And they can be messy and disgusting, especially in the bathrooms. Not every guest, of course, but most of them. It's as if they don't care, as if they know someone will clean up after them so they don't bother to show any respect for the space.

I find it a little insulting.

I've been almost two weeks on the job and have developed strong feelings about this. I've had to pick up dirty underwear, scrub wine spills from a sofa, peel an upside down slice of pizza off a bed sheet, and mop up day-old vomit from a bathroom floor. If I open a door to a particularly pigpen-esque scenario, my first thought is to run. Find a different job. Now.

But there are positives too. I work independently, giving me lots of time to ruminate, to try to understand the hypnotic effect the island has on me. The best part is that all the rooms in the hotel have terraces that look out over the ocean, so when I slide open the patio door, I take time to soak in the view. Every day, the sky and the water are different. Sometimes they change as I go from one room to the next. Clouds become fluffier or disappear, light changes in color and intensity, waves become more violent or tame. I store the images in my mind, for a time when I can paint them. I listen to the birds, the surf. I close my eyes and inhale the outdoors. It centers me.

And then I turn to the room. Other than the disgusting

messes I have to tackle, the work is easy. Already I feel like a pro. I'm pretty much doing what I've done at home every week for the twenty-seven years of my marriage to Dan. Of course, no one at our house, neither Dan nor Carly, ever left a mess the way some of these people do. And making twenty beds and cleaning twenty bathrooms does make it seem like one long housecleaning day every day. By four o'clock, when I get back to the camper, I'm done in. Augusta says it'll get better. That soon I'll be used to it and actually have energy left over when I finish my shift. I hope that's true, because right now I'm wondering why I ran away from my life in Toronto to this.

Before doubt takes over too strongly, I shake it from my head and gaze at the ocean. Today is sticky and hot. Opening the patio door doesn't air out the room because there's not a bit of movement out here. The ocean looks like glass. And I'm moving slow. Room 40 is the last on my roster and I'm hungry and tired. Reluctantly I turn back inside.

In each of my rooms, I play a little detective game. How many guests? Male or female? What do they do? I don't snoop in their stuff, mind you, only try to guess from what they've left about. This room is currently occupied by one man. I can tell because of the lack of paraphernalia in the bathroom. He's using the hotel toiletries, for Pete's sake. Only a man wouldn't bother to bring his own toiletries. I wonder if he's here for business? There aren't any other clues. As I make the bed, I am thankful that this particular hotel guest appears to be tidy and considerate. A shirt is neatly hung over the back of the chair, a newspaper is folded into the trash, and the towel is hung up in the bathroom. I'll get through here quickly.

However, something about this room makes my neck prickle. I can't put my finger on it. Maybe the smell? Or perhaps that navy T-shirt on the chair. It looks the same as one Dan got from the Reeboks sales rep, and that gives me the willies. I spend most of my time trying not to think about Dan. The heat must be getting to me.

I've just finished vacuuming when my brain kicks in gear. Why didn't it register before that the T-shirt could be Dan's? And the black suitcase in the corner.

Impossible. Dan couldn't be...No, Dan wouldn't be here. He'd never leave his precious store. Oh my God. Is Dan here?

My mouth dries up and I can't swallow. I scramble toward the suitcase to check the label.

A noise at the door startles me and I jump back before I get a chance to see it. My heart beats like an African drummer.

"Housekeepin'." Augusta's voice sings through the door as she taps her key card against it. Not Dan. The relief I feel is palpable and my hands start to shake from the adrenaline release.

"Come in, Augusta. It's me. No guest here." I exhale a loud breath.

The door opens and Augusta's energy fills the room. She's a mere five feet tall, with velvety dark skin, and is round and huggable, with a personality to match. I liked her from the first, when she smiled at me with her warm chocolate eyes.

"I knew y'all was here." She folds her arms across her chest. The gold cross around her neck catches the light and twinkles. "But, remember, we always hafta knock. Even when you know the room's empty."

Whenever Augusta is with me she gives me instructions, but I'm not resentful. When I think of how things could have been, with Floyd for a boss, I welcome her directives.

"Right. I'll be sure to remember."

"I came to help y'all finish. It's your last room, ain't it?"

"Oh. Thanks." I wonder why she's here. On my first day she helped me with the first few rooms, when she showed me the routine. But since then I've worked alone. "There isn't a problem with my work, is there?"

"No, no. Your work is good. But everybody's waitin'

in the kitchen. Mason got an extra catch of shrimp today and he made jambalaya for us. Girl, you ain't had nuthin' 'til you tasted Mason's jambalaya. He won't serve it 'til everybody's there."

An unexpected perk of this job is that chef Mason cooks a meal for the staff every day. He tries out new recipes on us, or uses up leftovers from the restaurant specials. We, the staff, enjoy a delicious repast, all sitting around a big table. It's been a great way to get to know my co-workers. And it's certainly helped my budget.

"Oh. I'd better hurry up and get down to the kitchen then." I take up the vacuum cord, not thinking at all about food. My stomach is clenched tighter than a fist, leaving no room for appetite. I need to check out that suitcase label. "I'm pretty well done, just gathering my stuff."

"Good. It's already quarter past three."

"I didn't realize it was so late." I finish wrapping the cord, then walk over to the patio door to slide it shut, noticing a dark cloud on the horizon. Glancing at the suitcase, I try to think of a legitimate reason to check it. I suddenly know it's Dan's but need to make sure. I mean, maybe it isn't.

Augusta picks up the wet towels I'd tossed on the floor and takes them to my cart. With her attention off me, I move toward the corner.

"All done?"

Her voice makes me jolt, and I almost trip over the vacuum. Righting myself, I wheel around. "Uh, maybe I should turn on the air conditioning?" The control is right near the suitcase.

"No, no. Save electricity. Let's go."

Pushing the vacuum to the hall, I glance back at the suitcase, staring hard, as if doing so will confirm or deny that it's Dan's. It seems to beckon to me, but I sense Augusta's impatience and reluctantly pull the door closed behind us. Queasy and apprehensive, I follow her down the hall.

In the kitchen, the staff are seated at the long table.

Our arrival is greeted with cheers. Nathan taps his glass with a fork.

"Yay, Anne's here. Now we can eat."

"Not so fast, Nathan." Mason brings over a pitcher of iced tea. "This here's a special day for Anne."

"It is?" I have no idea why it would be. Then I think of the room I just left and my stomach plunges to my shoes. Did Dan actually find me? Maybe these people think they've got a surprise for me by presenting me with my husband. My hands go clammy.

"Yes," Augusta interjects. "Y'all survived your first pay period at Live Oak. It's your first payday. Congratulations."

"Here, here." Mason pours a glass and hands it to me. "A toast to Anne."

Relief washes over me. This is not about Dan. He's probably not even on the island. I've let my imagination run wild. I raise my iced tea to nine other glasses being held in the air. To think that thirteen days ago I didn't know these people at all, and now they're a part of my everyday life. Although I admit I still don't feel quite like part of the gang and often question what I am doing here.

"Too bad it's not alcoholic," Steffi wrinkles her nose as she puts her glass down.

Mason guzzles the last of his tea. "Ahh." A belch escapes from his lips. "'Scuse me." He smiles sheepishly at me. He's been the chef here for eight years so I know he's older than he seems, but he sure seems young. I wonder if he even shaves, his chin is so smooth. His bleached hair sticks up every which way, and in his narrow face, large green eyes sparkle like emeralds. The rest of him is thin too, and he's tall, not at all roly-poly, which is what I'd expect in a chef. Putting his glass down, he claps his hands. "Okay, jambalaya."

I take my seat beside Esperanza, the other cleaner who overlaps shifts with me by a couple of hours. A dark-eyed, quiet woman, her black hair has a silver streak running from her forehead to a bun at the nape of her neck. She's attractive, but an unsightly scar mars her right cheek and runs down to her chin. People say her husband cut her, but nobody really knows because Esperanza generally keeps to herself. They say it's because she only speaks Spanish, but I think it's because she's scared of life. I put my glass down and smile at her.

"Hi, Esperanza. Do you like jambalaya?" I speak English to her anyway because I believe she understands more than she lets on.

The corners of her mouth bend up, not exactly in a smile, and she nods and busies herself with her cutlery. Augusta slips into the seat on the other side of me.

"What y'all gonna to do on your day off tomorrow?" she says as she nudges me. "Got any plans?"

"No," I say, but actually thinking I'll do some detective work, find out if Dan's really here. And if he is, decide what I'm going to do about it. "I'll sleep in, maybe go to the beach. Recover from this week."

She laughs. "Oh, you'll soon get used to it."

A plate gets placed in front of me. Mason treats us like his customers, serving us. It respects the food, he says. Us too, I think. Even Wade and Harlene, the waiter and hostess, get to "respect the food" before they start the dinner shift in the restaurant.

He touches my shoulder. "You first, Anne. Tell me what you think of it." I believe Mason has a bit of a crush on me. During these meals, he tends to lean in close, giving me tidbits to taste, blushes when I compliment his food. I'm not quite sure what, if anything, to do about that. I mean, he's probably not much older than Carly.

I look down at my plate. Plump shrimp, chunks of ham, morsels of sausage, green peppers, tomatoes, all mixed in with rice and spice. The aroma is tantalizing, making my mouth water, even though a minute ago I had no appetite. I pick up my fork and scoop a shrimp and some rice into my mouth.

"Mm," I hum as I chew. "Really good. Awesome even."

Mason beams and scurries off to get the others' plates.

For a while, no one talks as they savor their meal. As appetites get sated and plates get emptied, bits of conversation begin. Wade and Harlene, at the other end of the table, lean toward each other, deep in a tête-a-tête. Wade's dark skin and hair are such a contrast with Harlene's freckled face and ginger ponytail, they're like a poster couple. There's something going on between them, I'm sure. Steffi kids around with Mason, laughing at some joke. Nathan is seriously discussing something with Dewain, the maintenance guy, and Jolene, the desk clerk with whom he overlaps shifts. Augusta is leaning behind me, struggling, in broken Spanish, to talk to Esperanza and Manuel, who does I'm not sure what at the hotel. From around the table, I catch words and phrases here and there but have no idea what anyone is talking about. I feel a little like an uninvolved participant in some weird kind of reality show. Disassociated. As if I don't belong and am not really a part of all this. Again, I find myself wondering what I am doing here.

"Well, how is everyone?"

Instantly everything stops. Floyd Hill, standing in the doorway, flashes us a slimy smile. Our response is dead silence as we all stare at him. He normally doesn't join us for dinner and chooses to eat alone in his office after we're all done.

"I see you're enjoying your little family dinner." He checks his watch. "Five minutes until the next shift starts, people. Harlene, Wade, is everythin' ready in the restaurant?"

"Yes, Mr. Hill." Harlene scrambles out of her chair and hurries away. Wade nods and follows. Mason slides behind the kitchen counter at the other end of the room.

Augusta clears her throat as she stands and pushes her chair toward the table. "I'll go get your share of the week's tips, Mr. Hill."

"Good. How's the new girl doing, Augusta?" He directs his gaze at me. "Any problems? Has she been handing over her tips?"

"Oh, no problem, Mr. Hill. She's good worker. And yes, she gives me her tips. Be right back." As Augusta rushes out, Mason approaches bearing a tray with a covered plate on it.

"Your dinner, Mr. Hill. A pretty good jambalaya, if I do say so myself."

"Thank you Mason. Bring it to my office, will you?"

I realize Esperanza has left too, and everyone else. Why didn't I notice them disappear?

I stand. "Well, I guess I'll go now too. My shift's done."

"Where do you go when you're not here, Anne?"

I shrug. "Oh, I've got a place." No way am I letting this rat know about my camper.

"You know that we have facilities for staff here." He shows his teeth. I am hesitant to call it a smile. "At a nominal rate."

I've seen one of the staff residences. Esperanza, Dewain, and Manuel each live in one. They make my camper look luxurious.

"I know. It's okay. I'm happy where I am." I've been moving toward the door and am almost there. "Well, bye."

I feel his fingers on the flesh of my bicep before I get through. I turn and glare at him, shrugging his hand off.

His eyes widen, all innocence. "Don't take it the wrong way. I only wanted to get your attention." Something in his face makes me wary.

"Saying my name would have gotten my attention." I attempt to keep my voice even. Being alone with him makes me want to take a shower.

"Well, that's the thing. Your name."

A quiver shinnies up my spine. I say nothing.

"A man checked into the hotel today, says he's looking for his wife." He stares intently at me. "She came to the island a couple of weeks ago."

My throat gets dry. I try to keep my expression neutral. "Why are you telling me this?"

"He's from Canada, like you." He pauses. I stay silent,

although my heart thuds. "But she's an artist, a painter or something." His eyebrows arch, almost to the top of his head. "You wouldn't happen to know someone named Lydia Burgess, would you?"

Suddenly I'm free falling, my brain whirling. I can't breathe. I swallow the rock that's become lodged in my throat and try to regain my composure. I shake my head and speak as calmly as I can. "No, I...."

"Here, Mr. Hill. Here's your money." Augusta almost collides with me as she comes through the door. I move aside and she hands him a drawstring bag. He glares from her to me, then at the bag in his hand. I need to get out of here, and fast, so I attempt to sidle past Augusta. Floyd opens the bag and peers inside.

"This is all?"

"We didn't get much this week. Cheap guests, I guess." She shrugs. She only gives him a portion of what she should, having told me emphatically that we earn the tips, not him. So instead of half, she gives him a quarter of what we get and lets us keep the rest.

"Maybe you should go the extra mile, do something special for them. That might increase the gratitude." He looks from Augusta to me and then back to Augusta.

"Give us chocolates," Augusta says. "We can put them on the pillow. Like the more posh hotels."

"Our hotel is..."

I don't wait to hear the end of this conversation. Touching Augusta's arm as I pass her, I mouth, "See you Tuesday."

I need to figure out what to do about Dan.

Chapter Seven

I arrive at the camper drenched, from sweat and from rain. The sky broke open as soon as I began pedaling away from the hotel. It seems only fitting to be pelted and deluged, symbolic of what I deserve after what I've done. What I'm doing. Running away from Dan. Avoiding consequences.

I walk the bike round back to park it under the shelter of the lean-to, out of the rain. Not that it matters. It's already soaked. Inside I peel off my clothes and lather myself under a hot shower. Under the streaming water I feel a little sick. Mason's jambalaya sits heavy in my stomach.

Dan's here. What should I do?

The question hangs in the air, and as the water pounds on my head, answers ricochet around the shower stall.

Find him. Face him. Tell him what you're doing.

No, no. Figure out what you want first.

Explain it to him. It's not fair to leave him hanging.

No, he'll talk you into going back before you're ready.

Back and forth the arguments oscillate, making my head ache. As the water starts to cool, a quieter voice floats above them. I go still and listen. You haven't yet figured what you are doing here, it says. You don't really know why you've done this. You've messed everything up.

And suddenly I'm crying. No, not crying, bawling. Shuddering with sobs and shivering under the now cold water, I give in to it, releasing emotions I can't even identify. When there are no more tears left, I turn off the tap and grab my towel. I rub it all over me, trying to wipe away the goose bumps, then wrap it around me and stare in the mirror at my red blotchy face. My eyes are puffy, my expression desolate. Taking a deep breath, I can feel that quiet voice calming me.

Follow your heart, it says.

A half hour later, I'm dry in my sweats with a hot mug of tea in my hands. The rain has stopped and through my little windows I see the sky begin to color with the setting sun. I should take my paints out to Twilight Beach, to try to capture the after rain sunset. But I know I won't. I haven't painted since Tilly was here, having somehow lost the desire.

Besides, I'm afraid to go outside. What if Dan is out there? I don't want to bump into him by chance. If I face him, it has to be on my terms.

I need some kind of disguise, to change my appearance somehow so he won't recognize me. Maybe I should cut my hair. That occurred to me while I was staring at myself in the mirror, but unlike people in the movies who run away, there is no way I'd take a pair of nail scissors to my head. With my straight hair, I'd never get it looking anywhere near decent. How do the TV fugitives manage to do the back of their own hair, anyway?

Perhaps I'll ask Agnes to help me.

A rock falls to the pit of my stomach when I realize the first person Dan would have gone to here on the island is Agnes. Thank God I didn't tell her about my trailer. She doesn't know about my job. Or my new name. All she can tell him is I've got her old bike.

I get up, suddenly unable to just sit still thinking about what to do. The camper has become warm and I remove my sweatshirt. As I take my mug to the counter, there's a rap at the door. It startles me and I slosh the now tepid tea over my hand and T-shirt. Has Dan found me? I freeze, holding my breath.

Rap. Rap. Rap.

I wonder if he can see my shadow behind the door. I don't move a muscle.

"Anne? Are you there? It's Bill. Bill Alpaca."

Relief flows over me like water. I wipe my hands on my pants and open the door. Bill has an expectant look on his face.

"Hi. Come in." I wave him inside. It's his trailer, after all.

"Actually, I wondered if you'd want to come out. Take a walk with me. I know the perfect cove with a beach where we can watch the sun go down. After that rain, the sky's going to be an awesome sight tonight."

"Oh, that'd be n…" I stop. What if I bump into Dan, and I'm walking with Bill, and Dan thinks I stayed because of Bill, and—

"Come on. I won't bite." He chuckles. "Although the skeeters might."

At his mention of mosquitoes, I step out and close the door. No point inviting them inside. I inhale the freshness. There's nothing like evening air after a cleansing rainfall. The heat has broken, and while it's not exactly cool outside, it is refreshing after the muggy heaviness of this afternoon.

"I don't know." I look longingly in the direction of Twilight Beach, where the sun has just begun to pastel the sky. "I was planning to stay in tonight."

"Is that why you're here on the island? To sit in an old camper on a beautiful evening?" He cocks his head.

"No, you're right. It's just that…."

"What are you afraid of, Anne?"

I can't meet his gaze. "Nothing." I straighten my shoulders. "Let's go."

We walk without speaking for a while, batting at mosquitoes as we make our way down the path to the road. They leave us alone once we're on the pavement. It's still light, but the trees and shrubs become shadowy, lit up in the headlights of a car that passes us. The evening sounds permeate the air. A chorus of cicadas is punctuated with leftover raindrops dripping from the trees. As we turn onto the trail leading to Twilight beach, varying hues of fire fill the sky. A quilting of clouds adds interesting shades and textures.

"Look at that," I say, pointing upward while keeping pace with Bill's long strides. "It's so amazing."

"The island is famous for its sunrises over the Atlantic, but here on the mainland side we get some inspiring sunsets." He starts to climb down the dune. "Ever been to this beach before?"

I follow him down, my steps careful in the dim light so I don't stumble in the thick sand of the dunes. "Once, a couple of weeks ago with my sister. We took a zillion pictures."

He stops and stares at me. "You have a sister here?"

"No. Well, we came to the island together. For an art course. Then she went home." I shrug. "And I stayed." I walk past him onto the beach and gaze out at the crimson ball sinking in the horizon, flaming the sky, silhouetting the mainland, and lighting vibrant ripples on the water. I take a deep breath, as if to inhale the splendor. This is why I stayed.

"Mesmerizing, isn't it?" Bill comes up beside me. His voice lowers. "Anne, I don't know what's going on, but I'm around if you need someone to talk to."

I nod and keep staring at the water. "Thanks. But I'm fine."

There are other people on the beach. Lots. Standing with their faces turned to the sunset. On beach chairs. Sitting on the sand. All watching the magnificent red sphere sink behind the water. In this light they are dark shadows, their features vague. The sounds I hear are muffled. Cameras clicking, laughter, bits of conversation. Suddenly I catch Dan's voice. "Yes, she's a painter. Dark hair, chin length. About five foot five. Her name's Lydia. Do you know her?"

My heart hammers. I look around, trying to identify him in the shadows of people. I want to find where he is. Not to confront him, just to see him.

And then I do. At the opposite end of the beach. He's talking to a man sitting at an easel. Frozen to the spot, I watch my husband as he tries to find his runaway wife. I am unprepared for the sympathy I feel for him and want to run to him, call to him. Here I am, Dan.

But I don't. I begin to tremble, my throat dries up.

"Are you all right?" Bill touches my elbow.

"Let's go." My voice sounds too loud. It resonates across the sand, across the water. Maybe Dan heard me or maybe he just felt me staring at him, but suddenly he looks right at me, his eyes gripping mine. I have trouble looking away.

No. Not yet. I'm not ready. I'm trapped. My head swivels left to right.

"Lydia." He starts to run in our direction, weaving his way around the people.

I take off, laboriously on the sand. I struggle up the dune and finally I'm on the road where I sprint faster than I've ever done.

Behind me Dan shouts, "Lydia," and Bill calls "Anne?" but I ignore them. Soon I'm on the main road and turn onto a side street, far enough from the beach that I no longer hear anything.

I'm flying in the direction of my trailer when abruptly I stop. If they're following me, I don't want to lead Dan there. A thought shivers down my spine. Are he and Bill having a tête-a-tête about Dan's deranged wife? Will Bill tell Dan where I live?

Glancing over my shoulder, I see no sign of Dan. Not understanding why he hasn't caught up with me but thankful nonetheless, I turn in the direction of the hotel. Then it occurs to me that since that's where he's staying, he'll eventually end up there as well. So instead I veer toward Agnes's house, checking behind me once more before taking off.

The road goes on forever, but finally I approach Agnes's neighborhood. Gasping, my pulse galloping, I sprint onto the sidewalk and round the corner to Agnes's street. I step behind a giant eucalyptus to catch my breath and peer out from behind the trunk. Someone is approaching. My heart stops for a second. I'm almost certain of it.

It's not Dan, but Esperanza, leading what looks like a

rat on a leash. As my breathing slows to normal, I wait for her to come closer. The rat, it turns out, is a Chihuahua with its tail perked up and its little legs moving so quickly he prances like a tiny dapper show horse.

"Esperanza," I whisper loudly.

Startled, she looks around.

"Over here." I glance down the road. It's clear so I step out from behind the tree. Keyed up and tense, I try to appear normal and unflustered. "Is that your dog?"

Her mouth forms the smile she makes when she doesn't understand what a person is saying, crinkling the scar in her cheek. But then she says, "Dis is Pepe. Hotel don't know I keep heem in my room. Dats why I walk here, 'way from hotel."

He's jumping up and down, his tongue hanging out, his tail wiggling. "Well, he's cute." I crouch down and pet him, casually looking back to keep an eye out for Dan. My brain is chugging away, trying to decide whether to ask for Esperanza's help or not. Pepe licks my hand. He's splotchy with tan and white patches. Chihuahuas are not my favorite dogs, with their bulging eyes and skinny bodies. But Esperanza obviously loves little Pepe so I can pretend. I've become good at lying.

"Pepe like my baby," she says. And then she looks so sad I decide I can't bring myself to involve her in my problems.

"I get that. Pets are family members, after all." There's still no sign of Dan, thank God, but I do need to get out of sight. Casually, I start to edge away.

She nods. "Specially when jou got no udder family." She picks Pepe up and buries her face in his fur, such as it is.

I like Esperanza. And it appears her English is better than she has let on. Here I'm presented with a good opportunity to reach out, be a friend to her, but I've got Dan on my heels. Not literally since I haven't seen him since I left the beach, but I need to be off the street.

"I'm sorry Esperanza, I'd love to have you over for a

chat, but I've got to be somewhere. Maybe another time?"

"Jou live 'round here?" There's surprise in her voice. Agnes's neighborhood is affluent, certainly not where a hotel maid would live.

"Oh, no. I, um, do some work for a lady here." My oh my, the lies come so easy. "That's where I have to be now." Giving Pepe a final pat, I quickly walk away. "See you at work."

I jog toward Agnes's house, hoping Esperanza won't run into Dan. With luck, if she does, she'll pretend she doesn't understand him as she does with most strangers, so she won't give me away.

The white BMW is in Agnes's driveway, which means her boyfriend is still there. I'll have to come up with a good story to intrude on the two of them. At my knock, the door is opened by a tall man with a wave of thick silver hair and eyebrows to match.

"Can I help you, ma'am?" His voice is deep and southern.

Boldly, I step over the threshold and pull the door to shield me from the road. I peer behind him into the house. "Is Agnes in?" Although he's wearing shorts and a red T-shirt with Georgia U in black letters across the front, he radiates a style that makes me feel like a slob in my sweatpants. I tug at my T-shirt.

He shakes his head and drawls, "No, ma'am. She's at her mahjong group. Won't be back 'til after nine."

"Oh, guess that's too long to wait for her." Darn. Now what? "Well, tell her that Anne, I mean, Lydia stopped by." I put my hand on the doorknob, knowing I should go, afraid to venture outside.

"Say, aren't you the gal whose husband was asking Agnes about? He thought you were staying here with Agnes."

"Uh, yes. Yes I am." I clear my throat. I'm getting antsy, not sure what to do now.

"Agnes couldn't say where you were. Said she hadn't seen you in a couple a weeks, not since you took her bike.

Did he ever find you?"

"He did, yes." I nod vigorously.

"Well, good. Can't have a man without his woman, now, can we?" He winks and then reaches for the door. "Can I give Agnes a message for you?"

"Oh. I, uh, I owe her some money. For that bike."

"I can give it to her." He smiles and the corners of his blue eyes crinkle. "If you feel inclined to give it to me."

"That's okay. I'll come back when she's home. I need to talk to her anyway."

He shrugs. "All righty. Try tomorrow after one. She'll be home and I'll be on the golf course then." He opens the door and I peer around him. There's no one on the street.

"Okay. Bye."

He puts out his hand. "Nice to meet you, Miss Lydia. Hope we run into each other again."

"Nice to meet you too, um..." I shake. His grip is strong. "I'm sorry, what's your name?"

"Rhett."

He's kidding, right? "You mean as in Butler?"

His laugh is like deep, dark chocolate. I can see why Agnes is attracted to him. "No, as in Sandusky. Rhett Sandusky." He shrugs. "And ma'am, I assure you, I was barely a suckling pup when Miss Mitchell gave a voice to that rascal Butler."

****

It has gotten dark, and the Live Oaks in Bill's yard look like shadowy sentries standing guard. A light shines through the living room window. I hope Dan isn't in there, having a drink or some such thing with Bill. I'm here because I need to find out what Bill told Dan and if it is safe to go back to my trailer. I've been wandering around, not daring to go home.

I peer in the window, hoping his neighbors don't call the police about a peeping tom. Bill's lying on the couch. His hair is no longer in a ponytail, and with it loose around his face he looks different. Younger, somehow, more worldly, kind of sexy in a Viggo Mortensen kind of way.

He's aiming the remote at the TV, and the screen flashes one channel after another. It appears even old hippies channel surf.

I don't see Dan.

Bill takes his time answering the doorbell. When he sees that it's me at the door he steps aside, holding it open.

"Come on in."

I feel like a child who is about to get in trouble with her parents. "I have some explaining to do. Don't I?"

"Only if you want to."

"I think I do." Anxiety percolates through my veins as I perch myself on one of the chairs. I run my fingers around the carved lines of the armrests. This gives me comfort somehow.

Bill lowers himself on the couch. Police sirens blare from the television. He picks up the remote and turns it off. "Want a beer or something?"

"No, thanks." I shake my head, impatient to know what I came here to find out. "Can you tell me what happened at the beach when I ran away?"

He gazes at me. After a moment he says, "When you took off, I managed to stop the guy that was chasing you. Dan, isn't it?" At my nod, he continues. "I had no idea what was going on so I wanted to give you time to get away." Again that stare, as if his blue eyes are infiltrating my hidden truths. He guides a strand of hair behind his ear. "We all have our reasons for doing what we do. It's not for me to judge."

I give him a thin smile. "I appreciate that." In my mind, I try to picture the two men on the beach. Bill challenging, Dan politely trying to get away to find me. "How was he?"

"That's hard for me to answer." He frowns. "Kind of confused, I guess, uncertain as to what was going on. Obviously I don't have all the facts, but he seems like an okay guy."

Oh God, he's going to take Dan's side in this. "He is, I guess. But Dan's not the reason I'm here." I exhale. "You told him about the trailer, didn't you."

"Anne." He looks at me pointedly. "Or I should I say, Lydia. I've told you I'm your friend, that I would help you if you needed it." He clears his throat. "I didn't tell Dan anything. I pretended I'd only just met you."

I suddenly feel much lighter. "Really? So he doesn't know where I live?"

"Nope."

"Thank you." I am almost giddy, and then I sober. "Now I've got you lying too."

"Would you like to tell me what's going on?"

How do I start? What kind of explanation do I really owe this man? Although I had earlier said that I wanted to explain, I realize now it isn't true. I simply came here to find out if it was safe to go home to my trailer. And at this moment, I just want to be there. Yet I at least owe Bill something, since he helped me at the beach. "The thing is, I'm not exactly sure myself."

He studies me but says nothing.

"Well, I was here with Tilly. That's my sister. This island is so amazing, it bewitched me. The giant Live Oaks, the Spanish moss, the beach. It somehow feeds my soul, makes me feel like me. Allows me to be me. To breathe. I couldn't stomach the thought of going back to Toronto with her, to the store, to my house. To my ordinary life." My voice goes quiet. "To Dan." I shrug. "I wanted something different, a new life, one that was about just me. One that this island offered me. So I stayed. It was as if Hyde Island made me stay." I realize that sounds a little crazy. "Not against my will, mind you. I'm a willing participant."

He frowns. "So you didn't run away from him because he abused you?"

Horrified, I shake my head wildly. "Oh, no, Dan isn't like that."

"He didn't give that impression, but what do I know." Bill clears his throat. "Why did you run away, then? Why not talk to him?"

I stare at the floor, at the weave of the jute rug, its strands running over and under, entwining and interlocking together. Memories crowd my head, from the time Dan and I met, of the big mistake we found ourselves caught in, and the resulting mesh of unhappiness through which I've woven the rest of my life.

I block those images, stem the flow of those recollections, not wanting to face any of it now. I can't look at Bill.

"The island," I say quietly. "That's why."

"Believe me, I understand about the seductive qualities of this place. But how could..." He heaves a big sigh. "Look, I've said before it's not for me to judge, but your husband doesn't get that about the island. He's come all this way looking for you and..." He shrugs. "It would be a shame if he went home without answers."

"You're right." I finger the armrests, reluctant now to leave. "I know the way I've handled things is unfair. I know I should talk to him. But I'm afraid that if I do, he'll convince me to abandon this." I wave my arms toward the window.

Bill raises his eyebrows. They arch above his glasses frame. "You found the courage once to stay here."

It's true, I did.

The room is silent. Bill sits calmly, watching me. He's so self-possessed that the air surrounding him seems to transmit serenity. Is that what is meant by one's aura? Willing some of that quietude to quash my agitation, I ponder what Bill said. Was it courage that enabled me to stay here? Or cowardice?

I nod, suddenly coming to a decision. "Okay, I'll go talk to him. Now. Before I change my mind." Resolutely I stand, quelling my apprehension. "Could you do me a favor, though?"

"Depends on what."

"Call me Anne?" I flash a small smile. "It's my island name."

He chuckles. "Sure, Anne." He opens the door. "He's

at the Live Oak Inn. Room 40."

"I know." At the threshold I turn to him. "Thanks, Bill, for being my friend."

He touches my shoulder. "No prob, Anne."

I step into the humid darkness, nerves clutching at my gut, and trudge in the direction of the hotel.

Chapter Eight

I couldn't do it.

When I left Bill's house, I had every intention of showing up at Dan's door to explain my behavior, to tell him why I couldn't go back with him. Maybe ask forgiveness, although that I wasn't so sure about.

I did go to the hotel, but instead of knocking on the door of room 40, I snuck around the back to spy a bit first, to try to look into Dan's room through the patio doors and see him at a distance before confronting him. I followed the path toward the sound of the surf, and when I turned the corner of the building, there he was, standing on his patio with his hands in his pockets. The glow from his room lit his silhouette.

I stopped mid-stride, crept slowly back and hid behind a cluster of palmettos, where I watched him staring at the moon reflected on the water. He looked so forlorn I almost weakened and went right to him, but I held back, trying to think of what I would say. I began playing the scenario through in my head, and all I could hear were recriminations from Dan, anger and entreaties, and I didn't know how to respond to it all. In the end I just wasn't ready to face him. So I turned around and left.

Call me heartless. Call me a coward. Call me cruel and callous. I did, all that and more, for the rest of the night as I slept fitfully on the thin foam mattress in my stuffy camper. Finally I got up, even though it was still dark. I paced a lot, drank three cups of coffee, and all the while my conscience wrangled with itself.

Eventually, of course, the sun came up. I took a shower, got dressed, had breakfast, and waited.

Now, finally, it's time to go to work. I jump on my bike and take off, but am so jittery that my cycling is unsteady, and I almost tumble a couple of times. Sweaty and out of breath, I make it to the hotel unscathed. I walk the bike to the staff parking area, looking all around in case Dan's out here.

Things are quiet in the service part of the hotel, other than the sounds coming from the laundry room. Usually when I arrive, Augusta is working at the supply cupboard, inventorying our carts, making sure we're in on time. Today no one is here. And the carts are already stocked, my unadorned one and Esperanza's with the keychain hanging from the handle. The keychain has a little frame in the shape of a heart containing a tiny photo of two adorable little boys, one grinning with a gap where his two front teeth should be. Those two boys have piqued my curiosity since I first noticed that picture, but Esperanza has been so reserved I've never found the nerve to ask her about them. I can only imagine how she feels about being here on Hyde Island while they're not, considering she keeps their images close while she works. I don't even entertain the idea her situation might in any way parallel mine.

I punch in my time card and see I'm ten minutes early. An unexplained prickle creeps along the back of my neck. Where's Augusta? With inexplicably shaky fingers I stick the card back in its slot. The locker room door opens.

"Anne." Without warning my arm is grabbed and I'm pulled into the locker room.

I struggle to regain my balance. "What the?"

"Shh." Esperanza holds her finger to her lips and shuts the door. "Wad jou doing here?"

"I'm coming to work. Why else would I be here?" My head swivels around. "What's going on?"

"But ees jour day off."

"My...." Oh my God, I don't have to work today. I slap my forehead and groan. "I can't believe I forgot."

"Jou should go. Dere's a man here, I teenk he's jour—"

The door suddenly opens and Augusta rushes in. "Esperanza, he's in room 40 and," she blurts out and then stops abruptly. "Anne, what are you doin' here?"

I smile sheepishly. "I kind of forgot it was my day off."

"You have to hide. Your husband is here." She turns the lock on the locker room door and lowers her voice. "He's been askin' all round, described y'all perfectly. He said your name's Lydia Burgess."

I plunk down on the bench. Of course Dan would have asked around the hotel. He was practically doing a survey at the beach.

Esperanza's eyes darken. "He ees jour hosbun', si?"

I nod. "Yes, he's my husband, but—"

Augusta clasps me in an embrace, then quickly lets go. "We are so glad he didn't find you."

Esperanza clutches my arm. "We no let heem hurt jou, Anne. I *comprendo*. I had bad hosbun' too." Her hand touches the scar on her cheek. "We *te protegeremos*...how you say...protec' jou."

I exhale loudly. "My husband isn't bad, Esperanza. He doesn't hurt me."

Puzzled furrows cross her brow. "Den, why jou run away?"

Why indeed. I gaze at this woman who has been through God knows what in her marriage, who would look at the life I left and grab it as fast as she could. I don't know how to answer her.

"Yes, why're you workin' here?" Augusta's tone is also confused. "Why get a new name? Why's he lookin' for you?"

"It's complicated." Suddenly there is a jostling of the doorknob. The three of us go still and stare at it. The door rattles as it is pounded upon.

"Hey, y'all, let me in."

Augusta blows out in relief. "It's only Pearl." She opens the door and in bursts a large woman wearing a maid uniform, panting as if she'd been running.

"Lawd, Augusta, why you lock the door on me? Is'at what y'all do when we's late now?" She yanks open a locker and pulls out a pair of white leather shoes. Plunking herself down on the bench she unbuckles one of her sandals.

"Sorry, Pearl. This is Anne." Augusta pulls me over to the woman. "Anne, this is Pearl."

"Hello." I stretch my hand out.

She looks up at me with wide eyes and clasps my fingers in her large dark hands. "Welcome, Miss Anne. You mus' be the new cleaner takin' Rosita's place. Thank the Lord you came, 'cause I shore don't wanna work more 'n three days a week."

Augusta touches my shoulder. "Pearl works here when you and Esperanza are off."

"That's right." Pearl finishes tying her shoes and casts her eyes around the room. "Why y'all here? Ain't I s'posed to be relievin' one a you?"

I shrug. "I, um, forgot and came in today."

"Anne ran away from her husband." Augusta says, and then tells Pearl about the man staying at the hotel who's been asking about me, calling me a different name. "I saw him." Augusta turns to me. "Your husband. I knocked on his door just now. You cleaned his room yesterday. He says he's checkin' out tomorrow mornin' when he flies back to Canada. Then you'll be safe." She smiles.

"Jou from Canada?" Esperanza asks in a surprised tone.

"Yes. From Toronto. We...he lives there. I came here on holiday and...and I stayed. I was..." My gaze shifts from Esperanza to Augusta to Pearl. I can't tell them my absurd belief that the island bewitched me. "I was unhappy and I wanted a new life." I stare at the floor.

"Workin' here?" Disbelief peppers Pearl's voice.

Esperanza touches my shoulder. "No matter why. She one of us now. We help her."

"Esperanza is right." Augusta turns toward me. "You don't want him to find you, right?"

"No, I don't. I—"

"Then we gotta hide you. 'Til tomorrow, 'til he goes."

A discussion ensues, in which I have little part, about the best way for me to stay out of Dan's way. I think about stopping them, telling them I can deal with it myself, that Dan's not a threat and that a part of me actually thinks I should talk to him. But sitting on the bench in this locker room, I am enclosed in a circle of caring that nourishes me. I don't want to break it open just yet. And really, I don't want Dan to find me. So I allow myself to be swept up in this tide of helpfulness and ride the current.

The three women concur that hiding from Dan would be more successful if I change my appearance. Having had a similar thought yesterday, I agree. Pearl suggests that since her sister is a hairdresser, we could take care of that right away. Augusta nods. Esperanza nods. I find myself nodding too.

Then I protest. "Wait. What kind of hairdresser is Ruby? I don't want just anyone..." I touch my hair.

"She's really good," Pearl interrupts. "Does most ever'one in my church. Does mine too." She pats her head.

I scrutinize her hair. Despite her natural tight curls and the fact that my hair would never do what hers does, the cut is even and stylish. I lift a few of my straight, silky locks. "But would she be able to work with my type of hair? And how much does she charge? I don't have any money here with me."

"Course she can do your hair. She's a wizard, girl. And don't worry 'bout the money. We'll work it out."

I think for a moment but cannot come up with a reason not to do this. I shrug. "What the heck. Okay."

Pearl calls her sister on her cell phone. "Ruby? You got anybody in the chair this mornin'?"

Esperanza pats my hand. Augusta stands with her arms folded across her chest. We listen as Pearl explains my situation and wait quietly while she listens to her sister's response.

"Thanks, girl. We be right there." She smiles widely, her teeth shining like a string of pearls in her beautiful dark face. I am struck by the appropriateness of her name. "Ruby can take you right now. She ain't got a customer 'til noon today." Abruptly her smile disappears and her hands slap her cheeks. "Lawd, Augusta, what about my rooms? If I take her to Ruby's, I'm gonna get behind, and I don't wanna stay later than three. I don't want no trouble from that Floyd."

Augusta picks up her clipboard and flips a page. "I'll start your roster, Pearl. But come back real fast."

I feel like a fugitive, sneaking out to Pearl's car while looking over my shoulder, and then hunkering down in the seat as we drive off the hotel property. Pearl keeps up a running conversation, about how men are no good, how we women need to stick together to empower ourselves. I don't know why she's going on like this, since I had told her it isn't Dan's fault that I'm here. I contribute little to the conversation, which is really just a tirade, but she doesn't seem to notice my silence.

It is beyond belief that I am in this car with a woman I've just met, heading off to get my hair cut by another woman whom I've never laid eyes on. How did I allow myself to be talked into this? I should be in my camper, figuring out how to deal with Dan and trying to bolster the courage to face him. Not allowing some stranger to enable me to stay hidden. Not letting others take charge of my situation.

Yet it's easier to do this, to let someone else take over for a bit and guide me along. Besides, getting a new look for Anne Cooper appeals to me, Dan or no Dan.

We drive to a part of the island I haven't been before. The street is lined with small wooden cottages painted a variety of colors. Dwarfing them is a forest of enormous Live Oaks, Spanish moss hanging from their branches like laundry. The yellows, blues and greens of the houses diffuse the gloominess of the muted sunlight, and the neighborhood exudes a cheerful atmosphere despite the spooky giants.

When we pull up the driveway of a green house with white shutters, the door is flung open and a clone of Pearl bursts out of the house. She throws her arms around Pearl, who, after extricating herself, introduces me.

"You take good care of her," Pearl says through the car window as she drives off.

I stare at the house, wondering what I'm doing here. "Ruby, this is your house? I thought we were going to your shop."

"This is my shop, honey. I got a corner of my kitchen set up jes' like a beauty parlor."

Sure enough, past the kitchen counter and behind a bright blue screen painted with daisies is a small, one-person hairdressing salon.

"Sit yourself down, sugar, and we'll figure out what to do." She runs her fingers through my hair as I stare into the mirror at my anxious expression. Shifting my gaze, I look into Ruby's confident eyes. She could be Pearl's twin.

"Twins?" She smiles a pearly smile when I ask. "Lawd, I'm a good six years older'n Pearl. And we got another sister between us, and a brother. We all look the same, 'ceptin' our brother, Garnet. He's tall and skinny, not endowed like us girls." She laughs then, a sparkly, joyful chuckle. "My mama called us her precious jewels, so that's how she named us. First me, then Opal, Garnet and Pearl. Don't know what she'd a done with another boy. Garnet ain't too bad a name, but there ain't many other gemstones sound like a man." She then proceeds to snip away at my hair, causing large chunks to fall to the floor and apprehension to fall into my lap.

Two and a half hours later I sit mesmerized by the face gazing back at me from the mirror, unable to recognize myself. And if I don't, then Dan sure as heck won't either. I reach up and touch the short blond points, amazed that my smooth brown bob has become this streaky, spiky hair.

"I think it suits ya, honey." Ruby rips open the Velcro on the protective cape I'm wearing and shakes it out. "Makes you look tough and soft at the same time."

"I like it." I stand up. "It's unlike anything I've ever tried before." I shake my head, enjoying the sensation of lightness. I glance at myself again, noticing that my eyes seem larger. It occurs to me that this hairstyle is similar to

Agnes's but despite that, it makes me look younger. "The new me," I say. "Anne Cooper."

Ruby's smile is reflected in the mirror. "Your husband ain't gonna know you from anybody else on the street, but he might take a second look 'cause you're so beautiful."

****

It's almost one by the time I get back to the trailer. I found my way with the help of a map Ruby drew for me, but it was a long walk, and more than once I thought longingly of my bike sitting parked at the hotel. At first I tried to keep my mind blank, not wanting to think too much about Dan. I was mindful of the trees, the birds, the sky, but Dan crept into my thoughts regardless.

Why did he come here? Why couldn't he just leave me alone to work things out? Does he hope to persuade me to change my mind? Drag me back against my will? I wrote him that letter, making it clear I was finished with my life in Toronto. Surely he should have understood from my words that I wanted to be left alone. Perhaps I was too subtle. Perhaps he is too obtuse to understand the words *I'm not coming back*.

As far as I'm concerned, Lydia Burgess is gone, replaced by Anne Cooper. With a new look, thanks to Ruby. If I can hide out in my camper until tomorrow, Dan will be gone. I won't have to confront him, or deal with any of his arguments against my choices.

Arriving home exhausted, sweaty, and hungry, I chug down two glasses of water and forage in the fridge for food. I end up making a cheese and lettuce sandwich, but when I take a bite, it feels like sand in my mouth and I can't finish it. How can one be hungry yet have no appetite? I plunk down on the couch.

Despite all my rationalizations, I know it's time to face the consequences of what I've done. Dan is here. Having come all this way, he deserves to see me and to talk to me. To be fair to the man, he has done nothing wrong, and I shouldn't be punishing him like this. If Carly were behaving this way, I would be chastising her and forcing her to accept responsibility for her actions. Why should I expect anything different from myself?

But if I stay in my camper until tomorrow, he'll be gone, back to Canada. I wouldn't have to face him yet. I'd have time to figure all of this out. I squeeze my eyes shut, willing away those thoughts. Man up, Lydia.

Anne, I mean.

I stand up and pull out cloths and the bottle of Fantastik and get to work, rubbing and polishing until there isn't an inch left that hasn't been cleaned. The fridge gets wiped out, the little oven scrubbed, the burners on the tiny stove scoured. I work the dirt out of the bathroom grout with a toothbrush. I organize my paint box, arranging the jars and tubes in sequence of the spectrum and the brushes according to length. Opening the storage bench, I stop still for a minute at the sight of my cell phone and laptop. But I shake it off and arrange everything in the space, books, power cords, papers. When I'm finally spent, when I can find nothing more to clean in this compact home, the light coming through the window is dusky, almost dark. The sun has set. I marvel that cleaning this tiny camper has occupied so much of my time.

Gazing out the window, a shadowy image of my face stares back at me, trees and dunes and grasses superimposed, their images distorting my features in the reddish purply sky. It's as if I have become one with the island.

How crazy is that? I shake my head and turn away.

I know I cannot avoid it any longer. No matter how clean I've made my surroundings, my psyche remains sullied. I must go talk to Dan.

Slowly I head for the shower. Stinky and damp, I want to refresh myself before facing my foibles. "You're going to talk to Dan. You're going to talk to Dan." I repeat it over and over so my resolve doesn't weaken.

In the bathroom, I am momentarily unnerved by my reflection, which is much clearer and more defined than in the window. The blond spikes are so strange, so not me.

But then I realize they are me, the me I've become. And I do like the haircut. Even though its purpose is moot once Dan sees me, I'm glad I did it.

After my shower, I gel it the way Ruby showed me, and it looks cute. I put on a skirt, the only one I brought to the island, and mascara. Anything to help bolster my confidence.

Stepping out of the trailer, I try to quash the flutters in my stomach by taking a few deep breaths. Then I hear Pearl's voice in my mind and I falter for a second. *How can you do this?* she demands. *After we've turned you into a new person he won't recognize. Don't go.*

But my inner voice is stronger than that of my newfound friend, and I lock the door and walk into the night.

Chapter Nine

I stare at the number 40. When I was outside this door yesterday, I was here to clean the room. This time I'm here to clear my conscience. My hand shakes as I reach up to knock and I touch my hair instead. It feels jagged and stiff with the dried gel. I take a deep breath to calm my jitters. *Just do it.*

I tap lightly. "Dan?" I clear my throat. "Are you there? It's me, Lydia." My real name glides off my tongue with ease, as if I haven't been answering to Anne for the past couple of weeks. This scares me. What if, when I speak with Dan, I just slide back into the old me and lose Anne Cooper and Hyde Island?

The door is yanked open. "Lydia. Thank God." His eyes widen as he takes in the new me. "Whoa, what happened to your hair?"

Instinctively, my hand reaches up and I quickly lower it and shrug.

"It doesn't matter. Thank God you're here." He comes forward to hug me but I step away. He frowns and pulls back. "What the heck is going on with you?"

"I came here to explain. Not to go home to you." I lower my gaze from his scrutiny, hating what I'm here to do. Squaring my shoulders, I look beyond him to the room. On the table sits a bottle of Scotch and a half-filled glass. A baseball game is playing on the television. Good God, it's like I've stepped right back into Lydia Burgess' life. Involuntarily I shudder and direct my eyes to the patio doors at the end of his room. "Can I come in?"

He says nothing as he goes inside and turns off the TV. He picks up the glass and takes a long drink, grimacing as he puts the emptied glass back on the table. "Want some Scotch?"

Why would he offer me Scotch? He knows I can't stand the taste of it. I shake my head no. Closing the door, I lean my back against it and keep my hand on the doorknob behind me. The familiarity of him engulfs me, his dark hair graying at the sides, his bushy eyebrows shadowing rimless glasses, his lean physique with just the hint of a belly.

"Dan, I'm sorry about all this. I didn't mean to hurt you."

"Really?" His stare radiates anger. "How could this not hurt me, Lydia? You're my wife and I want you home. I don't understand why you're doing this."

I clench the doorknob, tempted to turn it to open the door and run from here. "I explained it in my note."

He pulls a folded paper out of his pocket and holds it up. "This didn't explain anything." Tossing it on the table, he takes a step toward me but then stops. "You wanted to come inside. Come in then. Sit."

Reluctantly, I leave the security of the doorknob and stand by the chair on the opposite side of the table from him. Then I decide I'd rather not be so close and move to the far corner of the bed, perching myself on its edge.

Dan shakes his head. He picks up the bottle and pours his glass full almost to the brim. Half sitting on the edge of the table, he brings the tumbler to his lips, keeping his eyes on me. Memories crowd my head, of all those empty evenings at home. Not that he's an alcoholic, but more than occasionally, after a long day at the store, he'd plunk himself in front of the TV with a bottle of Scotch and turn on a hockey or football game or whatever happened to be on TSN. One drink would follow another until he'd end up snoring in his La-Z-Boy. Now, here, I'm worried he's going to get buzzed before I say my piece.

Whatever that may be.

"Please don't get drunk right now, Dan."

"I can do whatever I want. You don't have the right to tell me anything anymore." Defiantly, he takes another sip.

I'm having trouble reading him. I expected hurt, even

anger. Not this churlishness. "You're right. I don't, but we can either talk or I'll leave and you can get drunk. Your choice." I stand.

"Shit." The word comes out as a loud sigh. He puts the glass down and folds his arms across his chest. "Why don't you tell me what's going on with you? I mean, this all came out of nowhere. One day we're discussing whether to add to our inventory of Team Canada shirts, and the next you're here on this island and I've lost my wife." His eyes glisten. "What happened? What did I do to make you hate me that much?" He takes off his glasses and pinches his nose. My heart is tugged, but I won't let myself weaken.

"I don't hate you, Dan. I just…" Shaking my head, I sit back down on the bed. "This isn't about you or our marriage." I stop and try to find words that will make him understand. "It's hard to explain."

"Well, you owe me an explanation. Twenty-seven years we've been married, Lydia. Twenty-seven years. How can you just throw it away like that? How can this not be about our marriage?"

"I don't…" Damn. Tears are pricking my eyes. I blink them back.

"Is this some kind of menopausal midlife crisis thing? Maybe you should take hormones."

I stare at him, mouth agape. Surely he remembers I finished menopause early, about three years ago. "Can you just let me say what I came to say without interrupting? Please?"

"Fine. Go for it. I've got nothing else to do here but listen."

"Okay." I take a deep breath. What did I come here to say? How do I explain something I barely comprehend myself? "When I was here with Tilly—"

"Yeah, Tilly doesn't get this either. Do you have any idea how upset she is? It was so damn selfish of you to force her to be your messenger."

I flinch. "Please, Dan, just let me talk."

"Whatever. You're calling the shots here."

"Right." I get up and walk to the patio doors. It's so dark outside I can't see the beach or the water. Instead, the room and Dan are reflected in the glass. I close my eyes and remember how the ocean looked through these doors yesterday, remember why I stayed. "While we were here for the painting week, Tilly and I both fell in love with this place. But for me it was different. The island got a hold on me, Dan. I've never experienced anything like that before, not when we were in Mexico or Vancouver Island. This place expanded me, made me feel light. As if anything is possible. I had to stay because I felt it wasn't finished with me." I turn to face him. "I couldn't go home."

"Oh, please. Give me a break. Are you telling me this island has special powers? Like on that TV show *Lost*? What do you take me for? Do you think I'm stupid?" He stands right in front of me. His chestnut eyes grab mine. I can't look away. "Are you telling me you'd throw our marriage away because Hyde Island isn't finished with you? What the fuck does that mean?"

His profanity slaps me in the face. I back up, trying to regain my composure. The glass from the patio doors feels cool on my back. "I know it sounds stupid. I don't understand it myself." I return to my perch on the bed. "All I know is that I need more time here."

"Okay, so you need more time here. Why didn't just tell me that instead of disappearing? I don't know where you're staying, how to reach you. You don't answer my phone calls or emails. You've pretty much deserted me."

"I'm still trying to figure out what I'm doing. I was afraid if I talked to you…" I swallow. "I was afraid you'd talk me out of it."

"You're damn right I would've talked you out of it. I'm your husband."

I lower my head.

"So what am I supposed to do while the island—" He makes air quotes with his fingers. "—finishes with you?"

"Just go back home. Live your life." It sounds feeble even to my ears.

"I thought my life was with you."

I don't answer. He stays silent for a moment. Then he lowers himself beside me on the bed and asks, "What is it you want, Lydia? A separation? Divorce?"

What I don't want is to answer that. Because I know if I do, then there's no going back. Despite the fact that I'm committed to the choice I've made, the scattered doubts I've had this past week are enough for me to not close any doors. Not yet, anyway. "Dan, can you please find it in your heart to just go along with this? For now?"

"What the hell do you mean, for now? Are you planning to come back? How long do you expect me to wait?"

I shrug.

"Look, you can't play with me like this. I can't go along with something I don't want. With something open ended at your whim. Surely you get that. Besides, I love you." His voice cracks and he clears his throat. "I want to be married to you, live with you, run the store with you." He takes my hand. "You're my best friend."

His words bewilder me. We've been so distant with each other over the past several years that I didn't know he'd felt this way. I pull my hand away. "Dan, if that's true, why do I feel so lonely?"

"What?"

"You act like we're roommates, barely acknowledging me when we're together. You never hear me when I try to talk about us. You spend so much time at the store, it's like you live there. And when you're home, you're staring at the TV or falling asleep in front of it. We don't share anything. I don't feel like we're best friends anymore. Maybe we never were."

"That's what this is about?" His eyebrows arch, creasing his forehead.

A squiggle of doubt worms its way into my thoughts, but I blurt out, "No." I furrow my brows. "It's about discovering myself on this island. I want to focus on me for a change, live a different life now."

"A different life? What the f…" He shakes his head, closing his eyes. "You mean without me." He spits out the words. "What do you have here that's better?"

I consider my crummy job at the hotel, my stifling trailer and Agnes' rusty bike, and bite the inside of my cheek.

He reaches over and lays his hand on my thigh. His touch unsettles me. I want to brush him away, but am momentarily rendered immobile from the warmth of his contact. In a calmer voice, he says, "I didn't know you were unhappy. But I flew all the way out here to find you. Doesn't that prove I care?"

I gaze down at his hand on my leg, thinking about how much I wish he hadn't come. I've been telling him about my unhappiness for years. Why is he only hearing me now, when I've found a different way to be? A sigh escapes from deep inside me.

"Lyd, I still want us to be married. I love you, and I want you back. Come home with me and I'll change. I'll listen to you, spend more time with you." He gently squeezes my leg, the way he used to do when we were younger and driving somewhere. He'd have one hand on the wheel; the other would reach over and make my leg tingle. It propels me out of my paralysis.

I push his hand away and my thigh suddenly feels cold. Raising my eyes to his face, I see how hard he's trying to hide his anger and plead his case. "I know you're sincere, Dan, and I know you'd try. But I'm not here because I'm leaving you. I'm here because I'm here. That's what you're not getting."

"Whatever reason you say, you'd still be leaving me." Standing, he reaches out. "Just come home."

I shake my head. "I can't."

His stare chills me and I cross my arms.

His eyes slide away first. "Well, if you don't want what I want, I can't make you. I don't want to make you." Returning to the table, he turns his back to me and picks up his drink, taking a gulp. Neither of us says anything. His shoulders are hunched. From behind, with his thinning hair, he reminds me of his dad, who always seemed to have more interest in me than Dan ever did. He would ask about the books I'd read and we'd talk about art or gardening. He was kind, attentive, engaged. Dan is not at all like him, no matter how much he looks like him.

There is no easy way to end this conversation, so I get up and slink toward the door.

"I have to say this, Lydia, because I don't want to be made a fool of."

I stop mid-stride and face him. "Okay."

"If you don't come home with me now." He takes a deep breath, exhaling loudly. "I don't think I want you to come back at all."

Something inside of me breaks and I almost topple over. Dan is at my side in an instant with his arm around my shoulders, steadying me. He hugs me tight and kisses my head. "Lydia, please come home with me. I'll forgive you. We'll work it out."

"No." I push him away. "Dan." Tears gather in my eyes and I let them trickle down my cheeks. "I don't understand what is happening to me. But I want to keep on with what I'm doing right now. I need to." I wipe at my face. "I may not come back, but don't give up on me yet. Just in case? Please?"

He blinks several times. "I can't do that. You have to choose. This." He sweeps his arm around the room. "Or me."

I stare at him. I'm in the middle of a bridge, like the one that connects Hyde Island to Brenville. If I go one way I'll cross over, back to Dan, back to the store, back to being Lydia Burgess. Turn the other way and I'm safe on Hyde Island. Anne Cooper, hotel maid. I know which way most women would go, which way I should go.

"Goodbye, Dan," I manage to choke out. Before he can say anything else, I hasten out of the room, running down the hall and outside, not looking back. In the bushes I bend over, leaning my hands on my knees, and retch, purging my system of the contempt I'm feeling for myself.

"Lydia." Dan's irate voice jumps into the night.

"Please go away. Leave me alone." I straighten but do not turn. Trying to regain my equilibrium, I gulp in air. "Just go home."

"I have letters to give you."

I whip around. "I don't want any letters."

He's holding out envelopes, glaring white in the moonlight. "Fuck what you want or don't want. You have a daughter and a sister. You have obligations, the least of which is to read what they have to say. They have a right to be heard."

"You told Carly?"

"Of course I told Carly. You told Carly. You wrote her a note, remember?" He shakes his head, his expression one of disgust. "You have no idea what it's been like since Tilly came home. Do you even care?"

I want to answer no, that I don't care, but I can't. Because I love Carly and I love Tilly. And while I still believe in my reckless move to start a new life without them, this past week my commitment to it has weakened. I'm starting to miss them.

Dan pushes the letters at me. "Here."

Afraid for what will happen to me, to Anne, if I take them, I put my hands behind my back. "I don't want them. Tell them I'm sorry."

Exasperation explodes out of him. "Lydia." He purses his lips and stares at me. "I don't know you anymore," he says in a low voice and spins around. As he passes the bench on the other side of the path, he places the letters on its seat. "You'll regret it, you know, throwing us away like this." At the hotel door, he slams his fist, pushing it open. "And answer your damn cell phone."

I stay where I am, staring at the envelopes. They seem to pulsate. I am drawn to them and find myself picking them up. There are three. Nothing is written on the outside. All of them are sealed. I clutch them tightly as I head back to the trailer.

Chapter Ten

In the morning I am up and wide awake at five o'clock. I hardly slept a wink and am exhausted. The foam mattress seemed particularly thin and hard in the night. My back aches. My head throbs. My heart hurts.

I can't stop thinking about Dan, about him leaving the island today. Maybe he's gone already. I keep seeing the anger and hurt in his eyes. The letters, which I'd put on the counter, draw my gaze constantly, as if they're calling me. I wonder whom the third one is from, since Dan only mentioned Carly and Tilly.

I pour my second cup of coffee and start cutting up a grapefruit. My appetite is non-existent, but I know I need to eat if I'm to get through today. I'm glad I have work to go to. Cleaning toilets and making beds will keep my mind off the devastation I've left in the wake of my impulsive decision. Off all the guilt and shame in my heart.

A sharp pain slices through my thumb, causing me to jerk it back. I stick it in my mouth and then inspect it. A crimson line runs just above the joint. For a moment, the blood oozing out mesmerizes me. I carefully run the serrated edge of the knife alongside the cut. The acidic juice on the blade soaks into the gash and the stinging brings tears to my eyes. The pain feels good. And deserved.

When the blood starts dripping onto the cutting board and into the grapefruit I pull myself together, hold my thumb under water, and clean up the mess. I try to wash away my remorse with a shower, turning the water so hot it reddens my skin.

Dressed in a clean T-shirt and capris, with a dry Band-aid on my thumb, I feel better. Having ditched the bloody grapefruit, I fry myself an egg and eat it, all the while staring at the white envelopes on the counter.

What am I afraid of? If I managed to not capitulate to Dan in person, why would I expect a letter to weaken my resolve? I pick up the one on top and, before I change my mind, rip it open. The page is typed.

Dear Lydia, If you get this letter it means I haven't found you.

I run my eyes down to the signature. *Dan.* Of course. I don't want to read anymore. I heard enough words from him at the hotel. Crumpling the paper in my hand, I toss it on the floor and barely see where it lands before reaching for the next envelope.

Dear Lydia,

Tilly's handwriting accuses me.

I hope that by the time Dan gives you this letter you'll have come to your senses and I'll be seeing you at home soon. Since you're not responding to my emails, I thought I'd—

From her opening lines, I can tell there will be no understanding. I cannot read her recriminations. All my life I've had to listen to her and be judged by her. Our mother died when I was six and Tilly was fourteen. Barely a teenager, she practically became an adult overnight and took charge of the household and of me. Our father was content to let that play out. More often than not he deferred to Tilly's mothering decisions about me. I don't know if it was because of his grief or because he was naturally inclined that way, but I only remember my father as an aloof and unemotional man, uninvolved in our lives and wrapped up in his own. Tilly provided the nurturing in our family, not our dad, but she raised me with strong discipline and unattainable expectations. Even as an adult, I've been continuously subjected to her guilt-tripping and criticism.

Not anymore. I scrunch her letter and pitch it to land beside Dan's. The last envelope I hold against my chest for a minute, knowing it's from Carly. My poor dear girl, I did not want to hurt you. I open it slowly with shaking hands.

Dear Mom, What's going on? I've tried to call you, left messages, but you're not responding. Are you getting my emails? I know I've been out of touch since we met that day at the clinic, but I needed time to work through what I'd done. I'm really sorry if I hurt you with that.

But I think that what you're doing now is worse. When Daddy told me that Aunt Tilly came back without you, that you weren't coming home, I went to him right away.

Damn Dan. Why did he involve Carly so soon?

Dad is a mess. And I've never seen Aunt Tilly so upset.

I look away. My vision has blurred and I blink. I want to scrunch this up too because I know what's coming. More of what Dan was saying. Echoes of Tilly's viewpoint. But this is Carly, and what Dan said was valid. She has the right to speak her piece, and I deserve to hear her. So I begin reading again.

Your letter made no sense, Mom. The island made you stay? What does that mean? I don't understand how you could do this to the people who love you. Why didn't you call and tell Daddy in person? Why don't you answer my calls? Why won't you talk to us?

I'm really hurt that you don't care enough about me to share what you're going through with me. Me, your only daughter! (Although I understand not wanting to share certain things, having done it myself, but Mom, this is about OUR FAMILY!)

A tear drips on the letter. I blot it away and then wipe my eyes and continue.

But having said that, I also want to say something else. I've been taking your side against Dad and Tilly.

She has? I exhale a breath that I was unaware of holding.

While I don't agree AT ALL with how you've handled things, I can understand how you want to try a different life. I've often looked at you and wondered how you could put up with the way you and Dad live. I know you hate the store. I know you'd rather be doing something different but you're stuck with it. And Daddy can be so obtuse. He never engages with life unless it involves the store.

I love him, but since I've left home I notice a lot more than I did while I was in the middle of it. Then it was always about me, why didn't he pay more attention to me. But lately I realized that you must have been asking the same question for years. I wonder how you could accept that in your marriage for so long.

I suddenly feel very weak and place the letter on the counter. Propping my chin in my hands I continue reading.

This may sound weird coming from a daughter. What kid wants their parents to split up? I don't, Mom, don't get me wrong. I DON'T! Still, I kind of get why you're leaving him.

But please, don't shut me out of your life. I'm your daughter. Don't make me lose my mother. I still need you, even though I told you different a month ago. I understand that you don't want to come home to Daddy, but do you also not want to come home to me? Or Aunt Tilly?

Please, Mom, call me!

I love you, Carly.

Overcome, I dart to the bathroom and pull at the roll of toilet paper so I can blow my nose. I would never have expected to find an ally in my daughter. Independent Carly who's been so remote. I finally feel vindicated.

Wiping my eyes, I reread the letter, then fold it and put it back in the envelope. I must convince her I haven't left her. I pick up the crumpled letters on the floor and smooth them out, folding and placing them into their envelopes. Lifting the seat of the storage bench, I lay the three letters on top of my laptop and pick up the cell phone.

****

Somehow I manage to get through my workday. I avoid everyone, giving only cursory greetings to whomever I meet, striving to smile when they comment on my haircut. I clean through my roster like an automaton. Room 40 is vacant, meaning that Dan, thank God, has checked out and left the island. I excuse myself from the staff dinner, feigning a headache. When I get home, I grab an apple and head outside, striding purposefully to nowhere.

The beach is a balm. Waves lap on the shore, tugged into the sea with the receding tide. Sanderlings scamper back and forth following the rippling surf as seagulls soar and dive. In the glaring sun, the water shimmers. The air is still, but the heavy heat I've become accustomed to has given way to a comfortable warmth. As I walk, my feet crunch tiny shells washed up earlier by the tide, and I keep my gaze on the undulating designs etched into the sand. I focus on all of this to clear my head, endeavoring to push out all thoughts of Dan and Carly, and the self-recrimination and shame that are dogging my steps.

My phone call with Carly did not go the way I expected. Despite her written support of my decision, she was less than receptive to my determination to stay on the island and not return home with Dan. Apparently he'd phoned her after seeing me, rallying her sympathy at my unwavering obstinacy to remain here. Although I was adamant that she is still very important to me, she cried and railed at me, washing away any sense of acceptance I'd felt after reading her letter. It deflated me. Like Dan, she couldn't comprehend that my choice is about this place. That Hyde Island enticed me to stay.

I stop and watch the ebbing tide, feeling its draw. Waves edge up the shore, yet the ocean pulls them back. Those waves are like me and the ocean like Hyde Island, tugging at my psyche and luring me to stay.

"Really?" A voice inside my head slams me with how preposterous that is.

I drop to the sand and my knees thump on its compacted surface. No place, not even Hyde Island, should have the power to convince a person to fling off everything that is meaningful in order to pursue some unknown ideal. I force myself to examine the harsh reality that Hyde Island is the vehicle, not the cause, and in actuality I am leaving Dan and a life that is unfulfilling and joyless. How in God's name could I have convinced myself my actions were precipitated by some mysterious influence of this place?

A chill shivers through me, and then a flash of heat, as the truth assaults me. I never truly believed it. I hid behind it as an excuse. Falling back until I lie flat, I stare into the blazing sun, wondering how long a person can do so before becoming blind. My eyes tear up and I am forced to close them.

Oh God, what have I done? How can I continue this charade of being Anne Cooper, illegal alien and hotel maid?

This is not a life I would ever have chosen.

But then, neither was the one I left.

I don't know any more what to do, what I want to do. Did Dan mean it when he said he didn't want me back? If he'd relent, would I go? Could I go?

A shadow blocks the heat of the sun on my face. Opening my eyes, I see an elongated version of Bill. What an odd way to look at a person, from the bottom up. Hairy legs, bony knees, his paunch protruding a little over his belt, stubbles on the underside of his chin, dark hollows in his nostrils. I can't help staring.

He squats down beside me. "Hey, how are you?"

I push myself up to a sitting position and brush the sand off my shoulders. "Okay, I guess."

"Interesting new look. I like it." He gently pats my spikes.

"Thanks."

"I just checked some late turtle nests in those dunes over there." He points behind him to an area surrounded by yellow tape. "Want me to show them to you?"

I shake my head. "Maybe another time."

He scrutinizes my expression. "Wanna come over for a drink then?" He reaches his arm out. "You look like you could use it."

A drink is probably the last thing I should have, considering I've eaten nothing but an apple since breakfast, but I extend my hand. As he grips it, I flinch at the pain piercing my thumb.

"Oh, I'm sorry. You're hurt."

I stare at the Band-Aid, its furling edges stuck with sand. "Yes, I was slicing grapefruit and cut myself." The dual-edged implication of my explanation doesn't escape me, and my intentional gash throbs.

"Oh, just a little boo-boo, then." Bill smiles indulgently, as if I'm a child who needs placating.

I nod, wagging my hand, causing my thumb to throb even more.

"How'd things go with Dan?" He directs us to the

steps over the rocks. "If it's okay for me to ask, I mean."

A flush warms my cheeks as I think about how gratifying it is to have a man offer to listen to me. If Dan had been willing to hear me over the last several years, even once, I may not be here now.

"Not well. He was very angry." I look back at Bill. "He's justified, though. I've treated him badly."

"Hm."

"I've got myself into quite a situation, and right at this moment I'm not sure how to get out of it."

"Do you want to?"

His question triggers a wave of dizziness and I stop, bending down and pressing my hands to my knees. I inhale deeply.

"Are you all right?"

The light-headedness passes and I straighten and shake my head. "I'm fine. Just guilt attacking my equilibrium." I push back my shoulders and start walking. "The thing is I don't know what I want. Only what I don't want."

"And that would be Dan?"

My mind flashes on Dan's look of disappointment and betrayal. "And my insipid life."

"Here, let's go this way." Bill takes my wrist and steers me away from the road.

His hand feels warm on my skin. My pulse quickens and I hope he doesn't notice, since he's got his fingers right on it. Then I see where he's taking me. "Through the golf course?"

"Sure. It's a short cut to my place." As we step onto the fairway, he drops my hand.

I am unexpectedly disappointed as my arm falls to my side. "Just watch out for golf balls, right?"

"And gators. There's a big one that lives in the pond by the thirteenth hole."

"You're kidding me." I stop with my mouth agape. "Golfers play with an alligator on the course? Are they nuts?"

"Come on." He pushes me forward. "Gators don't

bother you unless you threaten them." His eyes slide to my face and a smile dimples his cheek. "Or unless they're hungry."

I should have known there was danger on this island. "Let's go the long way. I hate alligators. I saw a program once that said they could outrun a horse and crush bones in their jaws. And they have those cold eyes and big teeth." I shuddered. "They're disgusting creatures."

"Anne, they don't attack anything taller than a couple of feet. And these guys are well fed with all the deer and raccoons on the island. We won't get that close anyway." He walks ahead. "Besides, the golf course is a lovely place to walk."

As I quicken my pace to catch up to him, I warily check out the brush alongside the fairway. Fans of palms sit low to the ground, crowded by leafy bushes. Palmetto trees with their straight trunks tower near swooping oaks. The foliage is thick and dark, creating shadows where I'm sure a gator could hide. Something rustles behind me and I spin around. I see nothing at first, then a shadowy mound in the shrubbery.

"Bill, do you see something in there?" I point, as he looks my way.

"Nope."

"I thought I saw something move in those bushes."

We both stare but all is still. There are only trees, shrubs, and shadows. Bill shrugs. "Maybe a deer. Or a golfer looking for a ball."

"Not a gator?" I try not to sound unnerved.

"Naw. They only hang out by the water and there's no water there. Let's go. A cold one is calling my name."

Looking back over my shoulder one more time I continue walking.

"So your life in Canada is boring?" Bill's question startles me, and then I remember our conversation before we veered onto the golf course.

"Well, that's not the whole—" Again I hear leaves swishing and crackling, and I whirl around. "Did you hear that?"

"Yep." He cups his hands around his mouth and calls, "Hey, who's there?"

Everything is still. A bird twitters and another responds.

"Is somebody there?" Bill strides toward the greenery. Suddenly branches crackle and something, or someone, bounds away. The foliage obscures my vision and I can't make out any details, just a blur of brown, and then it's gone.

Bill heads back toward me. "Well, there was something, but not anymore. Probably a deer."

"It's like it was following us. What would…" A tendril of uneasiness takes hold. "Oh my God. Dan. Do you think Dan's still here? Following me?"

"I can't answer that. Is it something he'd do?"

"No. That's not like him at all." I walk quickly, wanting to get out of sight. "But I didn't tell him where I'm living or anything, so he might be trying to find out." I conjure up an image of Dan hiding in the bushes, spying on me at the beach, following me as I walk with Bill. It doesn't jive. Dan would confront me, ask questions. Subterfuge isn't his style. "No, it wasn't Dan. I'm sure of it. Besides, he's checked out of the hotel and is probably on his way home as we speak. He wouldn't stay away from the store that long." As I say this, I realize I have no idea how long he's been away. Still, I'm almost certain that whatever was in the bushes wasn't him.

****

Bill hands me my fourth beer and I wrap my fingers around the cold can. He settles into his Adirondack chair, stretching his long legs across the flagstones. The late afternoon sun lengthens across his patio, painting shadowed splotches on everything and shooting streaks of light through the trees. I lean my head back and close my eyes. Birds twitter. In the distance a dog barks.

This is the most relaxed I've been since I became Anne Cooper. The beers have given me a quiet buzz, and I am

100

enjoying the sensation.

Initially I was reluctant to sit out here, exposed like this. What if I'm wrong about Dan, and he's still out there somewhere? Bill convinced me being outside on the patio was better than cowering indoors. I'd already faced Dan, he said. What's the worst that could happen? I didn't have an answer to that, so here we are. Bill was right. It is so much nicer outside.

"This is the life, huh?" His voice steals into my consciousness.

"Mmm."

Our conversation to this point has been mostly trivial. I was glad not to revisit the discussion we started at the beach, ashamed about having to admit out loud I've been living here under false pretenses. We drank our beers, turned our faces to the sun, watched the birds and listened to nature's sounds. Bill brought out salsa and tortilla chips, and between the bag crinkling and the chips crunching, we made small talk. I told him about my job, and what a jerk my boss is. Bill knows Floyd apparently, from some kind of fishing competition, and concurs with the jerk designation. We discussed the weather, the trees on his property, turtle hatching season, how much fun it is to ride around the island on Agnes' ratty old bike. It was good, this chitchat, reinforcing in my mind some of the positive reasons for having stayed here and filling me with buoyant optimism.

Nonetheless, when he went inside to refresh our beers this time, I was glad for the respite. Bill is an attentive listener, and his undivided attention has me experiencing an ill-advised attraction to him. It occurs to me I should leave, but I can't seem to pull myself out of the chair.

The current silence is good because I don't want to talk anymore, having prattled on about everything except the one topic I hope to avoid. It hangs in the air like the Spanish moss on the trees.

"So, do you expect to be working at the hotel a while then?" Bill's question yanks down the moss. All the tension that I'd managed to drown in beer comes sputtering to the surface, and I am instantly and uncomfortably aware of how much I've drunk.

I open one eye. He tips the can to his mouth and stares at me expectantly. His blue eyes are like pieces of sky, shining through his glasses.

"Uh, I'm not sure."

He tries again. "What are your plans?"

"I don't have any." Why is he challenging me? I sit straighter and my head spins. I squeeze my eyes shut for a minute to still its motion. "Just be here, I guess."

"Can I say something? I understand that marriages fail, but to walk away from one without plans, without going to something seems so, so…" He twirls a hair on his beard.

"Irresponsible?" I shift in my seat. "But I did go to something. The isla…" I stop myself, not wanting to hide behind that lie anymore. Bill doesn't say anything, just gazes at me, his eyes boring into mine. I bite my lip. Why do I feel so compelled to unburden to him? "The island gave me a way to escape, a place to run to."

"But isn't that drastic? You haven't just run away from your husband, but also your life, your family." He quickly shakes his head. "I'm not judging you. It's just…I…" He exhales loudly. "Look, here's me without a speck of family and—"

"No family at all?" Somehow that seems impossible.

He shrugs. "I'm an only child of parents who were both only children, and they're both dead. And my Vera's gone too. We didn't have kids." He stares at the beer can in his hand. "So when I see you just walking away from all these people in your life—"

"Stop." I can't hear anymore. "You really don't understand. People in your life are great, but the demands they create. They pull at you from all different directions until you lose yourself."

"What does that mean?"

"All the choices I make, everything I do is for them. Not for me." I shrug. "Dan and I should never have married." As I say this, I understand that I've felt this for most of my life. "We met on a holiday in Cancun. I was young and stupid and I got pregnant." I can't believe I'm telling him this. No one except for Tilly knows it. "We hardly knew each other, but Dan did the honorable thing. I was terrified my dad would find out, so I married him to escape the embarrassment. To escape his judgment."

"I guess there were no other options?"

"What? Why are you...?" I frown. "Of course there were other options. That's not the point. The point is I should have made different choices. I left school to get married and have a baby long before I was ready. All this time I've been in denial about it being a mistake, but living on this island on my own has made me realize it. I've decided I no longer have to accept a marriage that's unfulfilling and a life where I'm a shadow. I've finally taken charge. It's time for me now."

Bill seems taken aback at the vehemence of my outburst. I shrug. "Sorry."

"Was there nothing good about your life?"

"Uh...of course there was." I blink. "Carly. Being her mother is amazing, she's the sunshine in my life. But she's all grown up, doesn't need me anymore." Carly's letter pops into my head. The phone call. Maybe she does still need me. I toss my head, shaking away that thought. "And after Carly started school I took bookkeeping courses and worked at a bank. That empowered me somewhat. But then we bought the store, and everything became about the store. Hockey, golf, baseball, football, soc—"

"So it was your forced career change that started your dissatisfaction?"

"No, not just that. And it wasn't forced." I pause. Now I'm defending a life I've chosen to discard. "Dan is a detached sort of guy, who doesn't know how to put himself out there for someone else, doesn't open up, or listen. Not like you." Bill's eyebrows go up, higher than the gold rim of his glasses. My cheeks get warm and I clear my throat. "I...I mean everyone needs somebody for emotional support, you know? Someone who hears you." What am I saying to this poor guy who has nobody? Sheepishly, I calm my voice. "Anyway, when you're married, that person shouldn't have to be your sister who always judges you. It should be your husband." I take a deep swig of beer and watch Bill. He rolls his can between his hands. Does he understand? Am I explaining it right? "I just accepted my life for a long time and expected to do so forever. But when I came here I realized that I've lost myself in the process. I've become the shell of someone Dan wants for a wife instead of the person I want to be. Here I can become that person. That's why I stayed."

Bill scrunches the beer can. "There's something about this island that makes you face your truths, isn't there?"

He does understand. I smile at him and nod. He stands and gazes in the direction of the sun, now a piercing, glaring ball hovering just above the trees. The electricity in the air between us is unmistakable. He must feel it too.

I get up, ignoring my alcohol-induced wooziness, and move beside him, turning my face to the sky. The blaze of the sun is blinding and I drop my eyes to look at Bill instead. He touches my arm and stares right at me. "Anne, I think—"

"Oh, Bill." He does feel the same spark. Dropping all restraint and giving in to impulse, to what I want, I reach my arms around his neck and kiss him.

"Whoa." He clasps my forearms and presses me back. "No. Anne. What are you doing?"

"But I thought...you were...we..." Oh God, I've messed up again. I squeeze my eyes shut. Squiggles of light burst behind my eyelids and the patio stones move under my feet.

"Anne, I never meant...we're just friends, right? It's not that you're not attractive. But you've got a lot to figure out." He lets me go. "I'm sorry. You should go. I have stuff to do."

I open my eyes. Silhouetted in the glaring sky, Bill's expression is indiscernible. "I have stuff to do too." I run and stumble over a chair, banging my shin in the process. I gasp at the pain but keep moving. Tearing down the sidewalk, I don't slow until I'm around the corner of his street. Only then do I stop and look back.

Bill doesn't come after me. I rub my throbbing shin and catch my breath. Stupid, stupid, stupid. Dizziness almost topples me. Maybe Bill will realize I'm drunk and excuse my foolish behavior. Maybe I won't have lost my only real friend on the island, the only person who knows my truth.

Chapter Eleven

Work the following day feels like slogging through a deep marsh. It's as if I'm one of the island's turtles, sluggishly plodding forward, carrying the weight of my life on my back. This is not only because I'm hung-over, although that would explain the lethargy and raging headache that started my day. Nor is it because of the dreams that disturbed my sleep: images of Dan chasing me with a hockey stick while Carly tried to pull me back by ropes tied to my arms. When they caught me, they tied me down like Gulliver, and Tilly started painting me with invisible paint, eradicating my feet, then my legs. "Stop." I cried, and Bill walked over with an alligator on a leash. Just as the alligator crawled over my torso, its sharp claws digging into me and disgusting belly sliding over mine, I jolted awake. Needless to say, I did not sleep much after that.

No, the main reason for my despondency is that any enthusiasm I felt for my Hyde Island escape has ebbed out of me. The seduction of this place has lost its power. The island seems small and gray. By facing the truth of why I've really stayed, I no longer feel confidence in my choices. And I recognize that I have handled everything very badly.

To put it mildly.

Compounding the remorse I feel for my reprehensible action is the shame I bear at my behavior with Bill last night. How could I so completely have misread his cues? How could I have been so foolish as to believe I have any appeal whatsoever to anyone and humiliated myself like that?

I grow warm thinking about it; my whole body radiates heat. I bang shut the door of my locker, where I've hung my uniform, and plunk myself on the bench beside Pearl, who is taking off her shoes. Billowing my T-shirt, I blow out my cheeks and lower my chin to my chest.

"You havin' a personal summer?" Pearl says as she drops a shoe to the floor with a thud. "Lawd, I'm so glad to be done with all that."

This is the first time I've worked the same shift as Pearl. Not that we saw each other much while we did our jobs, since we cleaned in different parts of the hotel, but her energy livened up the staff supper today, making me glad she was there. Still, I found myself wondering what Esperanza was doing on her day off.

I shake my head. "No, just burning up from my own mortification."

"Lawd, girl, what d'you mean by that?" She straps sandals onto her feet and pushes herself to stand. When I shrug, she touches my shoulder. "You were shore quiet at supper. Everythin' okay?"

I sigh. "I don't know what to do anymore, Pearl. I've made such a shambles of my life."

She throws her purse over her shoulder. "Ever'body does that one time or 'nuther. I've messed up my life more times 'n I can count. But 'ventually I always figger how to clean it up. I'm sure you will too."

Her optimism barely penetrates through my despondency. "I don't think my mess is cleanable."

"Course it is." She heads for the door but stops with her hand on the knob. "The mess don't matter once it's cleaned up, and when you figger how to do that yourself, you become a better person. You just got to buck up, honey, decide what you gotta do, then do it." With those words of wisdom she's gone and I find myself staring at a closed door.

In my previous life—that's how I think of it now—I'd head for the gym whenever things became unbearable. Some weeks I went there a lot and would pound the treadmill, row the machine, and stride on the elliptical, speeding away from whatever seemed intolerable. After a while the frenzy would abate, and my mind would begin to sort through what drove me there, eventually arriving at some decision or strategy for getting through another day.

That's what I need now. A gym. Pearl is right. I've got to buck up and decide what I want to do, and a good frantic workout will help me arrive at this decision.

Unfortunately, the only gym on the island is too expensive for my budget. The hotel has an exercise center, a small room with windows overlooking the pool, equipped with a treadmill, an elliptical, and some kind of all-purpose weight machine. Of course, staff members aren't allowed to use it so our key cards aren't programmed to open the door. Floyd doesn't trust us, I guess. I could go running outside, but today is too humid. Besides, I might bump into Bill and I'm not quite ready to face him after last night.

Lately, it seems all I'm trying to do is avoid men.

As I leave the locker room, I make a quick decision to see if Nathan, who has the afternoon shift at the front desk today, will give me a key to the hotel gym. He stands behind the desk, the phone wedged between his ear and shoulder, his head bent quirkily as he types on the computer keyboard while staring at the monitor. I lean against the counter, waiting for him to finish with the call. He acknowledges me with a roll of his eyes as he says, "No ma'am, we haven't had any problems with bedbugs."

Behind him, the door that leads to the offices abruptly opens and Floyd walks through. I do a quick turnaround, hoping he hasn't seen me, and make for the exit.

"Anne. Good, you're still here." His voice reverberates in the lobby, and I have no choice but to stop and turn around.

"Just on my way out. While the sun still shines." I smile feebly.

He approaches, followed by a short, dark-haired woman. "Glad I caught you then." He swipes his pudgy hand across his brow. "Lord, it's hot. I like what you've done to your hair, by the way. Have I told you that?"

Instinctively I touch the spikes on the top of my head. "Thanks. Did you need me for something, Mr. Hill? I have to be somewhere."

He sticks his hand in his pocket and jingles coins. "I've been meaning to ask, did you manage to talk to that guest? Mr. Burgess, I believe? Did he ever find his wife, do you know?"

"I don't..." I stop myself, wondering what the right answer is. What Floyd expects to hear. He narrows his eyes and I say quickly, "I think, yes, yes he did. He's checked out now. Left the island."

Floyd nods several times, then turns sideways and reaches his arm out to indicate the woman behind him. "This is Gaby, our newest maid. She starts work tomorrow."

Gaby has to maneuver around Floyd's sagging belly to come closer. She smiles shyly and bobs her head. "*Hola*," she says. "Hello." She reaches out her hand and I shake it. It's small and soft and warm. I give it a gentle squeeze.

"Welcome aboard."

"*Gracias*." Her head bobs again.

Floyd clears his throat. "Gaby's a cousin or somethin' of Esperanza's, just over from Mexico, so she doesn't speak much English. Do you mind takin' her over to the staff quarters, to Esperanza? I'm not sure she remembers how to get there. Augusta had to leave early, otherwise she'd be doin' it."

"I was just leaving, but I guess I could."

"Good, good. It's best if the management doesn't mingle too much with the staff, especially in their personal space." He splits his face with a slimy grin. "If you know what I mean." He turns to go but then spins around. "Leave by the back door, all righty?"

The staff quarters are at the rear of the hotel property, past the tennis courts and the landscaping shed. Almost hidden behind a large cluster of palmettos and other shrubs, they comprise a row of small, whitewashed wooden cabins, ten of them side by side, each with a window and a door facing front. I was in one of them once, when Augusta gave me my staff tour. They have one room, with a small three piece bathroom at the back. Under the front window is a small kitchen counter, with a sink, microwave, and miniature fridge, and they're furnished with a single bed, a table and two chairs, and a small upholstered recliner. I suppose one could decorate, and add bits to make it more homey, but I'm not sure how much that would improve the basic space.

Gaby walks slightly behind me, although she seems to know where to go. I wish I could speak Spanish, but since I can't, we walk in silence. The heat today is oppressive, even in the late afternoon, and the humidity heavy. When we're past the landscaping shed, I see Esperanza sitting on a green plastic lawn chair outside one of the cabins. Her Chihuahua, Pepe, lies at her feet. As we approach, the dog raises his head and emits a quiet growl. Esperanza pats his head and looks up, and then she jumps out of her chair and runs over.

"Gaby, *cómo fue?*" she asks as she throws her arms around her cousin. Stepping back, she looks at me. "I ask her how it go."

Gaby shrugs. "*Él es apenas como usted dijo.*"

"*Si, él es un cabrón.*" Esperanza grimaces. "She say Floyd not so nice. We know, don't we, Anne?"

I nod.

Pepe is hopping about, shaking his tail and yapping. I bend down to pet him, and he lowers his bottom to the ground, looking up at me with bulging eyes, his tongue hanging out one side of his mouth as he pants. I straighten and he remains sitting. "Good dog."

Esperanza touches my arm. "*Gracias.* For showing Gaby de way."

"No problem. It's confusing for a newcomer to find." At least it distracted me from my troubles for a bit. "I should go."

Esperanza waves her arm in the direction of the cabin where her chair sits. "Jou wanna have a dreenk?"

I shift my weight from one foot to the other. "I don't want to impose on your reunion with Gaby. And I'm sure she needs to settle in. I assume she's going to live in one of these cabins?"

"Si. In house beside me. But she get here dis morning, so we had rejunion already. Please, stay."

"Okay, then, just one drink. Thanks." I can exercise later. A brief sojourn with the two women might do me good.

I follow the cousins as they amble arm in arm to Esperanza's cabin. Pepe dances around my legs, and I have to be careful not to step on him. The two women chatter in Spanish as they walk. A couple of times Gaby looks back at me, so I assume Esperanza is telling her about the crazy Canadian woman who left her good husband to work here as an illegal maid. Gaby goes into the cabin to the left of Esperanza's, and I follow Esperanza and Pepe into hers.

What she has done to this humble abode is astounding. Bright floral curtains in shades of green and pink hang in the window and a Mexican blanket with the same colored stripes is spread across the bed. The dark green upholstered chair has two cushions splashed with sunflowers and on the table sits a vase filled with pink and white azaleas. Pictures cover the walls, a photograph of two little boys and one of a very old couple, and paintings of flowers and colorful fish. The place looks, in a word, cozy.

"This is great, Esperanza. You've really made this little house feel like home."

She shrugs. "Ees where I leeve." She opens the door of the fridge and brings out a carton of Corona and a lime. "Jou like *cerveza*? Or how jou say, beer?"

"That'd be great." I look closer at the photograph with the two boys. They are the same boys who are in the little photo that hangs from the keychain on her cart. Here they appear to be about four and six, both dark-eyed with wide grins on their faces, the older one having a big gap where his two front teeth should be. Staring out from the photo mischievously, they have their arms around each other's shoulders. "Are these your two little boys? They are so cute. You must find it hard to live away from them."

She comes up behind me. In a quiet voice, she says, "Dey are both dead."

Horrified, I turn to face her. "Oh Esperanza, I am so sorry. What happened?"

She shrugs. Her eyes glisten. "Is long time ago." With her finger, she gently caresses the faces of the boys. "I no like to talk about." She returns to the kitchen and rummages in the fridge.

I am afraid I have overstepped. "Can I help you with anything?"

She points at the table and chairs without looking away from the fridge. "Could jou take one chair ou'side? I be right dere."

I pick up a flimsy wooden chair and carry it through the door. When I step outside, I see that Gaby has brought over a second green plastic lawn chair and is sitting on it. I place mine beside her. "It's hot, isn't it?"

She smiles and nods vacantly.

"*Chaud?*" I say, having heard that French has similar words to Spanish. She frowns. Then, out of nowhere, the word pops into my head. "*Caliente.*" Suddenly I'm transported to Cancun, some twenty-eight years ago. I was a naive nineteen-year-old, a freshman at university. My friends and I were there during Christmas break on the lookout for fun. I met Dan, they met other guys and that was the end of our trio. Dan and I basked in the glow of wanton attraction. We sat on the beach, rubbing each other with baby oil, flirting. "*Cerveza, por favor,*" we'd call to the waiters at the bar. "*El frio, por favor, es caliente.*" And we'd snigger at our feeble attempts to speak in Spanish.

Tears unexpectedly prickle my eyes.

Thankfully, at that moment, Esperanza appears carrying a tray holding three bottles of Corona with a wedge of lime stuck in the mouth of each and a bowl of peanuts. I subtly wipe my eyes and take one of the bottles. Pushing the lime down into the beer, I clink my bottle against Gaby's and Esperanza's. "To friendship and womanhood." I take several swallows of the cold, effervescent brew, its carbonation causing more tears.

"*Qué?*" Gaby asks.

"Oh, sorry." I raise my bottle again. "*Salud.*"

With that we all smile and take a drink.

****

Having given up on the idea of working out in the hotel exercise room, I decide that instead of a run I'll go for a swim. Bill has told me he isn't partial to swimming, so as long as I can avoid running into him before getting into the water, I figure it's a safe place for me to exert myself.

The sun is lower by the time I get to the beach, but it's still bright and hot. A handful of people are sitting on the sand or walking along the shore. Some are swimming. One man is standing hip-deep in the water with a fishing rod. I throw my towel down and kick off my flip-flops and briefly gaze at the sun. As I pull off my T-shirt, I notice in the distance Bill sauntering in my direction, recognizing his distinct gait. Quickly I peel off my shorts, hoping to get in the water before he sees me. But as I'm about to run into the ocean, he stops mid-stride and shields his eyes, looking at me. I raise my hand in a wave. He waves back, and then slowly he turns around and heads back in the direction he came.

As much as I wanted to avoid seeing him, this rejection wounds me to the quick. I race into the water and begin to stroke furiously until I'm far out and too deep to stand. Winded, I stop and tread water.

I had no revelations while swimming, no insights into what I should do next. All I could think about was Bill, which is not where I wanted my mind to go.

The people on the shore seem very small. I dive under to touch bottom and realize I've swum very deep indeed. The pressure hurts my ears and my lungs feel as if they'll burst. I push my way to the surface and float on my back. The water is almost as warm as my body, and an opaque brown. I become a bit uneasy, not being able to see what creatures might be swimming around me, and I stroke toward shore.

"Hey, look. I caught a little shark." Ahead to my right, the fisherman is holding up his rod with his free hand grabbing the line on which a large dark fish is flapping. A woman splashes in to join him and I start swimming faster, now very eager to get out of the water.

Once on the beach, I lean over with my hands on my knees to catch my breath. Drops of water plop from my body onto the sand, and I watch them, allowing my mind to empty.

"Lydia? I almost didn't recognize you."

Jarred out of my daze, I grab my towel and straighten to find myself face to face with Agnes. She looks lean and spry in a hot pink one-piece bathing suit. Standing next to her is Rhett Sandusky. His paunch protrudes slightly over navy swim trunks and his upper body is muscular, although his legs are old-man bony, which seems a bit incongruous with his handsome face.

"Oh, hi Agnes." I wrap the towel around my shoulders. "Nice to see you again, Rhett."

Rhett puffs out his gray-haired chest. "I might say the same."

Agnes slips her hand into his. "We thought you went home with your husband." She glances around. "Is he still here?"

"No, he went back to Toronto. I..." My cheeks get hot. "I guess you don't know. I've left him. I'm living on the island now. Working here." The words leave my mouth, and it feels as if someone else has spoken them.

Agnes' eyes have gone wide. "Well, knock me over with a feather. I had no idea. Are you coping okay? Where are you working?"

"I'm fine, really. It, uh, it was a long time coming, but it's...it's for the best." I shrug to stop my stammering. "I work at the Live Oaks Inn, nothing great but it pays the bills." I rub the towel vigorously on my arms. I'm starting to feel a little chilled, standing here wet and dripping.

Rhett's brown eyes twinkle as he smiles. "Well, I'm sorry for your troubles, Miss Lydia, but your presence makes Hyde Island a better place." He turns to Agnes, touching her shoulder. "Dahlin', we need to have our swim before cocktails. Shall we get in the water?"

Agnes nods. "Stop by sometime, Lydia."

I almost correct her about my name, but the whole Anne thing seems kind of silly now. "I will."

They walk into the water hand-in-hand. They're so sweet, to be in love in their seventies. I am heartened by the sight. It also makes me feel inexplicably sad.

I finish toweling dry and pull on my shorts and T-shirt. As my head pops through the neck of the shirt, I'm startled to see Rhett standing in front of me.

"You're not swimming?" I gaze past him to the water. Agnes, in her hot pink suit, is doing a vigorous front crawl.

"Got a cramp." He pulls his left foot up behind him in a quad stretch. He barely sways, standing only on his right foot. For an old guy, he's got good balance.

I stick my feet into my flip-flops. "I'd better be off. See you."

"Wait." His foot drops to the ground and he reaches his arm out. The tips of his fingers touch my shoulder. They feel warm through the fabric of my shirt. Droplets of water cling to the gray hairs on his forearm. Curiously, I find the sight alluring and resist the urge to caress it.

For a brief second, our eyes hold one another's and I forget he's much older than me. Then I blink. "Yes?"

"I wanted to ask, we did, that is. Shall we get together for a coffee sometime? Tomorrow maybe?"

Again I look to the water. Agnes waves and I wave back. "I get off work around four."

Rhett also flicks his hand at Agnes and turns back to me. "Drinks, then." His smile crinkles the corners of his eyes. "Shall we say four o'clock at the hotel bar?"

I shake my head. The last place I want to socialize is the place where I work as a maid. Besides, the hotel doesn't really have a bar, per se, more of a counter in the restaurant where one can order a drink. "No, not the hotel. Somewhere else, okay?"

"How about The Fishing Hole." I must look puzzled because he adds, "It's by the pier, over by Sunset Beach."

I have not actually been to the pier but know where it is because it is visible from Sunset Beach. "Okay, I'll find it. I'll meet you and Agnes there around four-thirty tomorrow."

"Yes." He touches my shoulder again. "Tomorrow." Then he winks and heads back into the water, with no indication that any muscle is cramping anywhere. He splashes at Agnes and she laughs her throaty laugh.

I must have imagined that wink.

Chapter Twelve

Four-thirty arrives slowly the next day. Why is it that when you're looking forward to something time seems to drag? At least the anticipation of drinks after work keeps my mind off my problems. Instead of stewing over Carly and Dan and what I should be doing about my muddled life, my thoughts are on Agnes.

I actually don't know her that well. She's a casual acquaintance whom I've met a few times at art workshops Tilly dragged me to. What I do know about her I could write on a very small piece of paper: she's widowed and has two grown sons but no grandchildren; she's a retired accounting clerk; she lives somewhere in Pennsylvania but has a home on Hyde Island, and she's a very talented artist and portrait painter. Oh, and she currently has a handsome southern boyfriend.

Last spring, when she suggested Tilly and I rent her place here on the island for the art week, I think it was more about business than friendship, although I have the sense she doesn't rent the house to just anyone. We do get along great, in fact, something about our personalities click. Her wry humor compliments my cynicism, and our dialogue is often quick and witty. We laugh a lot when we're together.

So I'm looking forward to spending time with her. I could use a good laugh. Also, I'd be lying if I didn't acknowledge I'm anticipating seeing Rhett again. He's charming, friendly, and likeable. Not to mention he's nice to look at, as long as he's wearing a shirt. An evening out with friends and drinks, so I can cast off the cloak of indecision and self-condemnation that I've been wearing, is very appealing.

I regret that I've not been more in touch with Agnes.

The last time I saw or spoke to her was that weekend when I first decided to stay on the island. She lent me her car, gave me her bike, and then I simply ignored her. I'll try to make it up to her tonight, spring for a few drinks and an appetizer. Maybe we can set up a time to paint together. Lord knows I could use some inspiration, as I haven't picked up a brush since Tilly was here.

When I finish work, I stay for the staff dinner because I didn't have lunch and am starving, even though I'm itching to leave. I make my excuses as soon as I can and rush home, riding like mad. I shower, put on a pair of black capris and a sleeveless cream blouse and apply makeup, although I'm uncertain who I'm trying to impress. I can't get over how excited I am to be going out and don't really understand it. It's merely drinks with Agnes and Rhett.

The late afternoon is quite pleasant, not too hot or humid, and I decide to walk because I I'll be consuming alcohol and may not be all that steady on the bike coming home. Besides, it's not far and this way I won't arrive all sweaty.

The Fishing Hole is easy to find as it's very close to the pier. It peeks out from behind a copse of palmettos and other greenery, and I'm puzzled that I hadn't noticed it before. I guess it's because anytime I've gone to Sunset Beach, I was so focused on the water or the sky or myself that I simply didn't see it.

Set close to the water's edge, the patio overlooks the channel between Hyde Island and Brenville. I imagine that at night one can sit there and enjoy the twinkling lights of the mainland. It would be a fantastic place to watch the sunset, sipping a glass of wine while watching the sky blaze. It's only four-forty, though, and right now the sun is angled such that it glares right at tables, so it's probably a bit hard on the eyes. Agnes and Rhett aren't among the few patrons on the terrace, and since I'm ten minutes late I assume they're inside.

When I open the door, a cacophony of conversations strikes my ears at the same time as the stale smell of beer mingled with musty wood assaults my nostrils. It takes a second for my eyes to adjust to the relative gloom, and I scan the dozen people scattered around. Four scruffy guys in jeans and rubber boots stand at the bar, chugging beer and laughing loudly with the bartender. In the center of the room, two tables are pulled together around which a group of people is digging into plates of piled-high nachos. A pool table stands to one side, and a man dressed in black is helping a young women cue up to take a shot. She's squeezed into jeans and a T-shirt so tight I'm amazed her bosom doesn't pop out of her extremely low neckline.

Agnes and Rhett are on the other side, sitting at a table with their heads together. I head toward them, but realize my mistake when I see that the man and woman are several decades younger. I glance around. A lone man at a table in the corner raises a tumbler with golden liquid and I recognize Rhett.

"Is Agnes in the ladies' room?" I pull a chair over from the next table. I notice there isn't a glass at the place opposite Rhett.

"She couldn't come after all." Rhett smiles widely, revealing a perfect row of white teeth. "So we won't be needing that extra chair." He stands and moves the seat I assumed was Agnes' away from our table. "Now, what would you like to drink?" Behind me, he places his hand on my shoulder.

Somewhat disconcerted at the change in plans, I stammer, "Uh, a glass of Chardonnay please." I twist around to look at him. "Why couldn't Agnes come?"

He gives me a gentle squeeze and returns to his seat as he waves at the bartender. "Jimbo, my man, bring the lady a Chardonnay and another bourbon for me." Placing a hand over mine on the table, he says in his smooth southern drawl, "She asked me to convey the utmost regrets. She had a meeting at the art school, or bridge club, or some such group. I can't keep track of all her activities. She's busier than an ant at a church picnic."

His smile crinkles the corners of his eyes, intensifying

his handsomeness: that rugged chin, those thick silver eyebrows and wavy hair, the lines that etch the charm into his face. How can it be that I am attracted to a senior citizen? I squirm in my seat, uncomfortably aware that we are sitting side by side instead of across from each other. I consider moving my chair over to create some distance, but his hand over mine renders me immobile though it barely exerts any pressure. It feels warm and reassuring, and I like his touch. I stare at the wiry hairs on his arm, and am reluctant to have him remove it. Immediately as I realize this, a wave of guilt swirls through me and I pull my hands away.

"Oh, too bad." I try to keep my voice even. "I was looking forward to spending some time with her."

"And not with little old me?" He pulls a mock pout. "You and I can have a good time all the same."

"I didn't mean...I guess I can stay for one drink." I say this despite the little voice inside of me advising me to leave. I shuffle the chair a bit away from him, but it scrapes so loudly on the floor that I stop immediately and stay where I am.

"Good." He leans back and picks up his glass, draining the bourbon in it.

An awkward silence settles on us, at least it feels awkward to me. Rhett on the other hand, appears as relaxed and natural as a cat basking in the sun, observing me with ardent scrutiny. Although his regard flatters my ego, a pang of uneasiness strikes me. There is some kind of chemistry between us, an allure I'm finding difficult to resist. Careful Anne, I caution myself. Remember what happened with Bill.

Rhett leans forward. "Your new hairstyle is very attractive, Lydia. Has anyone mentioned that? It highlights your comely hazel eyes, which have little gold stars flaring out from the pupils, like fireworks on the Fourth of July. I find them irresistible."

A blush flames my cheeks and I bring my hands up to cool them. "I, uh, thank you." Clearing my throat, I blurt out, "I now call myself Anne, by the way. On the island? My name is Anne." I can't sit here as Lydia Burgess, not with this man, not feeling the things I'm beginning to feel—desired, aroused—sensations that have not surfaced in a long while for Lydia. Not without alcohol anyway. Lydia Burgess was Dan's wife, taken for granted and proper. But Anne, she's another story. As Anne, I can choose to behave any way I like.

At that moment the bartender deposits a glass of wine in front of me. "For you, ma'am," he drawls, and then he winks at me. Unnerved, I take a sip. He removes Rhett's empty glass, replacing it with a full one, its ice cubes clinking as he sets it down. "And your whiskey, Rhett. Y'all enjoy your evenin'." He gives us a sleazy smile that seems to say I know what you're up to.

"We plan to." Rhett chuckles. "Much obliged, Jimbo." He raises his drink to me. "Cheers."

I tap my glass against his. They ping like wind chimes, and a current tingles up my arm. I bring the wine to my lips, savoring the flaxen-colored Chardonnay. The spicy oaky liquid flows down to my stomach and calms me.

Rhett sets down his tumbler. "So you've changed your name? Why are you not Lydia anymore?"

I exhale. "New life. New persona. It seems to fit." It's a little embarrassing, having to explain this yet again. The more I do, the more stupid it sounds.

"Well, I think I can manage to remember." He wriggles his eyebrows. "Anne."

"Thanks. So where are you from, Rhett? Around here?"

He laughs, a velvety rich sound that draws me in like a magnet. "No ma'am. I'm an Atlanta boy, born and bred. Lived there all my life. Plan to be buried there too. I'm just visiting here because of Agnes."

"So how did you two meet? She lives in Pennsylvania, doesn't she?" I'm happy to get on this topic. It will keep my perspective and help me to resist the attraction I'm feeling. Maybe keep Rhett's perspective too.

"On the Internet."

"The Internet? You mean through an online dating site?" I am incredulous. They are both in their seventies after all.

He leans forward, his arms resting on the table, hands hugging his drink. "You won't believe the number of women I've met online. There are an abundance of lonely ladies out there, just looking for someone to cuddle with."

"And out of all of them, Agnes was the one for you?"

"One of many." Pride sparkles in his eyes. "She's my island gal."

I frown. "So what you're saying is that you have more than one girlfriend?"

He nods. "And each of them is special."

"Does Agnes know this?"

"Now, why would I muddy the waters?" He sits back and takes a swig of bourbon. "We have a good time while I'm here, then I leave and go back to my life, she goes back to hers and we're all happy. We don't bother ourselves with what the other does when we're not together."

"Hm." I sip my wine. "It seems kind of deceptive, though, if she believes she's your only girlfriend."

"Frankly, my dear," he says, sounding just like Clark Gable. I wonder if that's his intention. "I'm not aware of what she believes in that regard. She may have more than one beau herself that I don't know about, and it wouldn't bother me a speck." He touches my arm lightly. "But why are we discussing Agnes when I'm sitting here with one of the most beautiful belles on Hyde Island?"

Oh, he's smooth. I sit back and gaze at him. It enters my consciousness that he never intended for Agnes to be part of this evening. His deviousness and manipulation grate at me, especially when I consider poor Agnes.

On the other hand, I could also take it as a compliment. This suave and elegant man is attracted to, and wants to spend time with, me. When that notion hits my brain, warmth washes over me.

Maybe he's right. He and Agnes are both consenting

adults enjoying life. And Agnes is no dummy. I should just butt out. Who am I to judge anyway? Lydia Burgess turned Anne Cooper, family deserter, illegal immigrant. I toss back the rest of my wine and plunk the glass on the table.

"Want another?" he asks, his eyes twinkling.

I had intended to leave, but what the heck. He is one good-looking man and I am a free woman. "Just one more."

One more glass of wine turns into three. What with the wine, and a heaping plate of fried shrimp and hushpuppies, I hardly notice the afternoon slip into evening. Rhett has charmed away any hesitation I might have felt, and I have to say I am having more fun than I've had in a long while. His southern drawl and colloquial metaphors make his amusing stories very entertaining. At the pool table, he teaches me how to hold the stick, how to bend my body so I could make the smoothest shot, how to tap the cue ball just so. With his arms encircling my shoulders and his hands curled around mine as it holds the pool cue, we sink four balls in a row.

Too soon, our turn at the pool table is over. We drift toward the door, not arm in arm exactly, but leaning in close to each other. I am caught off guard by how sexy I'm feeling. Sexy is a sensation I normally ascribe to the young. Certainly in my youth I was extremely frisky, but middle age and menopause extinguished any libidinal flame that may have been stoked. Now, though, basking in the heat of my encounter with Rhett, I wonder if that had more to do with my insipid relationship with Dan than my advancing years.

The intrusion of Dan into my thoughts tempers my ardor. This impact of my psyche on my physical state disconcerts me. How desire ebbs and flows. I certainly don't want Dan in my evening, and although I am uncertain how far I want this thing with Rhett to go, I grasp his hand in an attempt to erase Dan from my mind. Rhett squeezes my fingers and warmth suffuses me. Unsettled, I pull my hand back, causing Rhett to send me a puzzled smile before he pushes open the door.

Outside, the sky is velvety purple with a few stars dotting the sky. The lights of Brenville sparkle across the dark water. A subtle breeze cools the air and I imagine it to be an angel blowing on my cheeks. Letting it caress me, I close my eyes for minute. I feel a little unsteady from the alcohol I've consumed, and am reminded of a similar sensation not so long ago in Bill's backyard.

"It's a mighty fine evening." Rhett puts his hand on the small of my back as he guides me down the steps.

"It is." At the bottom of the stairs, I inhale the salty air and listen to the gentle lapping of the waves against the pier. I turn to face him. "I had a really good time tonight. Thank you."

"The evening doesn't have to be over." He touches my arm. "Let me escort you home. Who knows how much more fun we can have." The lights from the patio glisten in his eyes.

I am enticed. However, my misstep at Bill's is very fresh in my memory, and I know my prudence is compromised because of all the wine I've drunk. But, oh, I am so tempted. I lightly stroke his forearm.

"I don't know. I—"

"Excuse us. Could we please get by?"

We are blocking the stairs and two men want to walk up. Rhett and I step apart. As the men pass, I recognize one of them. Bill.

He must hear my intake of breath because he turns in my direction. "Anne?" He catches my eye in the dim illumination.

"Hi." I shift my weight from one foot to the other.

"Hey." He looks at me, then at Rhett and back at me. In the faint patio light, I can see him frown. He offers his hand out to Rhett. "I'm Bill Alpaca. A friend of Anne's."

Rhett shakes it. "Rhett Sandusky." His drawl seems more pronounced. "Also a friend of Anne's." He smiles.

"Well, have a nice evening." Bill directs a questioning glance at me before heading up the steps.

Damn. Damn. Damn. My sigh is so loud, the fish in

the ocean could probably hear it.

"A unique fellow." Rhett moves in close again. "Especially the ponytail." He points one arm in the direction of the parking lot while the other goes around my shoulders. "Shall we?"

I slide out from under his clasp. "I think I should go, Rhett. I really had a good time, but it's getting late and I have to go to work tomorrow."

"Oh." Disappointment radiates from his voice. "Is he a...special friend?" He points up the stairs.

I shake my head vigorously. "Oh, no, not at all. But I really do have to work tomorrow. And there's Agnes and all..." My voice trails off.

"I see. Well, then, I'm off too." He starts walking toward his car.

"Rhett," I find myself calling.

He turns. "Yes?"

"I'd like to see you again sometime." I mean to continue and suggest he and Agnes have dinner with me, but I leave the first statement hanging in the air.

"I'd like that too. How about tomorrow, at the golf clubhouse? I can take you on the course and show you that putting trick. Same time?"

I nod in agreement. "Four-thirty tomorrow."

****

It seems the bed in my trailer is just a vehicle for guilt feelings and self-doubts. I sleep fitfully all night, questions plaguing my rest. How can I have betrayed Agnes that way? Why am I on the verge of making the same mistake with Rhett that I made with Bill? Why do I run away from Dan only to run straight into the arms of the first man who pays me attention? What the heck is wrong with me?

When I finally rise in the morning, I decide to stand Rhett up. Instead of going to the golf clubhouse to meet him after work today, I will visit Agnes and reconnect with her. She is my friend. I should do nothing that will jeopardize our relationship and do everything to cultivate it. Especially if I intend to stay on this island.

I should probably tell her about Rhett, too, that he is a Lothario disguised as a southern gentleman, but how do I do that without hurting her? Without divulging my involvement with him? The answer eludes me.

The trouble with sticking to my decision is that all day at work I daydream about my evening with Rhett. I really like him and felt happy and relaxed when I was with him. The flirty undercurrent to our conversation and the game of pool kindled a fire in me I thought Dan had doused. Despite all the reasons not to, I want to meet him again. So after work, I change into my floral print skirt and a cute turquoise top and head for the golf course.

As I walk across the hills of green, I'm reminded that my last time here I was with Bill and I had frightened myself, thinking that Dan was hiding in the bushes following me. How ridiculous that was. Bill had also frightened me, telling me about the alligator on the thirteenth hole. I consider going around to the entrance from the road and walking up the driveway, but that's a long way around and it's almost four-thirty already. So I push all thoughts of the gator out of my head and continue to walk on the fairway.

I pass a foursome of men all wearing khaki pants and colored golf shirts. One of them is teeing off, and suddenly I hear Dan hissing, "Sshhh. Don't make a sound while he's concentrating." My ear can feel the hot air of his whisper, even though he's not even here. I listen to him all the same and stand quietly and wait. The guy is wearing a red cap that does not at all match his orange and green striped shirt, and it bobs up and down as he assesses the distance to the hole.

Impatiently I tap my foot, and my eyes wander over the course. In the distance, past a couple of sand traps, is a pond. It is smooth as glass, like a mirror it reflects the clouds and the trees. By one edge, the image ripples and I see a long shadowy thing slithering into the water. Repulsed and mesmerized, I stare at the spot where the alligator disappeared from view and involuntarily I shudder. Not caring whether Red Cap has hit his ball or not, I hurry on my way, making a wide berth around the pond.

The bar in the clubhouse is noisy with male laughter. I spot Rhett sitting at a table with two other men. He is impeccable, with his silver hair combed tidily and his pale blue cotton shirt crisp and pressed. He's listening intently to one of his companions telling a story. I hang back and watch for a moment, not wanting to intrude.

The storyteller is bald, and the little pendant lamp hanging over the table shines a spot on the shiny dome of his head. It glitters as he gesticulates.

"...and I wasn't going to let ol' Bubba take possession of my new Titleist," he declares. "So I stared him in the eye, wrapped my fingers around the ball and pulled it right out." He mimics clenching a ball and lifting it in the air.

"Well, if that don't put pepper in my gumbo. Ol' Bubba didn't do nothing?" The other man, in a golf shirt the same inky shade as his slick black hair, throws out his hands in surprise.

Baldy shakes his head and sips his beer. "Nope, he just winked at me."

Rhett guffaws, raising his thick gray eyebrows. The man in black slaps Baldy's shoulder. "You, my man, are a true golfer."

"And a brave fella." Rhett holds his drink aloft. "To you, my friend, a fearless golfer."

The three of them chortle and clink glasses. Disturbed by the déjà vu feeling that has crept up into my psyche, I wonder what I'm doing here. These men and their golf stories, it all reminds me too much of Dan. I turn to head for the door.

"Anne." Rhett's voice booms over the din. "Anne, wait."

I swivel back and Rhett is there, standing right in front of me. "Is it four-thirty already?" His blue eyes twinkle. He touches my shoulder. "You are looking mighty fine. Come, let me introduce you to my golfing buddies." He leans in and whispers out the side of his mouth. "I'll tell them you're my niece."

That comment makes me feel dirty. I now fully regret having stepped inside and wish I'd been quicker out the door. "I don't think this is such a good idea, Rhett. I should go."

"What?" His eyes widen. "I won't hear it. We'll just say how-do to the boys, and then find our own table." His fingers stroke my upper arm.

My face gets warm and I almost give in. "No, I'm going to visit Agnes instead."

He gazes at me for a minute. "I can't sweet talk you into staying?"

I shake my head and he drops his hand.

"Well, my dear, at least let me walk you out." He calls to his friends that he'll be back in a minute and then opens the door for me. As the afternoon sun hits my eyes I squint. The green on the fairways seems especially bright and the air is already clamorous with the chorus of cicadas. Beside me, Rhett offers his hand. I don't know why, but I take it and together we descend the three steps to the path.

"I was hoping for a repeat of last night." He squeezes my fingers gently. We amble to the driveway. "I had such a marvelous time. And you were picking up the nuances of snooker right quick."

That southern drawl of his chips at my resolve. "I had a good time too." I stop and look up at him. "I don't know what to tell you. It just didn't feel right in there." I nod my head in the direction of the clubhouse.

"Does this mean you don't want me to give you that golf lesson we talked about?"

I'm about to say yes, that's what it means, but then I have a flash of memory. Me bending at the pool table with Rhett leaning over me, his hands around mine as he shows me how to take a shot. A desire washes over me to feel encircled by him again, and heat spreads through my insides. I find myself saying, "Well, I do still want you to show me your special putting trick." As it escapes my mouth, the double entendre of that statement hits me. "Just not right now."

He brightens. "Tomorrow?"

"I'll let you know, okay?" I pull my hand back. "I'll be in touch." I walk down the driveway to the street, resisting the urge to look back while he watches me leave.

Chapter Thirteen

As I knock, I am pierced with a stab of anxiety. Will I be able to face Agnes without exposing my flirtation with Rhett? There's little time to consider the question, however, because she flings open the door before my hand has returned to my side.

"Lydia." She breaks into a big smile. "I'm so glad to see you. Come in. Come in."

"I thought it was about time we reconnected." I follow her to the kitchen. "I feel bad for being on Hyde Island all this time and not getting in touch with you."

"Oh, nonsense. I know you've been busy." She reaches into a cupboard and pulls out two tall glasses. "I was just about to make myself a gin and tonic. Want one?"

"Yes, please." I glance around the room, soaking in its familiarity from my time here with Tilly, a week that seems a lifetime ago. The place is a bit untidy. Dishes clutter the counter, tubes of paint and brushes litter the kitchen table, and upon one chair sits a stack of golf magazines. I try not to think about the fact that they are most likely Rhett's. In the corner by the patio door, an easel is set up, facing out so I can only see the back of the canvas. "Oh, you're working on something," I gesture toward it. "Can I look?"

The bottle of tonic in her hand jerks and some of it sloshes on the counter. Her cheeks flush crimson. "I'd rather not show it." She busies herself with wiping the spill and then she shrugs. "Oh, what the heck. Go ahead."

I lift off the cloth that covers the painting and heat rises to my face. It is Rhett, his naked masculinity portrayed in full glory. Agnes, the artist, has been kind to him, as the body of the man depicted is definitely much younger than the older guy I've gotten to know. However there's no doubt that the thick silver wave of hair and those blue eyes are his. Somehow, in his facial expression, she's managed to capture his charm.

I can't stop my gaze from continuously straying to the genitalia. "Wow." I am unable to come up with any other words to express my admiration.

"Do you think it's good?" She appears beside me and hands me a glass. The ice cubes chink. "I wanted to flatter Rhett, so I made his body more…" She clears her throat. "Vigorous. But I'm worried about the incongruity between his youthful physique and his face."

We stand side by side, studying the painting of Agnes's boyfriend, my dalliance. I look at his body, then his face, and then his body again. He is leaning back against the counter on one bent arm, the other arm reaching out and beckoning. His sinuous muscles and the warmth in his gaze don't seem incongruent at all. I am drawn to him, and find it difficult to scrutinize the figure as a work of art instead of a sexy portrayal of a man to whom I am extremely attracted.

"I think it works, Agnes. It's very good. Very realistic, especially the perspective you've achieved on his arm. He's literally reaching out. And you've captured the essence of him." I take a swallow of the gin and tonic to stop myself from revealing how familiar I actually am with Rhett. "I think. I don't really know him." I grimace at the drink's bitterness and study Agnes to see if she noticed my slip, but she simply stares at the painting and nods.

"Yes, well." She lowers the cloth, concealing my enchanter. "It isn't finished yet. Let's sit outside, okay?" She slides open the patio door.

In the pinking sky, the sun is not visible from Agnes's yard. We admire the colors for a minute and then lower ourselves into her plastic chairs. My hand is chilled from the glass, but I clutch it nonetheless. I've begun to feel a tad self-conscious with Agnes, having had her intimacy with Rhett thrust at me by her painting, and my mind gropes around for a conversation starter.

Agnes, however, has no such trouble. "So how are you

coping? Having left your husband, I mean." She takes a sip and places her drink on the table. "It seems to have come about quite suddenly. Or had you already left your husband when you came here for the art week with Tilly?"

"No, I hadn't left him then." I stare into my glass, watching the tonic bubbles rise up around the ice cubes. "I didn't know I was going to do it until I got here. Actually, not until it was time to go home. You see, this island—" I jerk my head up and look at her, remembering that I wasn't going to lie anymore about the island making me stay. I take a deep breath and continue. "That week I did a lot of soul-searching. This place seems to inspire introspection, don't you think?"

A frown creases her brow, but she says nothing. I wonder if I am changing her opinion of me.

I trace my finger in the condensation on the outside of the glass. "Anyway, all that navel gazing revealed to me how unhappy I was and have been for so long. Somehow I found the courage to walk away from my life and start a new one." I swallow. "A new life here."

"Just like that?" Agnes leans forward, disbelief edging her tone. "You mean you didn't…oh." She sits back. "Now it makes sense. That phone call you received when I'd just arrived. That was your husband?" She must have been musing over that phone call since she found out about me staying here. At my nod she continues. "You went outside with your cell. And then took off." She shakes her head. "You ended your marriage over the phone?"

"It wasn't quite like that. My marriage had been dying a slow death for years. I—"

"And you say being here was the catalyst for your decision?" Agnes gazes at the eucalyptus branch hanging over the fence. "You just never returned home."

Like her, I stare at the eucalyptus branch. I shrug.

"How is your family taking it? And Tilly?"

I squirm in my seat. "Not so well." I glance sheepishly at her.

"I can imagine." She stares intently at me and I look

away. I have no response. Her chagrin is well founded.

Still, who is Agnes to judge me? I feel like I'm sitting here with Tilly, who at least is more qualified to admonish my actions than Agnes is. I put my glass on the table. "I'm sorry if you disapprove of my choices, but you don't know all the circumstances that led up to them." I stand. "I should go."

She reaches out and touches my hand. "Hon, sit down. I'm sorry. I didn't mean anything. You do what you have to do. I can understand that. I was just surprised, is all. I only know you a little, but you didn't seem to be the type of person who would make such a rash decision."

This apology laced with recrimination doesn't sit well with me. Just what type of person does she think I am? Nevertheless, I return to my chair. "The truth is I don't know what to do anymore. I've handled things badly, but they can't be undone. Not that I necessarily want to undo them, but—"

The front door slams. "Agnes, darlin', I'm home." Rhett's voice resonates through the house. "I'm ready for a cocktail with my honey."

Agnes jumps out of her chair. "I'm out here, Rhett, but I'll come in and fix you a drink." Heading for the door, she turns to me, smiling. "Wait here. I'll be right back."

My pulse quickens. I can't sit here with Rhett and Agnes together. What if she senses something between Rhett and me? What if he gives away our little flirtation? Not to mention, I've now seen him naked. At least, naked the way Agnes sees him. My instincts tell me to leave, and I rise from the chair.

Agnes giggles inside the house. "Stop it, sweetie pie. We have company outside." Rhett chuckles, his laugh creating a little wiggle in my gut. No way am I walking in on whatever they're doing, so I'm stuck here. The only way out is through the house.

I strain to hear more, but their voices are too quiet for me to make out anything else. It occurs to me Rhett might be playing at something. When I left him at the golf club not a half hour ago, I had told him I was going to visit Agnes. Now he shows up here. Just whom did he mean when he said he was ready for a drink with his honey?

At that moment I resolve to stop messing around with that man. No more drinks with just the two of us, no more hand-holding, no special putting trick on the golf course. God knows I have treated my family badly, but I'm not going to betray Agnes. As far as I'm concerned, Rhett is history.

I return to my chair and pick up my glass. I sit as casually as I can, crossing one leg over the other, and stare at the multicolored sky. The ice has melted in my drink and I sip the watered-down gin. In the dusky light, a breeze whisks over my arms, making me wish I had a sweater. Abruptly the screen door slides open.

"Well, looky who's here." Rhett feigns exaggerated surprise. "Anne, isn't it?" He steps toward me with his hand outstretched.

Agnes places a bowl of pretzels on the table. "It's Lydia, silly. Of course, I can understand you getting mixed up. You only met her once or twice." She gives him a quick peck on the cheek and sits down.

I shake Rhett's hand, ignoring the way his touch unsettles me. Warmth spreads through my arm and then the rest of me. I no longer need a sweater. "Nice to see you again," I say in as calm a voice as I can manage.

He winks and gestures toward my glass. "Can I top that up for you?"

"No, thanks. I should get going." Yet I remain in my chair.

"Nonsense," Agnes says, crunching on a pretzel. "Stay and have a cocktail with us. You can even join us for supper if you like."

'That's very kind, Agnes, but I'll just finish my drink and go." I hold it up, noticing it's almost finished.

"Are you sure? You know you are welcome." She turns to Rhett, who has parked himself in a chair beside Agnes, but directly opposite me. "You met Lydia on the beach, remember? She's a friend of mine from an art class I took in Canada."

Rhett raises his eyebrows. "You're an artist? Are you as good as Agnes?"

"Oh, no." I shake my head. "I'm just a dabbler. Agnes is the real artist here."

"I know it. Did she show you her latest work?" There's a mischievous twinkle in his eye.

I blush as I recall Agnes' rendition of him. "Uh, yes, she did." I grab a pretzel and crunch on it. "It's a good painting."

"Now, Rhett, you stop it," Agnes scolds. "How was your meeting at the golf club? Did you get all the details settled?" She looks in my direction. "He's volunteered to help organize a tournament, even though he's not technically a resident of Hyde Island." She touches his knee. "That's just the helpful kind of man he is."

Rhett kisses her hand before placing it back on her lap. He shifts in his seat. "The tournament is shaping up, although the meeting didn't go quite the way I expected." He stares right at me. He brings his glass to his lips. "Do you golf, Lydianne?"

Agnes swats him playfully. "It's Lydia, you nut. Do you golf, Lydia?"

Rhett's cavalier attitude makes me a little nervous. He'd better be careful or he's going to give us away. I shake my head. "No, not really. I've only played in a couple of charity tournaments, but I'm not very good. I have been thinking about taking it up, though, since I live here now, but..." I stop myself before digging too deeply into this topic. The only reason I'd been considering golf at all was because Rhett had offered to show me some special strokes.

Agnes reaches for more pretzels. "I don't play either. I can't hit a ball for the life of me, can I, Rhett?" She laughs. "He's tried to teach me, but I'm hopeless."

Rhett tosses her a smile. "Hopeless only because your heart isn't in it." He looks at me. "I could give you a lesson or two if you'd like. Teach you a few of my tricks." His eyes pierce mine.

Agnes gets out of her chair and moves behind Rhett, putting her hands on his shoulders. She kisses the top of his head. "That's sweet of you, but I'm sure she's much too busy."

I break from Rhett's gaze and smile at Agnes. She smiles back, but with just her mouth. Her eyes are saying something else, like she's just figured out something about Rhett and me. I nod. "Yes, I am fairly busy with work, so I don't really have time. Appreciate the offer, though." Gulping the last of my drink, I stand. "I should be off. Thanks for the cocktail, Agnes."

"Oh, you're welcome. I'm glad you stopped by. Don't be a stranger, now."

"Yes," Rhett agrees. "Don't be a stranger."

****

Agnes and her canvas have inspired me. Not that I want to paint a nude Rhett. On the contrary, I decide to start painting again so I don't think about Rhett. Or about the look Agnes gave me. The next afternoon after work, I dig around in my storage bench for my brushes and paints. I have only one blank canvas, so I make a mental note to bike to Brenville on my next day off to pick up some more. I had brought just enough for the workshop that Tilly and I came to the island for. Was it really only three weeks ago?

I stop for a moment and stare at my computer and cell phone. It's been a while since I've turned on either of them, having stuck to my resolution of staying out of touch with my old life until I figure out this new one. Obviously, I can't ignore my family forever. I'm starting to miss Carly and Tilly. Plus, as disagreeable is it is, I must deal with the legalities of ending my marriage.

I'm just not ready for any of that yet.

So I close the lid on the storage bin and gather my art supplies and head for the beach. I'm glad my workday ends when it does, because there are still several hours of daylight left. I love how the sun sparkles on the water this time in the afternoon. It shimmers like diamonds and silver and I want to try and capture it on my canvas.

Despite delighting in the feel of a brush in my hand and playing with the goopy mounds of color on my palette, my inadequate attempts at reproducing the glistening ocean frustrate me. Why do I ever think I can do this? Notwithstanding Tilly's belief that everyone is an artist, I am not at all creative. Tilly has natural talent and effortlessly produces wonderful paintings. Of the two of us, she is the artistic right-brained one. I'm the logical sister, the one who is better at math and puzzles.

Then I hear her voice in my head. You're also the sister who always messed up. That is true. And she would always clean up after me, whether I wanted her to or not.

Still, Tilly got me interested in painting, and even though I'm not good at it, I enjoy it. I do appreciate my sister, but I would be lying if I didn't acknowledge the resentment I bear toward her for her constant interference in my life.

I apply more paint to my overworked canvas in an effort to get Tilly off my mind, but my brain continues to dissect our relationship. I realize it is fraught with contradictions. As a child I emulated her, and I still admire her. She was my mother, after all. At the same time, her bossiness and her belief that even now she needs to fix my problems grate on me. I love her and hate her. Do all younger sisters feel that way about their older sister?

I must admit, though, Tilly has always been there for me, and I am sad I've turned my back on her. Yet, while I miss her, I don't miss the sense of inferiority I've always felt in her presence. Maybe this escape of mine is not only about running away from Dan and my marriage. Maybe it's also about getting out from under Tilly's overbearing love.

My painting fills me with dismay. The ocean doesn't shimmer. It is thick and heavy with brush strokes. With a putty knife, I scrape off my work while the paint is still wet. The canvas is left with a shadow of the scene I was trying to represent. It is like an apparition, a vague dream of a beach scene. I almost like it.

A high-pitched bark causes me look up from my work. In the distance a dog tugs at its leash while its owner haltingly runs after him. It is Esperanza and Pepe. I pack up my supplies, fold up my beach chair, and walk toward them.

"Anne," Esperanza says when we are close enough to speak. "So nice to see you at the beach. Ees a beautiful afternoon." She glances at the canvas in my hand. "You are an arteest?"

I shrug. "I try, but didn't do so well today." Reluctantly I turn my painting toward her. "I've just scraped off what I spent the last hour doing." Pepe jumps up and down as if he's trying to look at it as well.

"Oh, *si*. Well, next time jou do better."

I can't explain the disappointment I feel from her response. Did I expect her to gush compliments over my non-painting? Crouching, I pet Pepe. He quiets and sits. There is comfort in petting a dog. And comfort in being with Esperanza. Impulsively I ask, "Esperanza, would you like to come over for a drink? I'm in the mood for some company." She would be the first visitor to my trailer. Not counting Bill, of course.

"Dat would be nice. Ees okay I bring Pepe?"

"Of course." I stand and point in the direction of my home. "It's not far."

As we start on our way, I mentally run through what I can offer Esperanza in the way of refreshments. I have no beer, but there's an opened bottle of chardonnay and a hunk of sharp cheddar in the fridge. Veering onto the path in the tall grass that leads to the trailer, I adjust my hold on the painting gear. "This way."

"Where jou live?" Esperanza asks behind me. I turn. She has stopped at the edge of the grass, reining in Pepe, and peers askance at the weedy field.

"Just at the end of this trail. In a camper."

She still seems unsure.

I retrace my steps to stand beside her. "Really, it's

okay. The camper is in a clearing, and there's a better path to the road over there." I point in its direction. "This is just a shortcut."

Pepe is tugging at the end of his leash, eager to get into the grass, no doubt enticed by smells I can't detect. Esperanza's arm is pulled ahead of her. "Okay, lez go."

Inside the trailer she oohs and ahhs over my tiny space. I put my painting gear in the bedroom, standing the messed up canvas against the wall to dry and head for the fridge. "Would you like a glass of wine? Sorry, but all I have is white."

Esperanza shakes her head. "No tenks. I no dreenk much. Wader ees okay."

I take out the bottle anyway, for me. "Sorry I have no beer. Shall I make you some hot tea?"

"Tea ees good. I no dreenk cerveza too much eider. I only had eet een de house when Gaby arrive. To celebrate, jou know?"

I nod as I plug in the kettle and pour wine into a glass for me.

She stares out the window. "Booze make people do bad teengs."

Despondency in her tone compels me to regard her more closely, but she doesn't turn around. I follow her gaze and see Pepe, whose leash we tied to the stair rail, chewing on a stick. The kettle whistles and I tend to our refreshments.

She holds the door for me and I carry the tray outside, dodging an excited Pepe who leaps at my legs. I place our snacks on the widest stump by the campfire pit, and am pleased to see that it is well supported and balanced. I sure wouldn't want cheese and crackers all over the ground inviting rodents into my yard. Not to mention wasting a glass of wine. I open my beach chair and offer it to Esperanza. "I don't really have any outdoor furniture. Just this. You take it. I'm happy to sit on a tree stump."

"Tenks." She lowers herself into the chair. "Ees like camping here, weet dat fireplace."

"It is." I take a sip of wine. "I haven't actually had a fire yet, because then I'd have to scrounge around for firewood. But it's nice to sit here even without it. At least until the mosquitoes come out."

She nods and reaches for a piece of cheese. Breaking off a morsel she feeds it to Pepe, who gobbles it up and waits expectantly for more. "Anne, I no unnerstan why you here." She looks at me directly, her brown eyes questioning.

"Well, I was looking for a place to live and found this camper. The rent is cheap and the landlord is good." I falter for a second, thinking about how I must try to reconnect with Bill. "It's off the beaten path and I like it."

She shakes her head. "No, no. I mean here, on Hyde Island. Jou are from Canada, a good contry, and now jou are in America cleaning hotel rooms weedout permit. Ellegal. Like me."

"How do you know I don't have a per...." Her gaze stops me. I shrug. And then I explain briefly about my unhappiness in Toronto, in my marriage. About how being here simply provides me with an opportunity to escape all that. "I don't expect to stay here," I say, realizing that it's true. "I know I'll eventually return to Canada and live a legitimate life. Reconnect with my daughter and sister." I take a deep breath and exhale loudly. "But not yet, because I'm not sure how to go back." I fall silent for a moment, wondering when and how it will all come about.

Esperanza's brow furrows. "Jou have a daughter?"

"I do. She's twenty-six and lives on her own. Doesn't need her mother anymore." I sigh, thinking about how I miss her. "Her name is Carly." Then I change the subject, because I don't want to talk about me anymore. I'm sick of talking about me. "How did you come to be here, Esperanza?"

She shrugs. "Jou know, een Mexico dere ees no good work. And my cozin, Manuel, he work here a long time, so—"

"I didn't know Manuel was your cousin."

"Si, he ees my mudder's uncle's seester-een-law's nephew. And he got papers dat say he can work in America. I no have dem yet, but Manuel ees helping me with dat. He got me dees job." She turns her mug in her hands and stares into her tea. "I have nutting left een Mexico. My cheeldren are gone. My brudders are gone. I only have one seester left, and she need to stay dere to look after my mudder. I sen' money to help. My mudder no remember me. She got dat Altimers."

"Oh, I'm so sorry to hear that, Esperanza." I touch her knee. "You've had a hard life."

"Si." Her voice is sad. She is hunched over her cup of tea in such a way that it makes me want to wrap my arms around her. The white streak in her hair seems like a reflection of the heartache she has suffered. She raises her head. "Jou have no idea." A tear runs along the scar on her cheek to her chin.

I hand her a napkin and she touches it to her face. Her life is none of my business and I should respect her privacy, but I am curious to know more about it. I think of the photograph I saw of her two little boys. "I don't mean to pry, but can you tell me what happened to your sons?"

She closes her eyes and shakes her head slowly. "Oh Anne, I no talk about dem for so long. Is too horrible." She exhales a quivering breath. "I mees dem." She reaches down and brings Pepe to her lap. "Sandro he be ten year ol', now and Luis eight. Dey were happy boys, and bode so good wid de footeball. Luis was keeking de ball de same time he learn to walk." A hint of a smile plays on her lips.

I nod, not daring to break into her narrative by saying anything. On her lap, Pepe lies on his back, and Esperanza hypnotically scratches his belly. He appears to be in bliss.

"Jou see dees scar?" With her free hand she touches her face. "De night my two leetle boys were keeled, my hosbun' do dees to me. Eet was bad." She stares over my shoulder and blinks rapidly a few times, then continues. "Dat night, Juan, das my hosbun', he not home for sopper. He always late on payday en den come home drunk and mean. We fight a lot when he drunk. Anyway, dat night, me en de boys have a happy sopper, en den I play wid dem a leetle before dey go to bed. I go back to keetchen en I jost feenish washing de deeshes when I hear noise outside. I look in weendow and Juan is dere on an old motorcycle. He almos' heet de house when he stop en he fell off. But den he get up and come eenside." She shakes her head. "We never had anyting like dat before. He say he buy eet. I get mad because we need de money. But oh, he so excited. He get my boys out of bed even dough I tell heem not to. En Sandro was so happy to see hees papa so happy. But Juan was very drunk, he cood not stand straight. He want to take boys for ride. I say no, no, tomorrow when he not drunk."

She takes a deep breath and puts Pepe down, then walks over to the fire pit. She is obviously struggling as she dregs up these memories. I stay quiet, humbled by the fact that she is sharing this with me. Esperanza stares at the charred bits on the ground. "We fight. He grab de boys en I pull back on dere arms. Dey cry en den Juan let go en dey fall. Sandro stand back up en he look mad at me but I pick up Luis. Juan yells at me en he has knife een hees hand. I no see dat before. He wave it een front of me en he almost cut Luis weeth eet so I put heem down and tell de boys to go to bedroom. Sandro say no, but Luis cry so Sandro take him." She returns to her chair and crosses her arms over her belly. "Juan, he mad. He heet me and heet me and knock me down. He keeck me in stomach en I cannot get up. He stand over me en…" She stops talking and with her finger she touches her scar. Her eyes glisten with tears.

What am I doing making her dwell on this trauma in her past? I can surely guess what happens next in her story so she needn't continue. I press on her arm. "It's okay, Esperanza, you don't have to keep going. It must be hard to relive that night."

She closes her eyes and shakes her head. "No, I feenish story." Picking up her mug, she drains the dregs of her tea and sits quiet for a moment before continuing. "I been hit a lot by Juan but he never use knife before dat night. He slice right here." She again brings her hand to her scar. "He put hees face close to me, so close I smell de booze and ceegarettes. Eet make me sick. He say, 'Don' ever stop me again.' I een so much pain and I bleed so much, I no realize he got de boys unteel I hear de motorcycle. I crawl outside en see dem ride away. If I close my eyes, I can steel see dem in my mind. Sandro holdeeng tight to Luis en looking back at de house, en Luis holdeeng tight to Juan, deir hair blowing in de wind." She picks up Pepe and snuggles into his fur. Her voice becomes muffled. "Dey go so fast, dey're gone before I can yell to stop. I go back inside en try to feex my cut and wait. I so scared, Anne. I worry about de boys en I no sleep. Later *la policia* come to de house to tell me dey had accident. Juan heet a tree going too fast. Luis en Sandro fly off motorcycle togeder en hit de road so hard dey get killed. Juan die in hospeetal. My family dead in one night." She wipes her hand across her eyes and stands. Walking toward the camper, she says shakily. "I go to batroom."

Her tragic tale weighs me down. I envision the scene with her and her husband fighting while the boys stand innocently by. Lord knows Dan and I fought often enough with Carly standing there. But Dan never hurt me, not physically, and we never fought over Carly. And if Carly saw us angry at each other, we always made sure she also saw us apologize. I shudder at the image of Esperanza and Juan yanking on the boys' arms, the boys crying, the parents shouting.

Esperanza has suffered such abuse, such loss. I can't imagine how she manages to carry on. And yet she does. Despite everything she's been through, she still greets every day with optimism. She approaches her menial job with integrity, she lavishes love on Pepe, supports whatever family she has left. Compared to her, I am a whiner. My complaints about Dan and my marriage seem trivial. How dare I throw my family away so easily?

I gather the snack things onto the tray and in my agitation I drop the wine glass on one of the stumps. That startles Pepe, who barks. I pat his head and pick up the glass, noticing a crack in the bowl that travels down the stem. It is no longer usable and the realization overwhelms me. Placing the glass on the tray, I plunk myself back down on my tree stump and weep.

Pepe yelps happily as the camper door slams. I try to pull myself together, running my hands over my face.

"Oh Anne, I so sorry. I deed not mean to make you cry." Esperanza touches my shoulder. "It was long time ago. I'm fine now, see?" And she smiles, but it is only with her mouth, not her eyes, which are puffy and red.

"I don't know how you do it, Esperanza. How can you still be such a positive person after all that?"

"I em always sad about Luis and Sandro, Anne. But I keep dem here." She places her palms over her heart. "Dey are gone but I em steel alife. I belief dat life ees a geeft, so I look for someting every day to be happy about."

"But sometimes a person's life—their gift—is something they don't want. Like you, losing your precious boys."

"Si, but den I do my best en try to make eet better. I can't change what happen, but I can change what I do. Jou do dat too, Anne. Jou are trying to feex jour life so jou can be happy."

I nod. Considering the horrible story Esperanza just shared with me, I am ashamed to feel so grateful for her understanding of my situation. "I guess I'm exchanging my gift for a better one," I say, but as the words come out I'm not so sure I believe them.

Chapter Fourteen

When I wake up, I instantly remember that it's Carly's birthday.

Twenty-seven years ago today, September sixth, I gave birth to my girl, held her in my arms and felt her squeeze my finger. I close my eyes and picture that first day. She was such a little thing, and I was so afraid of her, not knowing what kind of mother I'd be, not being ready to take on that role. Not even sure I wanted it.

I resisted the labor at first, feeling resentful about being forced into it, into the waves of pain that felt like they were ripping me apart. Dan wasn't there, neither was Tilly, and I had only strangers helping me, although the nurses were kind. Afterward, all cleaned up and in the hospital bed, I held my baby clumsily, looked into her trusting blue eyes, and I knew I would fail her. She nuzzled at my breast and I panicked, put her down on the bed in front of me and watched her flail about as she began to cry in a squeaky little voice.

"I'm sorry," I whispered to her. "I'm sorry for all the mistakes I'm going to make. I'm sorry I had you before I was ready." I picked her up again and hugged her but couldn't stop her crying, which escalated to a wail.

At that moment Dan burst into the room with Tilly right behind him. Dan kissed my forehead.

"Hon, I'm sorry I didn't make it in time. I couldn't leave the conference call." Carly thrashed in my awkward embrace, her face all red. He placed his hand on her head. "My daughter. Why is she crying?"

"Oh, what a doll." Tilly swooped her out of my arms and cradled her. Instantly, Carly stopped crying and stared into Tilly's face, listening to her cooing.

From that moment, it seems to me now as I relive it, I

knew my life was a mistake: getting pregnant, marrying Dan, letting Tilly in on the whole thing, having Carly. It set the pattern for how it always was. Carly creating some kind of confusion, Dan watching, not knowing what to do, me trying ineptly to deal with it, and Tilly coming to the rescue, smoothing things over while Carly gazed at her with adoring eyes.

Not that we didn't have special mother-daughter moments or good family times. I must be careful not to let my current state of mind distort my memories. I did grow to love being Carly's mother. What I told Bill was true. She was—she is—the sunshine of my life, as trite as that sounds. After my initial maternal awkwardness, I became reasonably adept at mothering. But Tilly always did it better. A part of me thought, knew, Carly loved Tilly more than me. That knowledge was reinforced after a rip-roaring argument I had with her when she was fourteen, over something I can't even recall. But I do remember the words she spewed out at me before slamming a door in my face. *I wish Aunt Tilly was my mother.*

Dan basically stayed in the background. Like my own father, I now realize, who gave Tilly free rein in mothering me and was barely involved. Dan would take Carly out for ice cream, or help her with her homework and coach her soccer team, but the raising of her, the decisions, the agonizing, he left to me. "I don't understand her like you do, Lydia," he'd say. Or, "Leave her be. She'll come round." And, "Of course she loves you. Tilly's just a really great aunt. But you're her mother."

Thinking about all that, reliving it, makes my bed suddenly uncomfortable. I jump out of it, not wanting to dwell on that aspect of our lives. I'd rather recall the proud moments, the happy ones. Carly's bright shining face when she sang a solo in third grade. Her nonchalance at being top of the class in algebra in high school. Her hug of comfort when she left home, whispering in my ear, "I'll always be your girl, Mom, even though I'm grown up."

I guess she's not my girl anymore. Not since I chose to

leave the life that included her three weeks ago. I made that choice, not her.

I sink to the floor. Would she forgive me if I called her? Would she be my girl again if I apologized on her birthday?

I rush into the living room and grab my cell phone out of the storage bench.

Its battery is dead and I have to plug it in so I can use it. My hand shakes when I push two on speed dial. I lean against the kitchen counter as I bring the phone to my ear, attached to the wall by the charger cord. The anxiety that I feel while listening to the ringing settles like a knot at the bottom of my gut. My brain is spinning while I try to work out what to say to her. Please don't let her voice mail answer.

"Hello?"

The sound of her voice tightens my throat. "Carly?" I croak. And then I do what I've done on the phone for her birthdays ever since she moved out on her own. I sing. "Happy birthday to you. Happy birthday to you. Happy birthday dear Carly." My eyes fill with tears and my voice becomes shaky, but I keep on to the end. "Happy birthday to you."

"Mom! I saw your name on the call display, but I wasn't sure it was you." Her words do not sound judgmental or accusatory or angry or even hurt. They just sound like Carly. "Oh Mom, it's so good to hear from you. How are you?"

The delight in her voice instantly dries my tears and I find myself smiling. "I'm all right. How are you?"

"I'm great. Especially now that I'm talking to you. I wondered if you'd call today. I hoped, but..." Her voice trails off.

"Oh Carly, I wouldn't forget your birthday. I may have vanished from my old life, but you're still my girl."

"Right. Well, tell me about your new life. Are you happy? Are you still planning to stay on that island? Are you ever going to come home?" And then she quickly adds,

"Not that I'm pressuring you in any way. I'm just interested."

"Things are good." My thoughts brush against images of Rhett and Agnes, Esperanza and Augusta, my job, and Bill, and I immediately feel remorse for lying to her. Carly is an adult after all and she deserves to be validated as such. If I'm to reestablish my relationship with her I need to be truthful. So I add, "Ah, to be honest, I'm confused. I wouldn't say I'm happy, but I'm not unhappy. Mostly I'm figuring things out, and that was my point in staying here. And I miss you tons." As those words come out of my mouth, I recognize how true that is.

"Well, you know where I live," she says in a rather disgruntled tone. My throat tightens. Then she softens. "Sorry, I didn't mean that. Listen, do you still have the same email address? I've sent you a couple of emails, but you haven't responded at all."

I glance in the direction of storage bench where my computer sits untouched. "I haven't been online for a while."

"You should get on. I know Daddy's emailed too. The other day he asked if you'd been in touch with me, because you hadn't replied to him. He said that there's financial stuff to work out." Her voice lowers. "He told me he's considering filing for divorce. Did you know? I said it was way too soon for that. You need time. I mean, it's only been three weeks. He shouldn't take such drastic action yet."

These details crash in on the joy I was experiencing simply from talking to my daughter. I swallow. "And what did he say to that?"

"That the action you took was pretty drastic too. But for my sake, he would wait to hear from you."

"Thanks for sticking up for me." I twirl the cord around my finger, accidentally pulling the charger out of the wall. I stick it back into the outlet. "It doesn't surprise me that your father is talking about a divorce." Strangely, the idea of it does not upset me. Instead I feel something akin to relief. "He alluded to as much when he was here. I hurt him badly and he was very angry about what I'd done." It seems strange to be discussing Dan as a husband with Carly, rather than as her daddy. "How would you feel if we got divorced?"

"Mom, this isn't about me. It's about you. You have to decide what you need to be happy in life and what to do about your marriage. But you're right, Daddy is hurting. This is about him too. I just wish you guys would communicate so I'm not caught in the middle."

"Oh, Carly, I'm so sorry. Do you feel caught in the middle?"

"Yes. Well, only because Daddy keeps asking me if I've heard from you. Aunt Tilly too. Will you be phoning her today?"

I shake my head, even though Carly can't see me. "No. Not yet. I'm not ready."

"Mom, I think she needs to—"

"Carly, let's not talk about it anymore. Why don't you tell me about you. Your life. How's work? Are you doing anything special for your birthday?"

She sighs. "Okay." And then launches into an update on her job and the promotion she's expecting. Shamefacedly, I recall the message she left on my phone when I first decided to stay on Hyde Island and didn't respond to. But she carries on without referring to that. I want to ask how she's feeling about things after her clinic appointment, but I daren't touch that topic. She probably wants to put it behind her, certainly not discuss it with me. So I let her talk without interrupting. She bought a new couch for her living room and painted the walls teal and loves the new look. Recently, she started dating a guy from work but is not sure where the relationship is going or where she wants it to go.

A sense of calm descends on me as I listen to her. She sounds content and active and mature. My desertion hasn't made her miserable. Her birthday plans involve going out with friends for dinner tonight. Tilly and Dan will celebrate her birthday on the weekend, no doubt with Tilly baking her a German Chocolate Cake, which is Carly's favorite. I am struck by a pang of dejection at the picture, the three of them being together, Carly blowing out candles on one of Tilly's amazing cakes, and me absent from the festivities.

"That sounds wonderful." I attempt to keep my voice bright. "I'm sorry I won't be there to celebrate with you all."

"Are you, Mom?" But she says this lightly, without rancor. "Anyway, I've got to run. I haven't even had my shower yet and I've got an important meeting this morning."

I'm reluctant to let her go. "Carly, it was so good to talk to you, to catch up. I am so very sorry for everything. I'll make it up to you some day."

"Mom, just get happy, okay? Do you know yet when you're coming back? Will you come back?"

I tug my earlobe. Again, images from my Hyde Island life hover at the edge of my thoughts and they are struggling to compete with Carly's vivaciousness, with my love for my daughter. "I don't have the answers to those questions yet. But I can tell you that my resolve to stay away is weakening."

"I'm really glad to hear that. But be sure, okay? Don't come back until you're ready. And Mom, I won't mention our talk with Dad or Aunt Tilly, okay? Not until you contact them yourself. That's what you want, right?"

Relief and gratitude sweep over me. "You're very perceptive, Carly. I'd appreciate it."

"Well, I'm not a little girl anymore. I do understand human nature somewhat. Now I really have to go. Will you promise to stay in touch with me now? Please?"

"I will." I truly mean it. "I love you."

When I put my cell phone away, I experience a twinge of sadness at having had to say good-bye. But more than that, elation and hope flow through my veins. I've reconnected with my daughter. When I eventually figure out what exactly I'm going to do with my life, Carly will definitely be a part of it. And that makes me practically bounce to the shower.

Chapter Fifteen

The following day I have off work, and I decide to hightail it off the island. For one, I am on a high because Carly is back in my life, and I want to do something special to celebrate. I hadn't realized how much I missed her until I heard her voice on the phone yesterday. All day, the idea of simply going back to Toronto hovered on the edge of my consciousness, but her words to me kept countering them. Don't come back until you're ready. I don't yet feel ready.

The other reason I'm going to Brenville is that the thought of spending the day in the trailer does not appeal to me one bit. I don't want to go out and about on the island and risk running into Rhett, or even Agnes. In addition, my art supplies need replenishing. Some new colors might help me recover my lost muse. The idea crosses my mind that I could also look for an Internet café in town and get caught up on emails on my laptop. Carly's comments about Dan trying to get in touch to settle things niggles at my guilt.

I cringe a little at the idea of dealing with that other life. It isn't only Carly's comments that have me thinking about it, though. My visit with Esperanza has also spurred me on. Her story and attitude, and her confidence that I will fix my life, pushes me to start considering my future. And in order to do that, I have to settle my past. The computer goes in my bag before I change my mind.

Outside, woolly gray clouds cover the sun. I hesitate for a moment, not wanting to be riding my bike in the rain. Brenville is a hefty ride away. While I stare at the sky, a cloud shifts and a few bits of blue peek through, so I decide to risk it.

In some ways, it's nicer to ride in this kind of weather. The hot sun isn't beating down on my back, and with the cooler air, there is less humidity. Pedaling along the main road toward the bridge that connects the island to Brenville, I feel invigorated.

And free. Carly's validation has revitalized me. I am euphoric about this flight from all the troubles swirling behind me: the mess I've made of things with Bill, the tangle of Rhett and Agnes, Esperanza's depressing history. Then there's my job, which I've grown to hate. I constantly grind my teeth at the inconsiderate sloppiness of tourists and their rude sense of entitlement. They don't see me as a person. They hardly ever make eye contact and shuffle past me and my cart as if I'm some kind of embarrassment. I am on the verge of one day calling out, "Look at me," and berating them for the mess they leave behind. Also of course, there is Floyd and his constant innuendoes and attempts to intimidate me, although he never acts on his words.

All in all, absconding from my troubles lightens my heart.

I nearly fall off my bike when it dawns on me that this desire to escape is just like the impulse that made me stay on Hyde Island in the first place. Breathing suddenly becomes difficult, and I pull to the side, even though I've only reached the middle of the bridge at the top of its arch. A car whizzes past me, honking its horn, but I ignore it.

Taking deep breaths I stare down at the water that flows between the island and Brenville. Small swells make it seem alive. I focus on them. Up and down, up and down. My breath slows as the water begins to have a hypnotic effect on me. Not enough, though, to take my thoughts away from the disturbing question that invades my mind. How is it possible I have deserted one life and exchanged it for another one that I desire to escape?

"What exactly do you want, Lydia?" I shout, disturbing a seagull that had been sitting on the railing about ten feet from me. His wings flap rhythmically as he flies over the water and disappears under the bridge.

Unable to answer, I get back on the bike and pump the

pedals hard, forcing myself to think only about what I will do when I get to Brenville. I'll poke around in the interesting shops I'd noticed when I went there with Agnes's car a few weeks ago, and with luck I'll find an art store. Maybe I'll find a gift I could buy for Carly. I'll have lunch at a not too expensive restaurant and then pick up groceries before heading back. Although the clouds still hang heavy overhead, the sun does poke out now and then, so hopefully I'll be back safely in my trailer before the sky opens up.

Finally I see the Welcome to Brenville sign and the Piggly Wiggly supermarket on the edge of town. I ride past it, since that will be my last stop, and continue on to the city's center.

The streets are relatively quiet. A few people stroll on the sidewalk and a truck whizzes by, causing my bicycle to sway. Four cars are parked along the curb. I make a beeline for the bike rack on the corner.

Taking my purse out of the basket I look around. Trees hung with Spanish moss border the sidewalks, along with planters overflowing with red and purple petunias and bright yellow marigolds. Lining the street are clothing shops, boutiques, antique stores, a few restaurants, and a café. Farther along, hanging from a doorway is a sign shaped like an artist's paint palette, so I assume it's an art store. I take that as validation I was meant to come here today.

Directly in front of me is an old red brick building with wide concrete steps leading to its doors. The brass edged plaque bolted on the wall beside the entrance indicates that this is the Brenville Public Library.

My bag feels heavy on my shoulder, and I remember the laptop. The library will probably have Internet. If so, I could download Dan's emails, not reading them but taking my time to decide how to respond to them back in the trailer. And maybe the librarian could hold onto my computer for a couple of hours so I won't have to lug it around town.

As the hefty wood door closes behind me, I am encircled by musty coolness and subdued light. The hush is like a welcome. My footsteps echo on the mosaic floor. At the checkout desk, a patron whispers to the librarian, and her undecipherable words resonate among the bookshelves, the s's reverberating off the dark wood paneling. After my alien life these past weeks, being inside this place fills me with a sense a sense of familiarity, of coming home. Does every library feel this way?

I wander among the shelves, running my hands along the book spines. It's been a while since I've read a good book. Maybe I could borrow one from here. The titles in this section are all to do with science so I glance around for the fiction shelves. A table with a bright yellow sign captures my attention.

Georgia Authors, it proclaims. *Read one of our own.*

I paw through the hardcovers and paperbacks, surprised at the number of writers who are from Georgia. The pile on the table includes books by Pat Conroy, Alice Walker, and Anne Rivers Siddon. Also Stuart Woods, whom I did not know hailed from this state. There are other titles by authors I've never heard of, like *Baby of the Family* by Tina McElroy Ansa and *The Violent Bear it Away* by Flannery O'Connor. I'm leafing through *Fugitive* by Marion Montgomery, thinking it might be an intriguing read, when a small green book catches my eye. The picture on the cover shows a turtle making its way across sand, impressions of its flippers leaving a trail behind it. The authors, rather than the title, inspire me to pick it up: *Loggerheads on Hyde Island* by Bill Alpaca and Vera Hodge. Could this be my Bill? I mean, the Bill who owns my trailer? He did tell me that his wife was named Vera and she'd been a turtle scientist like him. The back cover has a black and white photograph of a hippy couple. Sure enough, there is a young Bill. He looks exactly the same, only more youthful, with long dark hair, John Lennon glasses, and no wrinkles. His arm is draped around his wife's shoulders. I stare at her. She has a long braid hanging over her shoulder with a flower stuck in at the elastic and wears a peasant skirt and a tank top. She is very attractive.

Arguably the best documentation of the threatened Caretta-caretta species in one of its nesting habitats, says the blurb below the photograph. *After years of studying the growth, migration, nesting, and habitat selection of Loggerhead turtles, scientists Alpaca and Hodge chronicle their observations in a readable and accessible narrative. A must-read for anyone interested in the conservation of this remarkable species.*

I stare at the turtle on the cover. Poor thing, plodding along the sand with that huge weight on her back. If I recall correctly, turtles lay their eggs and then take off, leaving their young to fend for themselves.

The whimsical notion that I am like that turtle comes to mind. Didn't I carry the weight of my life on my back when I came to Hyde Island? Haven't I left my young to fend for herself? Immediately I discard the image. Carly was fending for herself long before I migrated to Hyde Island.

I take the book and find a table. While my laptop warms up, I open the slim green volume and flip through the cover pages. The acknowledgement section is essentially a list of unfamiliar names. There is no dedication. I turn to chapter one.

It is late spring, it begins. *On the beach at Hyde Island, in the silent dark of the night, a female loggerhead sea turtle swims ashore and crawls across the sand to dig her nest.*

A clamor interrupts my reading and I look up. At the table across from me, a teenage boy and girl settle themselves. The girl's hair has a streak of purple in it, and she wears tight-fitting jeans with a low cut red T-shirt that accentuates her abundant cleavage, bringing to mind endless debates with Carly about the appropriateness of her outfits for school. The boy's blue plaid boxers more than peak out from the waistband of his jeans, which are hanging so low I wonder how he can walk. Their easy laughter is incongruent with the turtle struggling up the sand, and I close the book. I will read this in the quiet of my trailer.

My laptop has finally booted up, and Carly and Tilly stare out at me from the screen, the wallpaper image a photograph of them at the Toronto Christmas craft show. The three of us went last December, our annual pre-Christmas outing to buy gifts and interesting knickknacks. I took this shot at the café where we had lunch. They're holding wine glasses in the air, their faces radiating joy. As I stare into my daughter's eyes, impressions from that day come over me in waves. Carly and Tilly sharing a private joke over something to which I had no connection. The two of them teasing me about how quickly I walked past the booths. I recall that whenever we found some interesting jewelry or wood carving or handmade bag, both Carly and Tilly would like the same rendition, while I tended to prefer a different color or design. Although it was an enjoyable outing, I remember feeling an undercurrent of resentment toward Tilly about her closeness to my daughter, and then berating myself for it.

Why have I always rejected what my heart felt?

Abruptly I pull open the Internet connection and see that a library password is needed to access it. Leaving the table, I approach the librarian, who is typing at her keyboard.

"Excuse me," I whisper. "Sorry to interrupt."

She looks at me over the edge of her purple-rimmed reading glasses and brushes back her snow-white hair. "That's all right, hon'," she says with a soft southern drawl. She isn't whispering, but somehow it seems as if she is. "It's what I'm here for. How may I help you?"

"Could I get the code for the Internet?"

"You need to register with your library card to use it." She sighs. "We implemented that last year. Before, when it was openly available, everybody and his mother, tourists and all, came in here using their computers. Nobody cared about the books, and it got so noisy you would think we were downstairs in the children's section." She holds out her hand expectantly. "Do you have a library card?"

I shake my head. "I don't, but can I get one? I live on

Hyde Island."

"You shorely can." She immediately brightens and sits straighter. "All I need is something with your address on it."

I consider my driver's license, which has a Toronto address and my real name. I don't even know what the address of the camper would be. I shrug. "I just moved here a few weeks ago and I don't have anything with my current address on it."

"Not your driver's license? Anything like a bill or letter that you've received in the mail?"

I slowly move my head from side to side.

"Then I'm sorry. When you receive some mail, come back. A phone bill or even a personal letter will do. Anything with a postmark on it."

"I guess I can't check out any books then, either." I glance at the table with my laptop and the books I was hoping to take home.

"Sorry. You need a library card for that too."

I lean in closer. "Couldn't you just let me have the Internet code anyway? I'd be very quiet, and would only stay for a few minutes to get my emails." I smile conspiratorially. "I won't tell anyone."

She frowns. "Rules are rules, ma'am, and I am not one to break them." She resumes typing. "I'm sorry."

As I return to the table I feel her eyes are boring into my back, but when I glance behind me she's looking at her computer, her fingers clacking away on the keyboard. I'm not too upset about being unable to access the Internet. It's a good excuse to not get my emails. Now I don't have to get sucked into Dan's need to settle financial matters. Not yet anyway. When I'm ready, I'll just use the hotel Internet again.

However, I am disappointed because I won't be able to take Bill's book home. I suppose I could sit in here and read it, but I have other errands to run, and I need to get home before it rains.

I glance around. The librarian is intently typing, and

the teenage couple is completely oblivious of me. He squeezes her knee and then runs his fingers up her thigh. She whispers with her lips close to his ear and they giggle.

Opening my bag, I slide my laptop into it and surreptitiously slip Bill's book in along with it. That I don't even hesitate surprises me, but technically this isn't stealing because I plan to return the book next week. I'm simply borrowing it without having an official library card.

Casually I sidle past the librarian and head for the exit. I don't even notice the sensors around the door until the alarm starts to beep. I freeze. Should I quickly run out?

"Ma'am, do you have something in your bag that you shouldn't?" The librarian approaches. How did she get out from behind her desk so fast?

"Uh, I don't think so. I have my laptop in there."

"That wouldn't set it off. Only the magnetic strips that we put in the books." She crosses her arms. "Could you open your bag please?"

I clutch it close to my chest. Over her shoulder I see the teenage couple watching us. "Are you allowed to do that? Invade my privacy?"

"Please open your bag, ma'am."

I pull on the zipper, frantically trying to remember which side of the bag I had placed the book. If I lean it that way, then maybe the laptop will cover it. She wouldn't actually reach into the bag, would she?

Reluctantly I hold out my purse, barely open. She pulls the sides apart and peers inside. "Could you remove that green book, please?"

I sigh apologetically. "Okay." I pull the book out and hand it to her. "I was only borrowing it. I'd bring it back next week. You wouldn't give me a library card." Even to my ears I sound petulant, like a child, and I soften my voice. "I'm sorry." I hang the bag over my shoulder and slink out the door.

Outside rain is pelting the road. The heavy clouds are now dark gray and they blanket any sign of blue in the sky. Dismayed, I glance at my bike slippery with rain and then peer down the road. The art store is too far to get to without getting soaked, but the café is just a short sprint from here. A coffee would taste good right now.

I dart down the steps and across the street, hugging my heavy bag to my chest and wishing I had an umbrella. When I enter the café, I'm soaked, but inside it is dry and cozy. Wooden tables and soft cushy chairs fill the room. Bookshelves line one corner, and hanging on the walls are watercolors depicting beaches and birds. The comforting whoosh of a milk steamer draws me to the counter, alongside which there is a case filled with cookies, brownies and cakes.

"Can I help you?" The barista has a tiny sparkly diamond in her right nostril, enormous brown eyes and short kinky hair.

"Yes." I read the menu board behind her. "I'll have a medium latte and a piece of that tasty-looking pound cake, please."

"That'll be six eighty-five. Can I have your name for the drink?" She holds a pen to an empty cup.

"Lydia," I reply automatically, and then realize I've given her the name on my birth certificate instead of the one I bestowed upon myself on Hyde Island. Why would that come out of my mouth when I've been Anne for the past weeks? Was it triggered by the photo of Carly and Tilly on my computer? Maybe my subconscious is telling me I need to rethink my Anne Cooper identity.

Not wanting to examine that idea too closely, I glance around the café. All the chairs and tables are occupied, many with customers engrossed in their laptops. Two women pick up the trash from their table and gather their belongings. I make a beeline for their spot and am startled when one of the women turns around and it's Agnes.

"Oh, Lydia, you've come to town." She catches the eye of her companion and almost imperceptibly nods in my direction. "Not working today?"

"No, I have the day off." I turn to the woman. "Hi, I'm,,." I hesitate for a second, hating that I am again grappling with my name. "Lydia. A friend of Agnes."

"Yes, Agnes has told me all about you. You're an artist, right?"

I shrug. "Not like Agnes. She's amazing."

"I'm Dorrie." The woman reaches out her hand, which I shake. Her grip is soft and she releases my fingers almost immediately.

"Rhett was very taken with you the other night," Agnes says. Her eyes narrow. "He seemed to know a lot about you. Had you met him before?"

My cheeks grow hot. "No. Only briefly when I stopped by your house and you weren't home. And at the beach that time, when you and he were there for a swim. Also of course, I saw your painting of him…" My voice trails off. Does she know about our rendezvous at the golf clubhouse? Perhaps Dorrie saw us there. Maybe that's why she and Agnes were having coffee, so she could tell her. I clear my throat. "He seems to be a very nice man. And he obviously adores you." I stop myself from laying it on too thick.

Agnes nods. "Yes, well, I'm crazy about him too." Something in her tone, and the look she directs at me, makes this sound like a veiled threat. No, I must be wrong. My imagination and guilt is causing me to interpret something that isn't there.

"Lydia, your latte is ready."

At the barista's announcement, Agnes and Dorrie edge past me. "Nice to see you again," says Agnes, touching my arm.

When I'm finally sitting with my coffee and cake, I exhale a long breath, unsettled by my encounter with Agnes. Although she was never a close friend, she has always been a kind one and does not deserve my betrayal. Now, due to my own stupid behavior, I feel uncomfortable in her presence and that absolutely affects my relationship with her. What is the matter with me? Since coming to Hyde Island, I've been behaving like a teenager, making one bad choice after another.

"That was a heavy sigh." A man's voice interrupts my self-recrimination. Glancing up, I am delighted to see Bill's blue eyes peering at me from behind his rain-spattered glasses. "Mind if I sit here?" He indicates the empty chair across from mine.

"Please do." I shuffle my bag over to clear space for the coffee he's holding. "I'm so glad to see you. I figured you'd given up on me after...after that night at your place...when I...."

He waves his hand dismissively. "That's all in the past. We can blame it on the beer. I told you on the first day I met you that you were my friend and I still think of you that way." He takes off his glasses and wipes them with a napkin. "I saw you on the bridge with your bike. Did you hear me honk?"

I nod. "I didn't realize it was you." I offer him some cake, which he declines, and break off a piece for myself. "I thought you were avoiding me, especially when you saw me at the beach a few days ago and turned the other way."

He turns his cup in his hands. "Yeah, sorry about that. I was foolish, afraid you'd hit on me again. But after thinking about it, I realized we'd both had too much to drink that night and wondered if maybe I'd sent you mixed signals. I figured you were as humiliated as I was apprehensive." Looking directly at me, he says. "Let's just start over and pretend it never happened." He extends his arm to shake. "Okay?"

The warmth of his hand encircles mine. I feel that same spark of attraction I experienced the first time I met him, but from now on I will pay attention to my inner voice, the sensible one. "Okay, thanks." I shake and pull my hand back. "I missed you, friend."

Crinkles appear at the corners of his eyes as he smiles. "So what brings you to town on this rainy day?"

"It's my day off. I thought I'd leave the island for a bit and explore Brenville. I hoped I'd beat the rain." I finger-comb my hair, which is still damp. The spikes I so meticulously shaped this morning have disintegrated. "By the way, I was just in the library and found a book you wrote about the turtles. I tried to check it out to read, but the librarian wouldn't give me a library card."

"Yeah, Coralee is a stickler for rules." He chuckles. "Vera and I published that little treatise a long time ago. It's out of date. I'm still working on a new edition." He rolls his eyes. "One of those projects that sits on the back burner for ages.

"I wanted to read the book, though, and was disappointed not to be able to take it home."

He raises his eyebrows. "I have some copies in a box at my place. I'll give you one."

"That would be great. Thank you." We sit quietly for a while, sipping our beverages. The folksy guitar music playing over the speakers and the hum of other conversations mask any awkwardness in our silence. I finish my cake and drink the last of my coffee.

Bill emits an odd vibe, not a tension exactly, more like an edginess. I wonder if, despite what he said, he still feels awkward around me.

I pick up my bag. The weight of it reminds me that I could try to log on to my email account since the café probably has WiFi, but with Bill sitting across the table I am disinclined to do so.

"I should go." I sling the purse over my shoulder and gather my trash. Glancing out the window I'm dismayed to see rain still deluging the street. It will be a wet ride home. I'll have to visit the art store another day. My shoulders sag.

"You don't want to ride your bike in that downpour. Let me drive you. I plan to stop in at the Piggly Wiggly, though, if you don't mind." He raises his cup. "Can you wait 'til I finish my coffee?"

I nod and sit back down. "Thanks. I need to pick up groceries too. Will my bike fit in your trunk?"

"No prob." Bill takes a sip and then says quietly. "Anne." His tone causes me to stare at him, and he holds my gaze for a brief second before he continues. "I've been wanting to talk to you about something that might be a little sensitive. Please don't take this the wrong way. I'm merely concerned. As a friend"

I frown. What could he possibly have to say that I could misinterpret negatively? "Go on," I encourage, although I'm not sure I want to hear it. I hug my purse.

"That guy you were with the other night, at the Fishing Hole. Rhett? How do you know him?"

I shift in my seat. My transgression with Rhett has come to haunt me yet again. "Um, he's a friend of a friend. Why?"

Bill scrunches his cup. "He's got a reputation as a lady's man around the island. Every year he comes here for a month or so, and always with the same woman. Agnes Merin. Is that your friend?" His blue eyes grip mine. I nod slowly as he continues. "This guy hits on anything with a skirt, young or old. He has a different woman on his arm whenever I come across him at a bar. I don't know why your friend Agnes stays with him."

"Maybe she doesn't know?" My mind is whirring. How could she not know in a place so small? Does she simply choose to turn a blind eye? Perhaps I was correct in thinking she was aware of my meeting with Rhett.

"It disturbed me to see you with him." Bill reaches across the table, touching my arm. "I'm just cautioning you. I'd hate to see you get hurt. Or caught in the middle of something you may regret. We both know you're in a somewhat vulnerable situation, and I've seen that man break many hearts."

I don't know how to respond. My emotions are ping-ponging. In part I am affronted at the audacity of this man who barely knows me and who thinks it's his business to warn me about Rhett. But even more, I am touched by his concern. And not a little discomfited, knowing his warning is well founded.

I gently pull my hand back. "Thanks for your advice, I guess. Just so you know, I had already come to the conclusion myself that he was bad news for me."

"That's good." He stands. "I've probably overstepped.

I don't have the right to tell you anything." He shrugs. "But I don't want to see you get hurt."

This man is a puzzle. "I don't get it. Why does it matter to you what I do? Really, we barely know each other." I give him the hint of a smile as we head for the exit. "Even though we're friends."

His cheeks flush. "This might sound odd, but something about you kindles my protective instincts. You sort of remind me of a baby turtle."

"Really?" I make a face, not at all flattered by this comment.

"I don't mean that badly. They're very cute," he adds with a twinkle in his eye. "They flounder on the sand trying to find their way home to the sea. I see you as struggling too, to find your way home wherever that may be." He pushes open the door and stands aside to let me pass. Magically, the downpour ebbs at that moment and abruptly the rain stops. "As you know, I've devoted many years to the conservation of the baby turtles on Hyde Island. You're like another baby turtle that I feel the need to protect."

His kindness touches me, but I can't help feeling that somehow I've betrayed myself. Do I really come across so helpless as to need protecting? I look at the sky.

"It's not raining anymore." Brightness is breaking through the clouds directly overhead. "Thanks for the offer of a lift, but I think I'll ride my bike."

"Are you sure? It's no trouble putting it in the trunk."

"I'm sure." I hoist my bag and straighten my shoulders. "This turtle can make her own way home."

Chapter Sixteen

When I finally cross the bridge to Hyde Island, the sun has burned away the clouds and is starting its afternoon descent. My bike carrier is brimming with bags from the Piggly Wiggly, the art store, a craft store where I bought a bracelet for Carly, although I'm not sure when I'll be giving it to her, and the Nearly New Shoppe. I found a blouse there that was so me, the Anne Cooper me that is, I just had to buy it. A shade of green that makes me think of palmettos, with an indistinct print reminiscent of Spanish moss. And the cut of it flatters my middle-aged shape. I hate to admit it, but when I tried it on I couldn't help but think that both Bill and Rhett might find me sexy in it. Almost immediately after that thought entered my head, I mentally slapped my wrists, remembering my resolution to not pursue anything with either of them.

The breeze brushes my cheeks as I ride past the golf course, and a contentment bubbles up that, for the moment at least, reinforces the belief that I'm where I need to be right now.

"Anne. Lydia." The names hurtle into my ears.

I brake and glance around. Rhett is driving a golf cart toward me across the fairway. It bounces on the undulating grass. He's wearing a blue cap, which gives him a youthful air. Lord help me, my heart starts to beat faster and I tug my T-shirt straight.

"I thought that was you riding by," he says when he reaches the curb. "The sight of you speeding along was finer than a filly winning the Derby." He glances at the bags in the bike basket. "You've been out shopping I see."

I nod and clear my throat. "I was. Better get these groceries in the fridge." I put my foot on the pedal and grip the handlebar.

"Now hold up, sweetheart." He puts his gloved hand over mine. "I was remembering about the golf lesson I promised you. If you come right back I could show you a few things. My buddies and I are finished with our round and on our way to the nineteenth hole." He raises his bushy gray eyebrows and winks. "That's the bar. But I can drink with those guys any time. I'd rather give you your golf lesson."

My hand feels warm under Rhett's glove but I don't pull it away. In the distance I see two men leaning on clubs, watching us. I lower my gaze to Rhett's cocoa-colored eyes and a part of me wants to melt right into them. "Okay," I find myself saying. "I can be home and back in about five minutes, maybe ten."

He grins. Lifting his cap by the bill, he strokes his silver hair. "Great. I'll meet you at the tee box by hole thirteen. You know where that is?" I shake my head and he points off to his left. "You can get to it from the road, just around the corner there. The tee box is to the right of the pond."

I hurry home and scramble to put the groceries way. The irony is not lost on me that one of the reasons I stayed on Hyde Island was to escape a life focused on sporting goods, only to now be anticipating a golf lesson with Rhett. Golf! Dan would never believe it. Of course, I remind myself, golf is not really the reason I'm meeting Rhett Sandusky in a few minutes.

It isn't until I'm buttoning my new blouse that I remember about the alligator in the pond by the thirteenth hole. For a minute I hesitate, but then I shake my head. People golf there all the time and nothing happens.

More than ten minutes have passed by the time I'm back at the golf course. There is only one small opening in the bushes to get onto the fairway of the thirteenth hole. I lay my bike down by the palmettos at the edge of the rough some distance from the tee box. As I start walking across the grass, I can't help but stare across to the pond. The alligator is lying in the sun on the bank like a big fat log, his nose almost at the water and his tail curved in the dirt. He's not moving at all, and I'm hoping he's asleep and stays that way for a long time.

I pull my eyes away and head for the tee boxes where Rhett is swinging his club at an invisible ball. He glances at his watch and then looks in my direction, startling as if I've surprised him.

"For a minute there, I thought you were Agnes. Thank goodness it's you. I worried that you'd changed your mind."

My mouth goes dry at the mention of Agnes. "It just took me a bit longer to put everything away. Sorry." I touch the spikes in my hair that I'd meticulously formed a few minutes ago. "Was it my hair that made you think I was Agnes?"

"That and your blouse. She has one just like it." He leans in close. "But it looks better on you. I appreciate that you prettied yourself up for me. You look as fine as Cherokee rose."

My cheeks get hot. "Thank you." I tug the blouse smooth, wondering now if it was Agnes who had donated it to the Nearly New Shoppe. Suddenly I don't like my new top so much anymore. Eager to change the subject, I gesture at the golf club in his hand. "I thought you were going to show me a putting trick."

"We can do that if you like." He waves an arm in the distance. "But it's a little more private here. If you're self-conscious at all."

"I've only golfed a few times in my life, and I'm not very good. So here is okay. I do need help with my tee shot too."

"Well, then, let me show you." Rhett holds out his club. "This is a driver. Have you ever used one before?"

I shake my head. "I've only teed off with an iron, and I don't even remember what kind." Memories of Dan trying to teach me about golf start surfacing and I push them out of my head. "Drivers always look too big."

"Well, they do have the longest shaft and the biggest

head." He waggles his eyebrows. "So you have to alter your stance a bit. Here, you take it and show me how you'd tee off with it." He passes it to me.

The grip is warm from his grasp. I take the driver to the tee and try to line myself up. The long club feels awkward and I'm not sure how far down to hold it or how far back to stand. Self-consciously I adjust myself. Then I feel Rhett's arms encircle me, his hands covering mine on the grip.

"Just relax, Lydianne," he whispers in my ear.

His fusion of my two names causes goose bumps to spring up on my skin, and I find myself leaning back into him. "Like this?"

His lips touch my earlobe. "That feels nice, Lydianne, but for a golf swing, you need to lean more forward." He presses his chest against my back and soon we are standing over the ball, his body spooning with mine. I can feel his heartbeat, and imagine other parts of him responding to our closeness. It is difficult to concentrate.

Slowly he lifts the club in the air to the right, extending his arms so that mine do too. His upper arm brushes the side of my breast. "You feel this upswing? Lift it up slow. Notice the position of your arms and shoulders? Now, keeping your head down, let's bring it down quickly and follow through to the other side."

The club whooshes across the grass. Encircled by Rhett, my upper body swings to the left. His hips thrust mine around. It's as if we're performing a dance, Rhett and me moving in unison. I am very aroused and must resist the impulse to turn in his arms and kiss him.

Abruptly, he lets go of my hands and backs away. I totter at the loss of his support and am disappointed to feel the breeze blow across my back. Trying not to reveal this, I readjust my posture as if to take a shot. This is a golf lesson after all.

"That's how you do it." He sticks a tee in the ground in front of me. "Now try it yourself. See if you can hit that tee."

I take a deep breath and clutch the driver as I stare at the tee. I lift the club high. Just before bringing it down I glance at Rhett, who winks at me. Swinging hard, I ram it into the ground six inches away from the tee. Pain shoots up to my shoulder. "Ow. What did I do wrong?" I gape at him. "Didn't I do what we just practiced?"

"Not exactly." He chuckles. "You took your eye off the tee and raised your shoulders when you swung down. You need to rotate your shoulders and swing your hips around, but keep the rest of your body still. Let me show you again."

He steps behind me and we do the golf dance together once more. As his body encloses mine, I try to pay attention to the actual movement of my arms and shoulders, but his proximity makes it too difficult to focus. My heart beats fast. Surely he must realize the effect he has on me.

When he steps away this time, I'm prepared for it but no less disappointed.

"Okay, try again." He brushes his fingers along my cheek before moving to the side. "This time, keep looking at the tee instead of me." There is a mischievous twinkle in his eye.

I will myself to aim my focus only on that little stick of wood in the ground. Directing the club up in the air, I extend my arms and rotate my shoulders. I swing down rapidly and swivel to the left, following through on the stroke, and to my astonishment, the club whooshes across the grass and flings the tee in the air.

"I did it." I jump up and down.

Rhett beams. "That was stupendous." He wraps me in a big hug and then pulls away. "Now, how about some balls? I happen to have some here." Again he waggles his eyebrows, and reaches both hands into his pockets. He pulls out a bright white golf ball. "These are special balls. I don't let just anybody play with them."

"Well, I'm honored that you are willing to let me play with your balls," I say giddily, caught up in this golf lesson suffused with innuendos and flirtation.

He makes a show of brushing his brow. "Phew, it's hot for so late in the day, don't you think?" He sticks another tee into the ground and balances the ball on top. "Are you ready to try this on your own, or do you want me to guide you the first time?"

I touch his arm. "Oh, please guide me." I can barely stand the suspense of waiting to feel his body wrap around mine.

When we do the golf dance this time, there is little pretense about it being only about golf. His pelvis pushes into my buttocks as we set ourselves up to swing, and I feel a hardness pressing in. I thrust my bottom back. When his upper arm brushes against my breast, it nudges in and I lean my head against his shoulder for just a brief moment. But remarkably we make a decent shot together. The ball doesn't go very far but it does soar, although not too high.

Rhett brushes his lips against the back of my neck and moves aside. "Now, I only have one of these special balls left. Do you want to try it on your own?"

"Okay, I'll try the one shot." I stare into his chocolate-brown eyes, knowing that I radiate desire. Against everything I told myself, and Bill, this morning, I say tentatively, "And then maybe we could go to my place?"

He exhales loudly and grins, showing his straight white teeth. "I was hoping for an invitation." He reaches into his pocket and hands me a tee and a ball. "Make it good."

I stick the tee in the ground. For some reason, I have trouble balancing the ball on it, but after several attempts it finally perches there, waiting for me to hit it. I line myself up, spread my legs to balance my stance, grip the shaft and stare at the little white orb. I bring the club back up over my right shoulder and swing down, hitting the ball.

It goes in the air, but not straight along the fairway. Instead it lands with a splash in the pond. On the opposite bank, the alligator opens one eye and slithers into the water. I stand frozen, watching the beast disappear from sight.

"Damn. That was a Titleist." Rhett's expression is

pained. "I didn't want to lose another one."

"I'm sorry, Rhett. I didn't realize it actually was a special ball." I touch his arm. "You shouldn't have let me use it if it was."

He looks at me and sighs. "Aw, never mind." He cups my chin in his hand. "Let's pick up the other one and get ourselves to your place."

He shoulders his golf bag and reaches out. We hold hands as we make our way across the fairway toward the first ball. The closeness of him and the anticipation of what I am about to get myself into send my emotions into a jumble of doubt and excitement. I quiet my inner voice, deciding to throw caution to the wind. I am living in the moment.

When we reach the ball, I stoop to pick it up for Rhett. Behind me I hear the whine of a cart motor and a whistle.

"Hey, Rhett, my man," a deep voice calls out. "That's a mighty nice view."

Quickly I straighten. Rhett's friends, the same ones from the bar the other night, stop their golf cart right beside us. The one with the black slicked-back hair steps out. "Are you going to introduce us to your charming companion?" His scrutiny travels the length of my body, making me a tad uncomfortable.

Rhett casts a glance in my direction and shrugs. "Gentlemen, this is Ly, uh, Anne. Anne, this is Carl and Eugene, my golf buddies. Eugene's the one with the shiny head." Rhett grins in the direction of the cart's driver.

"Well, you silver fox, we were watchin' you give a mighty fine golf lesson to this pretty little lady." Eugene clambers out from behind the steering wheel. "Hittin' that ball right into ole Bubba's pond." He claps Rhett on the shoulder. "You gonna let Bubba keep it?"

"Firstly." Rhett lowers his golf bag to the grass and puffs his chest out. "I didn't hit it there. Anne did. Sorry, sweetheart." He sends a quick look in my direction. "And secondly, it's just a golf ball. I have better things to do right now than fish a ball out of a pond." He holds his hand out.

"Shall we go, Anne?"

Eugene raises his dark eyebrows. "You ain't scared of an old gator, are you?" He crosses his arms. "You gonna chicken out in front of your new girlfriend?"

I am about to take Rhett's hand when he pulls it back and places it on his hip. I glance from Rhett to his friends.

Carl leans on Eugene's shoulder. "Was it one of your new Titleist ProV1x balls? Didn't you pay close to four dollars apiece for them?"

Rhett purses his lips. "Yes."

Carl looks at Eugene in mock surprise. "Have you ever known Rhett to give up on a ball so easily?" When Eugene shakes his head, he continues. "Eugene, my friend, I guess you're still the reignin' champ of Bubba's pond. Next time you tell someone your Bubba story, you'll have to add that Rhett was too yella to look him in the eye." They laugh.

"I guess we could check to see if the ball is reachable." Rhett starts off in the direction of the pond.

"Wait." I blurt out. "You can't go over there. I saw the alligator go in the water."

Carl puts his arm around my shoulder. "Bubba's harmless. This is somethin' a man's just gotta do, honey."

I shrug him off and run after Rhett. We push our way through the rough grass to stand at the bank above the edge of the pond. Under the water, three white balls sit in the silt at the bottom of the pond, about a foot and a half away from the edge. The alligator, his eyes and snout barely above the water, watches us from twenty feet away.

"Well, looky here," Carl exclaims when he comes up beside us. "Three balls. Could be your lucky day." He leans toward me and whispers, "In more ways than one, huh?"

I ignore him. "Let's just go, Rhett." I peer at the alligator, but it hasn't moved.

Rhett doesn't seem to have heard me or is ignoring me, and he reaches for the ball retriever that Eugene is handing him.

"Careful, Rhett," Eugene says almost gleefully. "Bubba's lookin' interested."

I quickly glance across the water. The alligator's snout is advancing slowly in our direction. Backing away from the tall grass, I say loudly, "Leave it, Rhett. You don't even know if any of those three is your ball."

"Honey," Carl says. "Don't get between a man and his balls." The three men guffaw. Then, as if he suddenly remembers me, Rhett looks in my direction.

"This'll just take a minute, Anne. And don't worry. That old gator is harmless."

Eugene and Carl egg him on as he climbs down the grassy slope to the edge of the water, somewhat encumbered by the ball retriever in his hand. I note his slow progress as he carefully finds his footing, and it suddenly becomes obvious that he is an old man.

What I am doing here? My flirty mood and desire has all but disappeared in the wake of this ill-conceived display of machismo. Not to mention my fear and disgust for the creature in the water that is coming ever closer to the group of us.

I am about to announce that I'm leaving when all hell breaks loose. Rhett slips down the embankment and his foot splashes into the water. The alligator suddenly is right there with his jaw open. He clamps down on Rhett's leg and Rhett screams.

Eugene and Carl shout at Rhett and each other, grabbing Rhett's arms. They pull but the alligator tries to drag Rhett into the water. The reptile appears to be winning this macabre tug-of-war as the other two men slide a few inches down the embankment. Its tail thrashes in the water. Rhett, still bellowing, kicks at the alligator's snout with his free foot but he misses. The churning water around him has red streaks.

I am frozen to the spot, unable to think, horrified by what is playing out in front of me. "Help!" I shriek, but no one else is about.

Eugene looks up at me, his face red at the exertion of trying to keep Rhett from going under. "Grab a club," he calls hoarsely. "Whomp the critter between the eyes."

I frantically spin my head around and spot the golf cart close by and run to it. Grabbing a driver from one of the bags, I sprint down to the men. Out of breath by the time I reach them, I hold out the club.

Rhett seems to have fainted. Eugene and Carl are still holding tight to his arms, having wedged their feet in the dirt, but they're losing ground as the alligator drags more of Rhett into the water. Carl keeps kicking at the gator but misses every time.

"We can't let go of him," Carl says, panting. "Swing that club down as hard as you can right between the eyes. Quick. And do it over and over until he lets go."

I slither down the bank and into the water. The alligator's disgusting snout is wet and bloody and his teeth are clamped around Rhett's knee. Without thinking about it, I raise the club and whack it down heavily on the alligator's head, aiming for the ridge between the eyes. I miss and hit him on the eye instead. He grunts, opening his jaws, and Rhett is pulled free. His two friends drag him away while I wind up to take another swing. The gator directs his gaze at me just as I smack him again, this time getting him right where I aimed. I drop the club and run like a madwoman.

Heart pounding, hands shaking, and nausea roiling in my gut, I don't look back until I reach the tee box, where the guys have driven the golf cart. The alligator has retreated to the middle of the pond, having swum away from the churned up bloody dirt. He's floating there like a deadly piece of wood.

I hold onto the cart and catch my breath, trying to calm my stomach. My knees quiver. Rhett lies on the grass unconscious, and Eugene wraps a towel around his mangled knee. Carl is on his cell phone. I kneel beside Rhett's head and push back a lock of his hair with a shaky hand.

"That was close," Eugene says in a trembling voice. "You were brave." He squeezes my shoulder. I close my eyes and sit back on my haunches.

"Ambulance is coming." Carl lowers himself across from me. "And the police and park ranger. This'll be the end of Bubba." He lifts one of Rhett's eyelids. "Man, poor Rhett. How's his leg look."

"Bad." Eugene shakes his head. "We shouldn't have ragged him about the ball."

Outrage spews out of me. "Some friends. You goaded him into doing that. Playing your macho one-upmanship games. Men are so stupid." I stomp to the cart and lean my back against it. Arms crossed, I glare at them, but I'm feeling as guilty as I make them out to be. Rhett wouldn't even have had a ball in the water if it weren't for me.

Rhett groans and moves his head. I rush over to him and stroke his forehead. His eyes stay closed and he whimpers. The towel around his knee is saturated with blood. In the distance, the wail of an ambulance fills the air. Eugene stands and looks in the direction of the sound.

"Carl, did you call Agnes? She'll want to go to the hospital with him."

Carl shakes his head. "Phone was busy. One of us should go to her house and tell her." He turns and looks at me. "You know her, don't you?"

Eugene nods. "Hey, that's right." He points his index finger at me. "You go and we'll take care of things here. It's better that a woman breaks the news to Agnes."

I press my lips together and shake my head. No way am I going to tell Agnes about this crazy accident. How can I account for being on the golf course with Rhett? Then I realize I'd rather not be here when the police arrive, and maybe facing Agnes would be better than trying to explain who I am to the police. "Okay, I'll go."

"Good girl," says Carl, but I've already turned my back on the two of them so I don't respond.

I ride as fast as I can to Agnes' house. The whole way I wonder what I'm going to say to her, but by the time I arrive, I've come up with nothing. I drop the bike in the driveway, run up her front steps and bang on the door, panting. When Agnes opens it, she looks startled to see me there.

"Lydia. Come in."

I shake my head. "No," I say between breaths. "You have to—"

"Nice blouse." She smiles, and then leans closer. "Is that blood?"

I glance down at the smear on my breast. "Yes, but it's not mine. You have to go to the golf course, Agnes. Rhett's had an accident."

Her face pales. "Accident?"

"The alligator bit his leg. Carl and Eugene are with him and the ambulance is probably there already."

Her eyes widen. "Is he all right? How badly—"

"Agnes, he's alive, but his leg is bad I think."

"But how do you know—" She stops. I hope she sees the urgency on my face, but not the guilt.

"Leave right now, Agnes. So you can go with him to the hospital."

"Let me get my purse." She returns in less than a minute, keys in hand. "Where on the golf course?"

"Thirteenth hole tee box."

She starts the car and backs up. Too late we both realize that my bike is directly in her path. The crunching sound is very loud, but Agnes doesn't stop until she's on the road. She pokes her head out of her window. "Sorry." In a burst of acceleration, she's off.

I watch her tail lights disappear around the corner and then pick up my bike. Its frame is bent, the seat crushed and the front wheel is no longer a circle. There is no way I can ride this home. Half wheeling it and half carrying it, I place it in Agnes' garage.

I don't need to walk past the golf course to get home, but something pulls me in that direction. Agnes' car is crookedly parked at the curb near the bushes where I'd laid my bike. In the dusky light, the shrubbery is engulfed in shadows, and I make my way into the rough. A gunshot rings in the air as I look for a clump of palmettos to hide behind. I turn in the direction of the pond, where a cluster of men stands, silhouetted by the sun low in the sky. Alligator, I think. Good riddance. I step behind a tall clump of plants when another shot bursts the silence.

Emotion overwhelms me and I begin to cry. Through a film of tears, I watch the paramedics load a stretcher onto the ambulance. Agnes hovers by the doors of the vehicle and when it starts up, she runs in my direction. I shrink in the greenery, but she doesn't notice me as she starts her car and follows the ambulance with its sirens wailing.

At the pond, men load the fat lifeless alligator onto the back of a truck. Eugene and Carl are speaking to a policeman who scribbles in a notepad. Eugene briefly glances in my direction, but I know he isn't looking at me because I am well hidden in the palmettos.

I back onto the sidewalk and run the rest of the way home.

Chapter Seventeen

Sprinting as if I'm in a race, I arrive at the trailer panting and sweaty. I lean over to catch my breath in the almost dark clearing. My hand trembles when I swat at a mosquito on my leg and I run to the door. A white plastic bag hangs from its handle. I grab it and take it inside, closing the door on the biting insects.

In the Piggly Wiggly grocery sack is a copy of Bill's book, with a note scribbled on the back of his receipt. *Sorry you weren't home,* it says. *I had some beers with me to share. Enjoy the book. It's yours to keep. Bill.*

Overcome with gratitude, tears run down my cheeks. Even as I wipe them away, I realize that my reaction is radically out of proportion to Bill's gesture and probably due to the trauma of Rhett's accident. I slip the note inside the book and place it on the counter. Shower first, then Bill.

Under the cascading water, my mind keeps playing pictures of the thrashing alligator with its jaw clamped around Rhett's leg. The whole scenario played out quickly, but in my mental replay it unfolds in slow motion. I shudder at the image of the alligator looking at me after I struck him in the eye. Where did I find the nerve and the strength to whack it on the head a second time? Leading up to it and immediately afterward, I was terrified of the creature, but in the brief moment when I struck him, that fear morphed into rage.

Then there was the golf lesson. If not for me hitting the ball into the pond and Rhett's friends goading him on, I might right this minute be in bed with that man. My face grows hot, even though the water is cooling. I turn it off, grab a towel and rub it vigorously over my skin. An intense relief floods over me. Thank God I am here alone and

Rhett is not with me. As horrible as the alligator attack on Rhett was, it stopped me from making a grave mistake, and for that I am grateful.

"Saved by the gator," I say aloud in the tiny bathroom. Then I am immediately repentant about the callousness of my comment. Poor Rhett is in a hospital, possibly undergoing surgery, maybe even losing his leg. The weight of that sinks me to the floor.

When I'm dry and wrapped in my robe, I make a bowl of oatmeal. While it cooks in the microwave, I leaf through Bill's book but my concentration is feeble and I don't feel up to reading about turtles right now. I sprinkle a liberal amount of brown sugar on the oatmeal and take it, along with a glass of Merlot, to the couch.

My hands are still shaky as I eat the warm comforting porridge. I consider phoning Bill to thank him for the book. It might be good to talk to someone, but after our conversation this morning at the café, I feel like I've let him down. I had assured him that I wouldn't get involved with Rhett, and then I turn right around and do so.

Shame turns the oatmeal in my belly into a solid lump of discomfort. I don't want to explain to Bill where I was when he stopped by. I don't want to tell him about my golf lesson with Rhett, or about the alligator attack. Of course, he'll probably hear that story through the island grapevine, but thankfully Carl and Eugene don't know who I am or where I live, so it's possible that Bill won't discover I was involved.

Then I berate myself. What do I care if Bill finds out? He's not the boss of me.

Yet deep down it does matter what he thinks of me. I want him to respect me. He extended his friendship despite all the crazy things I've done since coming to Hyde Island, and I want him to know that I'm better than that. I want to *be* better than that.

I place my unfinished oatmeal on the table and lean back with my wine glass. Tomorrow after work I'll stop by Bill's house, when I've got a sense of how the news has traveled around the island. I will thank him for the book then.

I take a deep breath and exhale slowly. My hands no longer tremble, but I can't stop the tears that keep filling my eyes, like a torn blister that oozes. The silence in the trailer, invaded only by the singing of the cicadas outside, envelops me. In this small space, alone, I crave the company of another person. Back in Toronto, in the life I left, I would call Tilly when I'd had an upsetting experience. Dan was never one for comfort. He would back away from anything emotional and disappear at the slightest sign of any neediness. But Tilly would always be there for me. I'd phone her and she would be over in a flash.

Should I call her now? Or maybe Carly?

The idea paralyzes me. I shake my head and drink the last of my wine. I do not want to involve them in my Hyde Island troubles. I do not want my two lives to converge.

Still, for the first time since I abandoned my daughter and my sister, I yearn for both of their company. Perhaps it is time to seriously consider going back home.

****

Remarkably, I dream of nothing and sleep as if dead. The call of a seagull outside startles me awake, and I immediately picture Rhett in the jaws of the alligator. I look at the clock and groan aloud. It's after eight. I must have slept through the alarm, which was set to go off at seven. I wanted to have time to stop by Agnes' house on my way to work to ask about Rhett. In frustration I shake the clock and discover that although I'd set the time, I hadn't actually clicked on the alarm.

By skipping breakfast, I manage to be ready by eight-thirty. I rush outside and when I lock the door, I remember my crunched up bike sitting in Agnes's garage. My shoulders sag. Walking will take me longer to get to Agnes's making me even later to work.

I don't care. I want to hear firsthand how Rhett is and if that makes me late, so be it. I'll avoid Floyd and apologize to Augusta. She'll understand.

Agnes answers the door just as I'm about to knock a second time. She looks terrible, as if she hasn't slept all night. Dark circles shadow her eyes, her hair is limp and disheveled, and without makeup her wrinkles are more defined. She grips a mug of coffee.

"Lydia," she says in a dull voice. "I figured you'd show up, but you're not welcome here." She makes as if to close the door on me, and I push my hand against it.

"Agnes, you have every right to slam the door in my face, but could you please tell me how Rhett is before you do?" It takes little strength to stop the door from shutting, and she drops her arm as if resigned to my intrusion.

"Fine. Come in." She turns her back on me and walks down the hall toward the kitchen.

I quickly follow and stand in the archway that leads to the kitchen. Her painting of naked Rhett is still on the easel, now uncovered and facing the counter, and I resist the impulse to gawk at it. Instead, I watch Agnes top up her mug. I'm hesitant to say anything, wanting her to take the lead. My stomach grumbles loudly. She stares at me with tired eyes. "Do you want some coffee?"

"You don't have to—"

"Never mind that. It's already made and you're here now." She pours coffee into a cup and passes it to me, then plunks herself in a chair by the table and leans her chin in her hands. "The doctor says Rhett's gonna live, but they're keeping a close eye on his leg. It was fairly mangled. They repaired it as best they could, but they're not sure how much he'll be able to use it. Apparently a person his age takes a long time to recover from something like that. And he might lose the leg if it goes septic, which it has a big chance of doing. An alligator's mouth is full of bacteria."

"Is he in much pain?" I take a sip of coffee, but it gives me no pleasure, and I place the mug on the counter.

"Yes. No. He's strung out on morphine or whatever painkiller they give him. I'm not family, so the hospital doesn't tell me the details. And I haven't been able to talk to Rhett himself yet. He was unconscious when I got to the golf course and hasn't been awake in my presence." She looks up at me, and her eyes fill with tears. She blinks several times.

Her distress is my undoing. I crouch by her chair and hug her. She stiffens under my touch, but I don't let go. Gradually she relaxes, and then she sobs on my shoulder. My own eyes fill with tears. "Oh, Agnes, I am so sorry for everything. I haven't been a very good friend I know, but is there anything I can do?"

She pushes me away. On my haunches, I almost topple over. I catch myself and stand. Agnes wipes at her eyes. "I think you've done enough. I can put two and two together. I can figure out why you were on the golf course."

My mouth goes dry. "I'm sorry. I don't know what got into me. I never meant for any of it. And nothing happened, I promise. We were only flirting a bit." My cheeks grow hot as I relate this understated description of my golf lesson, and I quickly continue before she notices. "It was all my fault." She already thinks badly of me, and the least I can do is to keep Rhett faithful in her eyes. "Rhett didn't—"

"Oh please. I've known Rhett for a long time and am aware of exactly the kind of philanderer he is. I'm no fool." She directs her gaze at me. "I just didn't expect a friend of mine to go off with him."

I hang my head. "I can't apologize enough. All I can say in my defense is that I'm in a weird headspace right now and am not exactly making sensible choices. Will you please forgive me?" I raise my eyes to meet hers staring coldly at me. She says nothing. I hug my chest. "If you know Rhett's like that, Agnes, why do you stay with him?"

She laughs, but without humor. "Oh Lydia, he's fun to be around. Surely you've discovered that. For the month that he visits me on the island, he adds color to my life. What he does without me is his business, as long as he's mine when I'm with him." She glances at the painting of naked Rhett. I follow her gaze. His legs look strong and healthy and I'm struck with a pang of sorrow as I remember the alligator's grip in his knee. I look away, finding Agnes staring at me. She says, "And when he's in this house, he's definitely mine." She pushes herself to her feet. "You'd better go. And please don't come back."

I nod silently and walk down the hall. Agnes is right behind me and grabs the door out of my hand when I open it. "Good-bye, Lydia." I almost expect her to shove me outside.

I stop on the threshold and pivot to face her. "Agnes, when you see Rhett, could you at least give him my regards and wishes for a quick recovery?"

She closes her eyes and shakes her head and then pushes the door. It nudges me and I step outside just before it closes. Deflated and ashamed, I stare at the house. "Bye, Agnes," I say aloud.

For a brief second I consider not going to work, but if I don't show up, Esperanza will have to do a double shift and that's not fair to her. I look at my watch and then start running because it's past nine-thirty. I don't want to arrive there all sweaty, but what choice do I have?

It feels good to move like this, though, and the run clears Agnes and Rhett out of my head. The cool morning air and breeze feel good. I pick up my pace. Augusta must be wondering where I am. I've never been this late before. I hope I don't run into Floyd on my way to the locker room. This time of day he tends to do walk-around inspections of the staff.

When I'm a half block away, a commotion in front of the inn slows me to a walk. Just outside the hotel entry, three people are clustered together, flanked by two men wearing official-looking uniforms. I recognize Manuel, Esperanza and Gaby. Some distance behind them stand Augusta and Steffi. Augusta fiddles with her apron. Her characteristic bravado has disappeared; I can see that even at this distance. Floyd shouts at a uniformed woman while gesticulating angrily, aiming his finger at Manuel, but I'm too far away to hear the words. On the driveway to one side sits a black van.

The tension in the atmosphere is palpable, rippling over to where I have now stopped at the entrance to the drive. My empty stomach clenches. I wonder if Floyd will be able to change the outcome of this situation. Probably not, given his volatility. He folds his arms across his chest as the woman speaks to him, pointing at a clipboard in her hands.

Transfixed by the scene, I don't know whether to continue toward the hotel or to back away and disappear. After all, I am an illegal alien too. Gaby wails, drawing my attention. Esperanza puts her arm around Gaby's shoulder and looks at Augusta and then glances around, her eyes widening when she catches sight of me. An almost imperceptible shake of her head and wave of her palm from behind Gaby makes my decision for me. As stealthily as I can, I step through the greenery that borders the driveway and hide behind a thick Live Oak tree.

Leaning against the rough bark, I make an effort to calm my breathing and steady my trembling hands. From behind the massive trunk I peer toward the hotel. The two men escort Esperanza, Gaby and Manuel to the back of the van. They pull open the rear doors and the three hotel workers climb in. One of the men follows them, closing the doors behind him. The other man gets into the driver's seat and starts the engine.

Floyd shouts something I can't make out as the woman hands him a piece of paper. He looks at it while she climbs into the passenger seat and slams the door. Floyd strides over to the van, but it heads down the driveway before he reaches it. With his hands on his hips, he stares after it for barely a second, then turns and shouts at Augusta and Steffi. They hurry inside.

I shrink behind the tree as the vehicle passes me. Its windows are tinted so I can't see inside, but I know they can see out and I don't want them to notice me. If my fake Social Security Number was flagged, then they'd be looking out for me too. The last thing I want is to be picked up by Immigration.

When the taillights disappear around the corner, I exhale in relief and glance back at the hotel. I should just leave. Go to the camper, pack my stuff, say good-bye to Bill and get the heck away from here. Hyde Island is full of pitfalls. I step away from the tree and cross over to the driveway, making my way toward the street. The image of Augusta twisting her apron makes me stop, and I change direction toward the service entrance of the hotel.

I try to be very quiet as I go inside. I lift my time card to punch it when I hear Augusta's raised voice behind the locker room door.

"You gotta stop hirin' them illegals. We can't keep losin' cleaners. I have to keep trainin' new people and jugglin' schedules. It's not good."

"Augusta," Floyd says in his smarmy voice. "I do my best to keep this hotel afloat. Send me some Americans and I'll be happy to hire them."

"You don't pay enough for them to wanna work here, Mr. Hill."

"Speaking of which, where's that Anne Cooper girl? Isn't she supposed to be working today?"

I press my back against the wall and bite my lip.

"I don't know where she be. She ain't never late. Iz a good thing she warn't here, though, since she's not legal neither, is she, Mr. Hill?"

Floyd clears his throat. "Call Pearl to fill in for Gaby until we find replacements for those other two. And if that Cooper girl doesn't show up, you'll have to take her shift today."

Before I can move, the door is thrust open and Floyd steps out. "Well, speak of the devil."

"Good morning. What's going on?"

"You're late," Floyd barks at me. "I'll have to dock your pay." Behind him Augusta is looking at me wide-eyed and shakes her head. She puts her finger to her lips.

I ignore her signal. "You know what, Floyd? I don't care because I'm quitting. This is my two weeks' notice."

He bursts out laughing. "Two weeks' notice. That's a

joke." He leans in close. The rank odor of his sweat assaults my nostrils. "You're fired for tardiness. And for disrespecting me. As of right now. Don't bother picking up your last pay check either." He heads for the elevator. "And it's Mr. Hill to you," he calls over his shoulder.

I holler after him. "Floyd, you really—" Augusta pulls my arm and yanks me into the locker room. She slams the door and turns the lock.

"Don't make him any madder 'n he already is, or he'll take it out on me."

"I'm sorry, Augusta. I didn't think." I sit down on the bench. "What happened out there? I saw Esperanza and Gaby taken away."

"And Manuel, too. Don't know why, he's been here so long." She plunked herself beside me. "Somebody called Immigration, of that I'm shore. Somebody always calls Immigration. Iz like they have it in for Floyd or somethin'."

"I can certainly understand that." I exhale loudly. "I thought Manuel had papers. That's what Esperanza told me."

She shrugs. "Guess they were fake."

"And now you're left with only Pearl to carry the workload. I feel bad for both of you."

"Ah, sugar, don' worry 'bout us." She stretches out her legs. Her scuffed utility shoes look more gray than white. "We been survivin' Immigration sweeps and ole Floyd long before you came around." Her hand touches my knee. "Were you really gonna quit before Floyd got your goat?"

I nod, realizing it's the truth.

"Why? I thought you were figurin' on stayin' a while longer."

"Things have happened that made me decide this is not the right place for me. And I need to go and take care of things back in Toronto if I'm ever going to move forward." As I speak the words, I'm overwhelmed with a sense of relief and certainty that I'm finally ready to go back.

"You mean take care of things with your husband?"

"My husband. My daughter. My sister. Besides, working illegally is too risky, isn't it?" I grab her hand and squeeze. "But Augusta, you've been such a good friend to me here. I am very grateful and I'm really going to miss you."

She wraps her arms around me. "I'm gonna miss you too. You were like a cool ocean breeze blowin' into this place."

I gently pull away and wipe my eyes. "Thanks. Could you say goodbye to Pearl for me? And all the others?"

"Of course, hon. They'll understand. A goodbye through me is more'n they usually get after an Immigration sweep."

I open my locker to clean it out, but there is nothing inside that I want to take with me. My uniform and apron hang from the hook, my shoes sit on the shelf, and that's all that's there. I slam it shut, experiencing a sense of jubilation that I've actually made the decision to go. I hug Augusta again. "Good-bye, friend."

"Good luck, Anne." She presses my shoulder. "Now I'd best phone Pearl and get her to come in to work."

For the last time, I leave the locker room and walk past the cleaning carts on my way to the door. Unexpectedly I am hit with nostalgia for this place and run my hand along one of the cart handles. Esperanza's photo keychain with the picture of her two sons swings at my touch. I unhook it and stick it in my pocket.

"Pearl, iz Augusta," I hear through the locker room door. "I need you to come in to work, girl. Immigration came here this mornin'."

I wish I could hear Pearl's side of the conversation, to experience her vibrant energy just one more time. In the locker room, Augusta exclaims, "Bitten by that ole gator? I knew it would happen one day." I feel a chill, knowing they're discussing Rhett's accident. I rush outside.

The sun is hot and bright, and I turn my face to the sky. My stomach grumbles, and I remember that I didn't eat breakfast and had only one sip of Agnes' coffee. I muse over what to do when I remember Coffee HydeOut. They make a great breakfast sandwich, and there's a shortcut past the staff quarters so I head in that direction.

When I walk by Esperanza's unit, a high-pitched bark comes from behind it. Pepe!

I wonder who knows he's here. I suspect only Gaby, Manuel, and Dewain, who are the only other staff members who live here. I remember Esperanza telling me that having Pepe in these quarters was against the rules, so probably no one else from the hotel is aware of him. What will happen to him?

Pepe keeps barking, as if he knows someone is out here. I sigh and walk around to the back. The dog is on a leash that is tethered to a stake. When he sees me, he runs as close to me as the leash allows and strains to be closer, getting pulled up on his hind legs. He wags his tail and quivers. I pet him. He sits.

"Poor Pepe, your mommy's gone. I'm pretty sure she can't come and get you." He gazes at me with his bulging brown eyes. "What's going to happen to you?" He gives one quick bark as if in reply. He *is* kind of cute, despite being a Chihuahua.

Something needs to be done about him. Esperanza loved this little dog, and finding a place for him is the least I can do for her. I can't leave him here, tied up. I doubt Dewain, who likes his liquor just a bit too much, will want to bother with a dog. Running loose on the island isn't a good idea, either. All sorts of bad things could happen to him. Alligators, for example. I can't keep him myself, especially because I'm going back to Canada and I have no idea what's going to happen there.

Then the solution hits me. I unfasten the leash from the stake. "Come on, Pepe, let's see if we can find you a new home."

Chapter Eighteen

It is amazing how walking a dog can boost one's spirits. I leave the hotel property plodding along under a cloud of despondency, but Pepe prancing at the end of the leash with his tail in the air reminds me that life goes on no matter what happens. Despite setbacks and crises, we can always look forward and find something to be positive about. How ironic that it takes a little Chihuahua to remind me of this.

Of course I am outraged and saddened by what just happened at the hotel. I'm distressed by yesterday's alligator attack on Rhett, and remorseful about my betrayal and loss of Agnes's friendship. Yet despite all of that, my mood lifts, and I find myself stepping lightly and counting my blessings. The sun is shining. I escaped the immigration roundup. I no longer have to work at that crummy job. And I will soon be going home.

As apprehensive as I am about returning to Toronto and having to face Dan to deal with the dissolution of my marriage, I also anticipate this new beginning. I will be back in a city that I know and love, a place I belong. Where I'll reconnect with Carly and hopefully Tilly too.

It seems as if Pepe knows where we are going, and he turns the corner onto Bill's street ahead of me. Bill is in his yard walking behind an old-fashioned push mower. Briefly I wonder what he does to earn an income, considering it's a Wednesday morning and he is home mowing the lawn. The question flies out of my thoughts as Pepe yaps, causing Bill to look up.

"Hi." I stop beside him.

He wipes his brow. "Hey. Another day off?"

I shake my head. "Not a day off. I quit." Bill opens his mouth to say something just as Pepe jumps at his leg.

"Pepe, sit." I pull on his leash. The dog stares up at me with his black marble eyes and wags his tail. I scan my brain for the Spanish word. "Sientese, I think." Pepe stands where he is, his tail swishing back and forth. I push on his butt and tell him to sit again. This time he does. "Stay." I hold my palm out to him and turn to Bill. "It's a long story. Do you have a minute?"

"Sure. Come on in." He glances at Pepe. "Where did you get the dog?"

"All part of my long story. Is it okay if he comes inside with us?" I ask this to gauge how receptive Bill is to a dog. I point to the Live Oak beside us. "Or I could tie him to that tree." That's an absurd idea, because the trunk is so thick the length of the leash wouldn't wrap around it.

"Naw, bring him in. Pepe, is it?" I nod. He leans down and pets his head. "I might just have a piece of salami in the fridge for you." Pepe yaps a happy little bark and follows us across the yard.

The aroma of coffee wafts out to us when Bill opens the door. "Hope you don't mind coffee that's been sitting a bit. I've got some bran muffins to go with it."

"Sounds great." My stomach reminds me that I still haven't eaten anything.

There is little room for conversation as I wolf down my muffin. Bill has Pepe on his lap and feeds him bits of salami while glancing my way. I take another muffin and nibble on it more demurely, between sips of very strong and bitter coffee.

An amused expression crosses Bill's face. "So, now that your appetite is satisfied, tell me your long story."

"Sorry for eating like a pig. I skipped breakfast this morning. I was in a rush and late for work."

"But you said you quit."

"Yes, but not until after I was late." Skipping over my visit to Agnes, I launch into the story of arriving at the hotel and witnessing the Immigration officials leading Esperanza, Gaby, and Manuel away. I describe how the events of the morning made me finally decide it was time to leave the island and get my life in order. "So when I bumped into Floyd and he was being his usual charming self, I just quit. And then he fired me. Without pay." I relate the details of my encounter with Floyd. "He owes me almost a week's pay, but what can I do? I was working illegally, so I don't really have any recourse. And I do not want to face that man again." I take a sip of coffee, grimacing at its bitterness. "Anyway here I am, unemployed and making plans to return to Toronto." For a reason that I can't explain, tears sting my eyes, and I quickly wipe them away.

"Wow." Bill methodically folds a muffin wrapper, as if he's giving me time to collect myself. "That seems sudden. But it's good that you're moving forward."

"Yes, it is. I'm finally maturing." I roll my eyes and gather crumbs into a small pile on the table in front of me. "I guess, as your tenant, this is my notice that I'll be vacating the trailer as soon as I have the details worked out."

"No prob. It was empty before you came and it'll be empty again when you leave. I should just sell the darn thing." He pushes his glasses up at the nose bridge. "I'll miss seeing you around, though. And I'll give you your deposit back, which should help recover your loss of pay." He strokes the top of Pepe's head. Pepe is curled asleep on Bill's lap. "But where does the dog come in?"

I smile at the picture they make. "He was Esperanza's dog, and now Esperanza is gone and there's no one to take care of him. Esperanza really loved this little guy. So I took him with me. I couldn't just leave him tied up behind her place, could I?"

He shakes his head. "No, you couldn't." He scratches between Pepe's ears. "I wonder how he'll cope in Toronto?"

"Actually…" I draw out the word. "I'm not planning to take him with me. I can't predict what my situation will be." I clear my throat. "That's really why I'm here. I know you have an inclination to protect needy creatures. Like you do the baby turtles. And me." I smile wryly. "Pepe is in need of a home and a friend. I think you'd be the perfect new owner for him."

He blows an airy whistle. "I don't know. Getting a dog has never really been on my radar."

"But look at how the two of you have bonded already." I gesture at the sleeping Pepe on his lap. "And think of how nice it would be for you to have the company. I'm sure he's hardly any trouble. Esperanza kept him in her staff apartment and left him alone whenever she was at work. And he seemed happy enough." I press my palms together like a supplicant. "Please? I don't know what else to do with him."

His gaze holds mine for a few seconds. "Anne, you have certainly been a trip. Tell you what. You can leave him with me. I may or may not decide to keep him, but at the very least I'll figure out some kind of permanent arrangement for him. Good enough?"

"Yes." I sigh in relief. "Thank you. That definitely makes me feel better. I feel like I owe it to Esperanza, you know? She's had such a tough life." I lean back in the chair. "What do you suppose will happen to her?"

"She'll get deported and not allowed back in the country. Probably won't return unless she somehow finds a way to get back in." He puts Pepe on the floor. "I guess we just never know what life is going to throw at us." At the counter he tops up his coffee, which must be sludge by now. Pepe's nails click on the floor as he follows him. With his back to me, Bill continues. "Like that friend of yours. Rhett Sandusky? Did you hear what happened to him on the golf course?"

Heat rises to my face. "Yes, I did. I was there when the alligator attacked him, passing by as I was coming home from Brenville yesterday."

He turns, and his blue eyes bore into mine. "Ah. You were the woman who whomped the gator between the eyes, freeing Sandusky's leg?" There is no surprise in his voice, as if he already knew it was I.

I nod slowly.

"How'd you get to the pond so fast if you were riding by on your bike?"

I lower my head and stare at my coffee mug. My mouth is dry, but I can't bring myself to drink. "I know I said I wasn't going to hang out with him anymore, but he was teaching me a golf lesson." I lift my chin and look right at him, challenging him to disapprove.

He raises his eyebrows. "I didn't know you had any interest in golf." He returns to his chair.

I shrug. Then I decide to come clean and tell him about Rhett flagging me down as I rode past the golf course, and his reminder that he'd offered me a golf lesson. Omitting the flirtatious aspects of our lesson, I recount how Rhett taught me to tee off using a driver, and then how I hit his expensive golf ball into the pond. "At first he was going to leave it there, but his so-called friends egged him on, and Rhett went to the water to prove how macho he was." I shudder. "The alligator got to him so fast." I describe the macabre tug-of-war between the gator and Rhett's friends and my clubbing the creature with a driver. "It was horrible."

"I can imagine. Good thing you were there."

I glance at his face to see if he meant that, but his expression gives nothing away. "You're wrong. If I hadn't hit the ball into the water, Rhett never would have gone to the pond. I should never have gone back to the golf course for that stupid golf lesson. He'd still have a perfect leg if it wasn't for me."

Bill reaches over and touches my hand. "Anne, you can't blame yourself. He chose to go into the pond. Stuff happens."

"But I just keep making mistake after mistake. And they impact other people."

"There are no mistakes if you learn from them. Then they're life lessons."

I smile ruefully. "I used to say that to Carly."

"It's a good adage that allows you to forgive yourself.

Heed its message."

I shake my head. "Me leaving Hyde Island is a good thing for everybody."

"Not necessarily everybody." He squeezes my hand and then lets go and busies himself with clearing the table.

****

It seems that traveling somewhere starts with laundry and cleaning. As I go about these chores, I ponder what exactly I'm going to do when I arrive in Toronto. Where should I stay? I have no desire to move back to my house. Dan probably won't let me anyway. Uncertain about Tilly's frame of mind, I hesitate to contemplate staying at her place. Carly lives in a small bachelor apartment that would be very cramped for two of us. I decide to find a hotel for the interim and figure things out when I'm there. Checking that off my mental list I consider the big issue I've been avoiding.

Should I tell them I'm coming?

I drop the mop and sit down hard on the bench. What can I possibly say to Tilly after I betrayed her the way I did? How do I face Dan after our awful final encounter? My resolve to go back has not wavered, but am I really ready? I have broken up my family. How do I fix things so that we can still be a family, just with me not married to Dan?

I open the lid of the bench, take out the cell phone and turn it on. It's still half charged from my call to Carly. Recalling my conversation with her strengthens me and I punch in Tilly's number. My heart practically beats out of my chest while it rings. And then Tilly's voice mail answers and my throat constricts.

"This is Tilly Cooper. Leave a message and I'll get back to you as soon as I can."

Just as the beep begins, I hang up. My hands shake and I find myself thinking, *Phew, that was close.* Right then I decide not to tell anyone I'm coming. I'll go back, find a place to stay, and contact them all when I feel ready.

But as I clutch the phone, Carly's name surfaces in my brain. Surely I can let her know. Would she keep my secret?

Could she contain her excitement and not let Tilly or her father know?

Should I put that burden on her?

I will wait. Wait until I know exactly when I'll be arriving. Wait until I know exactly how I want to handle my re-entry.

At nine the next morning I'm at Bill's door. He kindly agreed to let me use his Internet access so I can book my flights. It's the only place I can think of with Internet where I wouldn't run into anyone I'd rather not see, like Agnes or Floyd. I'm a little anxious about getting onto my computer because I will also access my email inbox, and the email that Carly said Dan sent looms over me like a final exam.

Pepe barks inside the house when I knock, and Bill opens the door almost immediately. Pepe jumps up and down when he sees me. I bend over to give him a quick pat.

"Right on time," Bill says. "I'm about ready to leave for the Turtle Center. We're mounting a new exhibit today. So you'll have complete privacy to do what you need to. I figured you might want it, considering you'll be working on putting your life back together."

"That's very considerate, Bill. Thanks. I shouldn't be more than a couple of hours, if that." Shifting the bag on my shoulder, I follow him inside. Pepe scampers around my legs as I walk to the kitchen, and I have to be careful not to trip or step on him. "How did Pepe do last night?"

"He's made himself right at home. Even slept in my bed. He's not the most beautiful sleeping companion I've had." He scoops Pepe up in his arms and the dog licks Bill's chin. "But it was kinda nice to have company there for a change. You don't mind him being here this morning, do you? I can't really bring him to the Center."

I shake my head. "Not at all."

The coffee maker spurts and he gestures toward the counter. "I just put on a fresh pot so you won't have to drink the mud you had yesterday. And here's the network code to log on the Internet." He hands me a piece of paper.

"Thanks." I pull my laptop out of the bag and plug it in. "Well, here goes."

"Good luck," Bill says as he heads for the door.

I open the computer and turn it on. While it boots up, I pour myself a coffee. Pepe follows me and when I sit down, he curls up at my feet. Calm settles over me in the quiet house. Sunlight filters in through the window over the sink and I can imagine how lovely it might have been for Bill and Vera to sit here every morning having breakfast.

Carly and Tilly's faces springs up on the screen, and the coffee turns sour in my stomach. "I am so sorry," I whisper to their smiles and open the Internet access window. I check Bill's piece of paper and type Caretta-caretta in the space for the password, remembering from Bill's book that it's the Latin name for the sea turtles that hatch on the island.

Bill is so passionate about those creatures. Not only did he develop a career around turtles, he wrote a book about them and still works to protect them. He's even decorated his house with them. I find such a focus admirable.

A little voice buzzes in my brain. Is that so different from Dan's passion for sports, which I consider a major factor in the deterioration of our marriage? Like Bill, Dan developed a career around his passion. But, I remind myself, Dan fills pretty much all of his free time with it, leaving little room in his heart for anything else, including me. Bill, by contrast, seems to open himself to other experiences and people. He is a kind and caring man who has always shown a genuine interest in whatever I have to say. He even took in Pepe when he didn't want to.

I imagine him across the table from me, picturing his sky blue eyes peering at me from behind his John Lennon glasses, crinkling at the corners when he smiles, his long gray hair tied in a ponytail. Even though he's not here in the flesh, I am extremely attracted to him as I sit at his kitchen. I wonder what would have happened if I'd met him twenty-seven years ago. I wonder if anything could develop if I stayed here on Hyde Island.

Pepe barks and paws my foot, as if he senses that my thoughts are derailing and venturing into areas they shouldn't. I pick up the dog and snuggle him to my face. "Thank you, Pepe. That kind of thinking will get me nowhere. There will be nothing between Bill and me. I'm going back to Toronto, no buts about it." I place him on my lap and he curls himself into a ball then seems to fall asleep immediately. I turn back to the computer.

My inbox is not as full as I expected, containing some spam and a few emails from my friend Jane. Of course there are several from Carly, Dan, and Tilly, their dates indicating they were sent soon after Tilly returned without me. I don't even open those, having no doubt they repeat the sentiments in the letters Dan brought with him. Then there's a gap of almost two weeks with nothing from them, but starting last weekend there is one from Dan, a couple from Carly and one from Tilly.

I just want you to know I'm missing you, Tilly writes. That's it, nothing more, as if she's accepted what I've done and won't challenge me on it again. Her short message encourages me, and I feel better about having to face her when I go home.

Carly's first email pleads with me to contact her, and coaxes me to work things out with Dan and put the family back together. The message changes in her most recent one, however. She wrote it after our birthday phone call, and her relief at reconnecting is evident in her positive words. I find myself smiling when I read, *I'll accept whatever you decide to do about your marriage, Mom. I am still a daughter to you and to Daddy, but that doesn't mean that you two have to stay together. I get it.*

I lean back in the chair. Carly's and Tilly's latest emails vindicate me. I know mending my relationships with them will have its challenges, but I can already envision a scene where the three of us are together, wine glasses in our hands, laughing over something innocuous.

I've saved Dan's email until last. Pepe's hot little body

is cloying on my lap, and I carefully move him to another chair so as not to wake him. He whimpers and then is quiet. I refill my coffee mug and stare out the window at the Live Oaks in Bill's yard for a few minutes before returning to the computer.

I open another Internet tab and search for flights to Toronto. It appears that I'll have to fly from Brenville to Atlanta, and then Atlanta to Toronto. If I want to go within the next few days, it'll cost me over three hundred dollars more than if I wait a few weeks. I should save the money and go with the cheaper flights, but since I've made the decision to leave, I almost can't bear the thought of staying on Hyde Island. The place now seems to be full of hazards and bad Karma. Not to mention that I'd have to hide out from Agnes, avoid the hotel, worry about Esperanza and want to visit Rhett in the Brenville hospital. Which would be a very bad move on my part.

I take out my credit card and book the flight for the next day.

Pepe barks, startling me. He stretches out his paws and jumps off the chair. Toes clacking on the floor, he goes to the dish of water that Bill has put out for him and laps it for a bit.

"Okay, Pepe, I've been avoiding it long enough." He looks up at the mention of his name and nestles down under the table. I open my email inbox again. "Time for me to read what Dan has to say."

Lydia, the letter begins. *I was very angry the last time we spoke, and justifiably so in my opinion. But in the weeks since you left me, my anger has morphed into sadness and resignation. Tilly has explained to me why you were so unhappy that you felt your only solution was to abandon all of us (although your reasons seem unwarranted and trivial compared to the repercussions of your desertion). You hurt me. You hurt all of us. I don't know if I can ever get over that.*

When I first came home from Hyde Island, I was so mad and hurt that I wanted to freeze our assets so you wouldn't have access to them, but the bank wouldn't allow it because the accounts are in both our names equally. Besides, Tilly said that would be a vindictive and non-productive thing to do. Later I decided she was right. I don't want to hurt you that way (even though you've hurt me).

But I'm not writing this email to tell you off. I'm writing it because I want us to try to salvage what we had. In that hotel room, I spoke in the heat of the moment when I told you that if you didn't come back with me then I didn't want you to come back at all. After having time to think about it, I realize I didn't mean it. I need you. I miss you. Please, can't we start over? I promise I'll try to change to become whatever you want me to be.

I gaze away from the computer screen and stare out the window to the yard where the trees and shrubs glow in the morning sun. A flash of red in the leaves of one of the Live Oaks catches my eye as a Cardinal hops a few inches along a branch. "Pur-dee, pur-dee," comes faintly through the window and then the bird flies out of sight.

None of this is fair to Dan, I know, but I cannot do what he asks, no matter what he promises. Starting over with him is out of the question. Even though it's been barely a month since I left him, being Dan's wife and living in the same house with him and trying to pretend I love him are tasks that now seem impossible to me.

"I'm sorry, Dan," I say aloud, causing Pepe to give a little yap, and I turn back to the computer screen.

We need to move forward, his email continues. *I can't stay in this state of suspension any longer. I hope you will move forward with me, that we can do it together. I would even be willing to go to a marriage counsellor (and am sorry I refused in the past). I want us to be together again, man and wife, and I'm hoping that in your time away you've come to realize you want that too.*

If not…

Well, I hope there's no 'if not,' but IF, then decisions need to be made. You need to finalize your plans, because what you do impacts me and your silence is unacceptable. We need to organize our finances and make arrangements about the store. If you really don't ever want to come home, then I need closure on all of this. (I have to tell you that I'm crying as I type this, and you know that I NEVER cry. Please, Lydia, come back to me.)

Anyway, if you don't want to get back together, you need to come back to Toronto so we can meet with a mediator. Jack gave me the name of the one that he and Tammy used when they got divorced. Or would you rather deal through lawyers? A mediator would be a lot cheaper and hopefully help us settle things amicably, although God knows you don't deserve amicability after the way you've treated me. But lawyer or mediator, we have to get things settled.

I've promised Carly not to take any action until I hear from you, and I hope that what I hear from you is that you want us to be together. But Lydia, I can only wait so long. I'll give you to the end of September, and if you don't contact me by then, I think I'll call a lawyer.

Please stop this stupid silence and contact me so I know where I stand.

The email just ends. He doesn't sign off with his name. The mixed messages in his words make me nauseous, as if I'm on a ship in a storm. He understands my decision, but he doesn't. He says he's not angry anymore, but he still sounds angry. He wants to get back together, but he's ready to call a lawyer. He wants to settle things amicably, but he doesn't think I warrant it.

Dan is justified. I know he is. The way I up and deserted him and our life is no way to end a marriage. My fingers poise to send him a response, but I don't know quite what to say. Should I tell him I'm returning to Toronto but not to him? Agree to a mediator? Should I thank him for wanting to settle things in a positive way?

My hands drop to my lap. If I start writing, I know I'll argue for myself even while I'm apologizing. I'd feel the need to explain that if I hadn't given in to the lure of Hyde Island and stayed behind, I would have remained stuck in that quagmire of unhappiness that was my life. If I'd gone back to Dan, I would still be looking at him and wondering if there were more to love, if there were more to life.

I don't know why I never had the courage to confront my situation before this. Why I lived it for twenty-seven years and just accepted it. Why I simply did what was expected of me.

I can't do that anymore. I won't. If I've achieved anything from my impulsive decision to stay on Hyde Island these past weeks, it's the awareness and strength to be true to me, Lydia Burgess. No, not Lydia Burgess. Lydia Cooper.

I close the laptop. I don't want to write a response that will put Dan on the defensive. I don't want to have to justify my actions. I just want my marriage to be over and look to the future. I'm grateful Dan is willing to accept that too. I will wait to reply to him until I see him in person. My mouth goes dry as I realize that will be very soon.

Chapter Nineteen

Perhaps it's obvious from the way I deserted my family, but I've never been very good at goodbyes. Taking leave of Bill is no different. I accept his offer to drive me to the airport, telling him to drop me off at the departure doors. It will be much easier to leave that way, not having to linger while we awkwardly find ways to say farewell.

However, he insists on carrying in my suitcase and the duffle bag containing my art stuff. In the tiny Brenville airport terminal, he waits beside me while I check in. When the luggage is gone we face each other.

"Well, I guess this is goodbye." He sticks his hand out for me to shake. "It was good knowing you. Best of luck with everything."

"Thanks, Bill, for all you've done. You've been such a great friend." Ignoring his outstretched hand, I reach up to give him a hug. I don't know if he was trying to avoid the embrace or if he misjudged the direction of my gesture, but our heads bump and my forehead knocks his glasses askew. As he reaches to straighten them, his elbow knocks my nose, and my eyes fill with tears.

Despite the pain, I laugh and he joins in. I reach out my hand to shake. "I guess this is safer."

He grasps it and the warmth of his grip sends tingles up my arm. "Good-bye, friend," he says in a quiet voice. "Hyde Island will miss you." He strides to the exit. I wipe the corner of my eye and watch him out the door, waiting for him to turn and wave one last time. He doesn't.

From the air, Hyde Island appears very green and lush with a light edge of beach on the open ocean side. As we ascend into the blue, I seek out landmarks I recognize, like the hotel and the golf course. I find Bill's street and then Agnes's, but can't spot the trailer I'd called home these past weeks. Gradually the island becomes a blotch in the ocean connected by a bridge to the mainland, and as it disappears behind the clouds I wonder if I'll ever go back there. I decide I don't want to. Its magic has fizzled.

When we arrive at the airport in Toronto, the line-ups at Customs seem endless. Although barriers organize people into queues, the hall is chaotic. A full flight from India must have arrived around the same time as ours, as well as one from somewhere in Asia. Children crying, conversations in languages I don't understand, officials in uniform directing people, colorful saris, haggard expressions. It's stimulation overload. After forty-five minutes of shuffling and stopping, shuffling and stopping, I finally stand in front of a Customs desk.

"Where are you coming from and what is your purpose here?" The Customs official is a man who seems younger than Carly, clean-shaven with short hair. He hardly looks at me as he takes my passport and customs form.

"Uh, I've just arrived from Georgia and I, um, live here." Why am I stuttering? I take a deep breath. "I'm coming home."

"How long were you away?"

"Three or four weeks?"

He looks up, a child in uniform. "What is it? Three or four?"

I think for a second. "I left Canada on August eighth to attend an art workshop in Georgia." That week seems a lifetime ago. Was it really less than a month ago? "I uh, stayed longer than I expected."

"Having too good a holiday?" He scratches numbers and letters on the customs card with his wax pencil and hands it back to me inside my passport.

"Something like that."

"Welcome home." He looks to the crowd waiting behind me. "Next?"

Lonely in the sea of people, I walk through the doors into the waiting area of the terminal and scan the crowd. I see many happy faces but recognize none of them. Trying not to be disheartened by that, I adjust my purse and the duffle bag on my shoulders and drag my suitcase in the direction of the doors that will lead me to the car rental desks.

By the time the sun starts its descent, I'm sitting in a warm bath at the Metro Home Suites. It's not the grandest of hotels, but it's clean. My room has a small kitchenette and sitting area, like a tiny apartment. Heck, this place is luxury compared to the camper I lived in these past weeks, and much more spacious. I can actually spin around in the bathroom with my arms outstretched. It's fairly cheap for a Toronto hotel too, considering it is only six subway stops from Union Station. Anyway, I plan to stay here just until I find a more permanent place of my own.

Earlier, at the airport, when I first got behind the wheel of the snappy red Hyundai Accent I rented, I had intended to drive straight to Carly's office. It was close to four-thirty, and I figured she might be able to leave work early to have dinner with me. But when I turned the key in the ignition, I somehow couldn't go there, feeling unprepared to face her right then. I was unsettled and uncertain, and grimy from my trip. So instead I checked into this hotel and then walked to the small grocery store down the street to pick up food that would keep me going for a few days. Feeling a tad nostalgic for the liquor aisle at the Piggly Wiggly, I was happy to find an LCBO on the corner and bought a bottle of Merlot too.

Immersed in coziness and comfort in the hot bubbly water in the bath, I sip the wine I brought into the tub with me and replay the past several weeks through my mind. It all seems surreal. Did I really try to adopt a new identity? I become fidgety remembering my original idea of disappearing without a trace, of living as Anne Cooper for the rest of my life. What was I thinking?

Being back in Toronto feels right. Hyde Island is certainly a unique and special place, with its beaches and palmettos and warm, humid climate. Those are what drew me to stay, but if I'm honest with myself, deep down I had a sense I didn't belong there. Here, in Toronto, I belong. Even though I'm in an anonymous hotel room. Even though my gut roils at the thought of what I've subjected my family to. Even though I have no idea what is going to happen from here on.

I finish the wine and plunge under the water completely, holding my breath until my lungs practically cry out to release the air. I burst up to the surface, splashing water over the rim. The bubbles have all dissipated and the water has cooled. My arms are covered in goose bumps. I pull the plug and climb out, wrapping myself in a large white towel. One thing about this hotel; its towels are thick, lush, and huge.

Wearing the towel like a sarong, I place a frozen dinner of Chicken Florentine in the microwave. Outside is almost dark, and through the one large window the indigo sky is a backdrop to the city's lights. I stand there, staring out at the view.

How am I going to fix my life here?

The microwave beeps and I pull the drapes closed. In the dim light of the room, I climb into the bed to eat my prefab dinner and finish the bottle of wine, escaping into episodes of house hunting and renovations on HGTV. When I finally turn the TV off and pull the covers up, I am numb enough that I expect to sleep soundly.

Which I do not. Worries about my upcoming encounters with Dan and Tilly, and even Carly, plague my rest. Different scenarios play in my imagination, and with each subsequent narrative I envision, I become more perturbed. In addition, the question of what I'm going to do now that I'm here plays like a bass line to the theme of facing my family. There is no way I can work in the store, and I don't want to be dependent on Dan. I need to find a way to be self-sufficient.

After more than an hour of unsuccessfully attempting to clear my mind of all thought, I flip on the bedside lamp and open my laptop. I am sweaty, despite being in bed naked, so I turn on the air conditioner. And then for what seems like the rest of the night, I search online for jobs and tailor my resume to suit the various applications I send out.

****

A tap on the door awakens me.

"Housekeeping." For a confused moment I think I'm climbing out of a dream, still on Hyde Island, and that Augusta is out in the hall. I roll over, willing myself awake. A clunk on the floor makes me sit up.

More taps on the door. "Scuze me. Housekeeping." The sound of a key card being inserted into the lock follows.

The clock says ten-forty. I scramble out of bed and just miss stepping on my computer, which must be what clunked. Thank goodness for carpeting.

"Just a minute." I hurry to wrap myself in the towel lying on the chair, shivering slightly in its cool dampness, and pull the door open on its chain. A slim woman, with dark hair pulled back in a bun and wearing a mustard yellow uniform, stands with her cleaning cart. Except for the color of her dress and the fact that she doesn't have a white streak in her hair, she could be Esperanza.

"I'm so sorry." I clutch the towel closed over my chest. "I know you have a schedule. Can you give me a half hour before cleaning my room?"

She nods. "Oh, no problem, miss. I'll come back later." She writes something on her clipboard and moves down the hall.

"Thank you," I say to her back. "And thank you for working so hard that we can have clean rooms."

She turns with a surprised look on her face. "Oh. You're welcome. It's my job."

"I know. But it's an important one, and I appreciate that you do it."

Her smile lights her face. "Thank you." She taps on the door next to mine, while at the same time calling, "Housekeeping."

Frustrated that so much of my morning has disappeared before I'm even dressed, I take a quick shower and then struggle with choosing my clothes. What does one wear for a reunion with a daughter she deserted? All that's in my suitcase is what I had packed for a week on Hyde Island in August, and the capris and T-shirts are hardly suitable for a crisp autumn day in Ontario. Only the jeans that I wore on the plane and my fleece cardigan are appropriate for this weather. Stupid me. Why didn't I think of that and do some shopping before coming back to Toronto?

I longingly consider all the clothes in my closet at the house and then it occurs to me that I could drive there right now. Dan won't be home because he'll be working at the store. On Fridays, he's always there from opening to closing, and since most of the neighbors work, I'm fairly certain I could be in and out without being discovered. I check the time. From here it will take a half hour to drive to the house, maybe less in the mid-morning traffic. I could gather enough clothing to keep me going for a while, and a few other odds and ends, and get to Carly's office in time for lunch.

I throw on my jeans and a T-shirt. In the bathroom, I spike my hair. It looks pretty edgy for the conservative Torontonian I used to be, but the style totally the suits new me I want to be. Even if I'm no longer Anne Cooper. What will Carly say when she sees my new look? And Tilly?

Unable to gauge what their reactions might be, I turn away from the mirror. In my purse, I unzip the pocket at the side to search for my house keys and when I find them stick them in my pocket. A few weeks ago, I believed that I'd never use them again. What a fool I was. I'm glad I kept them.

As I take the room and car keys from the table, I realize the room is a mess. Towel in the chair, last night's supper dishes on the TV stand, empty yogurt container on the counter, empty wine glass and bottle on the bedside table, underwear on the floor, bed all rumpled. I tidy up my things, clean up the kitchen and hang the towel in the bathroom. There. Now it's the kind of room I didn't mind cleaning when I was a hotel maid.

It is both unsettling and thrilling to drive along familiar streets to my house. Although I now understand I was unhappy for most of my life in this neighborhood, I do have many good memories of my time here. Passing Carly's old elementary school, I am filled with nostalgia for a time when I didn't know how to be anything other than Carly's mother and Dan's wife. I mentally shake myself. That time is over, never to return. I am not that person anymore. I know myself better now.

When I arrive at the house, I automatically drive up the driveway, but then back out immediately and park at the curb. What if a neighbor passes by? They wouldn't recognize this rental car, but might find a strange vehicle on the drive suspicious knowing nobody is home.

The street is quiet. For as long as we've lived here, Mrs. Canden next door has had bridge club on Friday mornings, so she probably isn't home. Louise across street is either working at the hospital or sleeping off the night shift. I'm pretty sure everyone else is at work too.

Still, I cautiously scan the street before getting out of the car, and then do it once more before unlocking the door and stepping inside.

I am unprepared for the emotion that overwhelms me as I close the door behind me and inhale the air in my house. My home. Despite everything else about my life, I love this place. We bought it after we'd been married a couple of years, when Dan's dad died and left us enough for the down payment. Over the years we renovated the kitchen and bathrooms, replaced the floors, built a deck, redecorated a few times. I should say I renovated and decorated. Dan was his usual uninvolved self who simply agreed to everything I suggested. The only project he became engaged in was finishing the basement for Carly when she was a teenager.

Still, this house has seen many happy times. We threw dinner parties and Carly had sleepovers. We regularly hosted Christmas dinner for Tilly and Dan's brothers and their families. It is a good house. A family house.

Not anymore. I have wrecked the family that lived here.

I touch the banister by the staircase. Leaving Dan means leaving this house. When I was on Hyde Island, I didn't give it a thought, but standing here, seeing the wall of family photos leading upstairs, the Persian runner on the shiny wood floor, the bookshelves in the living room, I am filled with an anguish that resembles a physical pain. A piece of me is in this house, and because of the path I've chosen, I must forever eradicate it from my life. Will I miss that piece?

I wander into the kitchen. It has a subtle coffee smell. The pot in the coffee maker is about a quarter full, and Dan's blue Leafs mug sits beside it. In the sink is a cereal bowl containing a bit of milk with some threads of shredded wheat and a spoon. The remains of Dan's breakfast. I take a deep breath and am about to rinse the bowl and put it in the dishwasher when I stop myself. I am not here to clean up after Dan. I don't want to leave behind any clue to indicate that I've been here.

Upstairs in the bedroom I head straight for the closet. The first thing I do is change into a pair of brown slacks and a cream sweater, socks and brown loafers. Then I grab clothes I think I'll need, throwing them on the bed as I pull them off the hangers. It occurs to me Dan will notice empty hangers, so I toss the hangers beside the clothes and even out the spacing on the rack so there are no gaps. I take a couple of pairs of shoes with heels in case I get job interviews. Extra underwear, socks, panty hose, some toiletries. With whatever I choose, I make sure its absence is unnoticeable. When I'm finished, I inspect the pile and experience a moment of panic. How am I going to get these back to the hotel? Why didn't I empty my suitcase and bring it with me?

I run down to the basement, somewhat agitated with how much time I'm spending here. What if Dan decides to come home for lunch? I make a beeline for the storage cupboard under the stairs. The first thing I see when I open the door is the black suitcase Dan used when he came to Hyde Island. My jaw clenches as I recall the panic I felt when I realized Dan had come looking for me. I cannot use that suitcase, so I dig in the back for the big gray one that Carly used when she moved to university residence. It's a bit ragged but can hold everything that I'm taking with me. I lug it to the second floor, awkwardly ascending both flights of stairs two steps at a time.

The suitcase is quite heavy when I'm finished. I wheel it to the top of the stairs and prepare to heft it down step by step, but I catch sight of my study in my peripheral vision and leave the suitcase for a moment.

The room is really just an extra bedroom that I claimed for my own, with my desk and a craft table and a cushy wingback chair. The bookcase behind the chair is filled with books, but the bottom shelf contains a number of craft projects I started and got bored with: a multicolored afghan only half-crocheted, a bin with card-making supplies, a calligraphy set, a box of pastels, a pad of origami paper. I'm not really a crafty person, but I used these activities as reasons to escape into this room. Mostly I'd sit in here and read or listen to music or surf the Internet on my computer. Anything to avoid Dan with his sports programs and booze in the living room.

This room is a haven, but it is also where I spent my loneliest hours. I simply cannot imagine slipping back into this life. To think I was that person a mere month ago.

On the top of the bookshelf are framed photographs. There is one of me holding two year-old Carly in my arms. Another of Tilly and me standing in front of the CN Tower. My book club group. Carly and I caught in a happy moment together at a friend's wedding. I reach up and take that one. I doubt Dan will notice it's gone. He probably doesn't even come into this room.

Then I recall the door was open. I always kept it closed. Maybe he stands in the doorway and stares at my things, wondering what happened to his wife. Perhaps he sits in my chair, bewildered by my actions. Did he go through the drawers of my desk, trying to find answers?

I can't bear these images and suddenly don't care if he notices the picture missing or not. I can't get out of the room fast enough. I stick the photo in the front zippered pocket of the suitcase and haul the case downstairs, drag it to the car and hoist it into the trunk.

I turn the ignition, and without glancing back at the house, drive in the direction of Carly's office.

Chapter Twenty

I've only been to Carly's office once, four years ago when she first took this job as a Junior Business Analyst. On that visit, she proudly led me on a tour. In her cubicle a photograph of her cat was pinned to the divider alongside a picture of Dan, Tilly, and me sitting in front of our Christmas tree. She introduced her co-workers and her boss, showed me the coffee room and offered me a cappuccino from the pod machine. "I've totally entered the adult world now, don't you think?" she asked, beaming as she handed me the coffee. Yes, I agreed, she had, although in my view she'd entered the adult world much earlier, taking charge of her life and decisions when she was a young teenager. Even before she was out of high school, Dan and I congratulated ourselves on having raised such an independent, self-sufficient and confident daughter.

The building is located at the edge of the city's downtown core. It seems to be constructed entirely from glass with windows that are darkly tinted, giving the structure the appearance of a gleaming black tower standing guard over the street. Inside, the lobby is black and silver and stark, with only a security desk and elevators. I smile at the man sitting behind the desk and check the directory posted nearby. Carly's company is on the twelfth floor.

While I wait for the elevator to arrive I bounce on the balls of my feet and inadvertently begin to nibble on my thumbnail, yanking down my hand when a ping announces the arrival of the lift. Its doors slide open and two men wearing suits step out, deep in conversation. They barely acknowledge me as they walk past.

Alone in the carriage ascending to the twelfth floor, I take a deep breath in an attempt to calm my nerves. It's only Carly, for heaven's sake. She'll be glad to see me.

There is no need for me to be anxious.

My reflection stares back at me from the glossy black doors, and I am very glad that I changed out of my jeans and fleece cardigan. In my slacks and sweater I almost look as if I belong here.

The elevator opens onto a hall with a set of double glass doors at either end. I push open the ones with the logo of Carly's firm etched onto the glass and as I step through, I have no idea where to go. Even if I could recall the location of Carly's cubicle, it may not be in the same place. After all, she has worked here for a few years now.

"May I help you?" The young woman sitting behind the reception desk smiles at me. Large hoop earrings glitter through her shoulder-length blond hair. Her turquoise V-neck sweater hugs her lithe frame.

I glance toward the cubicles on the off chance that I get a glimpse of Carly, and then approach the desk. "I'm here to see Carly Burgess." I use as decisive a tone as I can manage. "Could you point me in the direction of her office?"

"Is she expecting you?" Her hand reaches for the phone.

I shake my head. "No, but I'm her mother. I want to surprise her."

"Oh." Her eyes widen. "I'm sorry but I can't let you wander around the office. I'll have to call her to let her know you're here. You can wait there." She gestures toward a pair of chairs against the wall.

I stay where I am and clutch my bag to my chest as she punches a few numbers on the phone. "Carly? There's a woman here who says she's your mother. She's asking to see—" She looks at the mouthpiece, then at me and hangs up the phone. "I guess she's coming to meet you."

"Mom?"

I spin around and am suddenly engulfed in Carly's arms.

"Mom, I can't believe it. You've come back. When did you get here?"

"I flew in yesterday." A knot inside of me springs free as I hug her and instantly I'm glad I've returned. Tears prickle my eyes and I blink rapidly and then step back. "It's so good to see you, Carly." I clear my throat. "Can we talk? Do you have time for lunch?"

"You bet. Just let me get my purse. Be right back." She darts off in the direction from which she appeared.

"So you're Carly's mom." The receptionist draws my attention. "You were away for a while, huh?" Her expression tells me she knows something of my desertion.

I nod, not quite knowing how to reply. Luckily for me, Carly shows up at that moment. "By the way, I really like your hair, Mom. It suits you. Makes you look younger."

Instinctively I reach up to touch my spikes. "Thanks."

Carly clasps my elbow. "Let's go. I'll be back in a bit, Renée." She steers me out the glass doors.

In the elevator, I can't keep my eyes off my daughter. She looks happy, fresh, healthy. Her caramel-colored hair is longer than I remember, with bangs that almost reach her chestnut eyes. Dan's eyes. I touch her arm. "I was so nervous to come and see you."

"Why?" She frowns.

I shrug. "I abandoned you. Stayed out of touch without explanation. I broke up our family." Tears well up and this time I let them spill over. "I betrayed you and I wasn't sure how you'd receive me."

"Oh, Mom, I forgave you when you phoned me on my birthday." She strokes my shoulder.

I wipe my cheeks. "Thanks."

Her arms cross over her chest. "I mean, it still upsets me to think about those weeks when I didn't know what you were doing, when I couldn't get hold of you. For a while I hated you for being so selfish. You did betray us, and you hurt me. You hurt Dad and Tilly." She leans against the wall of the elevator.

I pluck at my sleeve. "I am so sorry, Carly. I know my actions were inexcusable, but it was…" I exhale. "I needed to—"

At that moment the elevator opens and facing us are three women waiting to board. They abruptly stop their laughter and step aside to let us out. I give them a half-hearted smile as I walk past. Carly and I say nothing more until we are out on the sidewalk.

I put my face up to the sun, drawing warmth from it in the chilly outdoor air, and then look straight at my daughter. "Carly, I—"

"Mom, really you don't need to keep explaining. Nor keep apologizing to me. We've been over it already, and I don't really want to go there again." Her arm goes around my shoulders and she squeezes. "Let's just put it behind us and move forward, okay?"

I nod, unable to speak.

"Now lunch. There's a new self-serve soup place that opened up just around the corner." She links her hand in my elbow. "You'll love it."

I had not expected Carly to take control of our reunion the way she has. I anticipated having to continuously apologize and justify my actions. So relieved am I by her mature acceptance of me that I practically skip to the restaurant.

It's a storefront café-like place with many tables and a long wooden counter on which there are numerous kettles of soup. The profusion of aromas makes my stomach grumble. I decide on a pumpkin-apple soup while Carly chooses tomato-spinach. We both take freshly baked multigrain rolls and pats of butter and bottles of water. Carly insists on treating, so while she pays, I take our food to the seating area and manage to snatch an empty table in the corner. It is extremely busy here, but in the warmth and hubbub, I am filled with an unexpected sense of peace.

When Carly arrives at the table, I smile at her. "This place is perfect. It has a comforting atmosphere."

"Really? It's not too noisy?" She butters her bread. "I was actually in the middle of something at work when you arrived so I really can't stay away too long. That's why I chose this place. It's quick."

"I probably should have let you know I was coming." I stir my soup. "But I made the decision all of a sudden, and then with tying things up on Hyde Island and booking flights, well, I just didn't. I'm sorry." I blow on the spoon and take a mouthful. The soup is delicious, tangy with a hint of ginger. I dip a piece of my bun into it.

"It doesn't matter. I'm really happy you're here." She unscrews the top of her water and takes a sip. "Does Aunt Tilly know you've come home? Does Daddy? Are you staying at the house?"

I shake my head. "I'm staying at a hotel for now."

She sets the bottle down so hard that a bit of water sloshes out. "Oh Mom, did Daddy—"

"No. You're the only one who knows I'm here." I reach for her hand. "Please don't call either Tilly or your dad to tell them. I want to do it in my own time. My own way. Okay?"

She nods, albeit hesitantly. "But Mom, Aunt Tilly—"

"Please? I promise I'll go see them both today. You won't have to keep my secret any longer than that."

She takes a deep breath. "Okay. And then what are you going to do? Will you move back home?" She eats her soup, not looking at me.

I frown. "No."

"Do you want to stay at my place?" Her voice is quiet, as if she doesn't really mean it but feels obliged to offer. She moves a strand of hair behind her ear. "Not permanently, because you'd have to sleep on the sofa-bed, but I suppose I could rearrange my stuff to give you a few drawers. We'd be crowded, though."

"That's a generous offer, sweetie, and I appreciate it, but I won't do that to you. We both need our space."

"What about Aunt Tilly's condo?" She scrunches up her napkin and tosses it into her empty bowl.

I scrape up my last bit of soup. "I'm not sure if Tilly would want that. I need to figure things out on my own. I'll find an apartment, I think. Maybe this weekend."

She nods and pulls her Blackberry out of her purse,

then thumbs some of the keys. "I really should get back." She inclines her head. "I'm sorry."

I know she has to return to work. I've intruded on her day. Yet I'm reluctant to let her go. "Let's have breakfast tomorrow, okay? So we can talk some more?"

She holds my gaze for a moment. "Sure. Call me in the morning. After eight." She gathers the trash from the table and stands. "And Mom? I am glad you decided to return. I just hope you can work things out with Daddy so everyone can be content. Because I love you both, you know."

I hug her then, squashing the disposable bowls between us. "I know you do. Thank you for accepting me back."

****

Because of an accident that tied up traffic for almost a half hour, I arrive at Tilly's school later than I'd planned. My strategy was to be waiting by her car before the bell rang. Tilly usually leaves school fifteen to twenty minutes after that, and I had a scene all worked out in my mind of me leaning against the hood, her walking over completely surprised, and us reuniting with hugs and apologies. However, by the time I get there, half the parking lot is empty and I don't see Tilly's car anywhere.

For a second I am flummoxed about what to do next but then decide to drive straight to her condo. It will be better anyway to spring my return on her in the comfortable atmosphere of her home, as we will both likely become emotional.

I park on the curb in front of her building, and when I step out of the car I'm suddenly filled with an anxiety that makes my stomach flip. What if she doesn't want to let me in? It's certainly possible. I haven't spoken to her or had any other contact since I sent her off alone to drive home from Hyde Island. Has she forgiven me? Will she want us to be friends again? I definitely do, despite my recent insight into the unbalanced dynamics of our relationship. I miss my big sister but I don't know how to go about mending the rift between us.

What I do know is that I have to make the first move.

In the lobby of her building, I punch in the number for her apartment. While her phone rings through the speaker, I struggle with what I'll say when she answers. Should I be happy and bubbly? Perhaps I should be reserved and apologetic. Or maybe just matter-of-fact.

The phone keeps ringing and ringing. I try the inner door, but as I expected, it's locked. Eventually I accept that she's not home. She could be anywhere really, out shopping, having a drink with friends. Who knows? I pull out my cell phone to call her but then decide against it. This should be done face-to-face. I'll have to return here later.

Back in the car I drum my fingers on the steering wheel, knowing I can no longer avoid facing Dan. It would probably be best to see him at the house, but with the store closing at nine tonight he won't be home until at least ten. That's too late. We'll both be too tired to effectively discuss anything.

So with reluctance, I drive in the direction of the store.

Chapter Twenty-One

I manage to snag a parking space on the street three doors down from Burgess Sport Shop. A sandwich sign perched on the sidewalk in front proclaims *Great Deal$ on Hockey Equipment*. Of course. It's hockey season, our most profitable period.

Shutting the door of the Hyundai, I click the lock on the key fob, but remain standing in the road. I stare at the store over the roof of my vehicle. For some reason I can't seem to move, even though cars whiz past me. It should be because I'm trying to figure out what to say to Dan, but instead my mind has transported me to twenty-seven years ago, when I went to tell Dan I was pregnant. Then, like now, I stood too long by the car on a busy street in Toronto. The way I'm feeling at the moment—with my misgivings about seeing him, my feet glued to the ground, the turbulence in my stomach, my dry mouth and cold hands—has triggered some kind of emotional time warp and I've become that scared nineteen-year-old girl again.

To say I was shocked when I discovered I was pregnant would be an understatement. I wouldn't believe it and bought a half-dozen do-it-yourself pregnancy tests because I kept hoping one of them would come up negative. It seemed impossible I was having the child of a man I barely knew and with whom I'd had sex only three times. I had filed away my vacation fling as something best forgotten and was fairly certain Dan had too. We'd had no contact since Cancun, and all I knew about him was his name, that he lived in Toronto, worked in an office, and he was ten years older than me. I could barely remember what he looked like.

My first thought, when I finally accepted the inevitable, was to have an abortion. No one need know, especially my father and Tilly. I could carry on with my life, finish school and figure out a career. In a few years I'd get married to someone I loved and have a baby when I was ready. Not while I was a freshman at university with uncertain plans for my future. And certainly not with a man I didn't even know.

I couldn't act on that decision right away, still somewhat in denial despite the evidence. Twice I chickened out at the entrance of the family planning clinic, unable to even cross the threshold. I wanted someone to come with me but didn't know whom to ask. My two best friends, Lori and Janet, were backpacking in China. At university, my friendships were still tentative, not intimate enough to share something this personal and traumatic. I barely knew my roommate, as she'd found friends she liked better than me. Besides, everyone was studying for midterms and we were all stressed to the max.

Then Tilly came to visit me in residence, bearing a box of Timbits and bursting with news that she'd been offered a permanent teaching job in the middle of the semester, after years of substituting in Toronto schools. We sat on my bed and munched on the donuts, Tilly happier than I'd ever seen her. I tried to share her enthusiasm but was apparently not doing too good a job of it. She was in the midst of extemporizing on how wonderful independence was, and how lucky we were to both live in the same city hundreds of miles away from our dad, when she abruptly stopped, as if someone had pushed a pause button.

"What's wrong?" She touched my knee. "You don't seem excited." She could read me so easily back then.

I was quick to reassure her. "Nothing. I'm thrilled for you. It's fantastic news. And I love that you'll be staying in Toronto." I shrugged. "I guess I'm stressed because of exams, you know?"

"Oh, you'll do fine. You always do." She smiled in her indulgent, maternal way, and then concern flashed across her eyes. "But I don't think that's it. You're distracted, almost distraught. Is everything okay?"

I stared at her and weighed the pros and cons of telling her about my condition. Was it worth subjecting myself to her disapproval and judgment, considering I wasn't going through with the pregnancy anyway?

Still, I really needed someone and there she was, sitting on my bed. My big sister. She was practically my mother. Emotions got the better of me and my vision blurred as tears swelled in my eyes. I screwed them shut, clamping down on my loss of control.

"Remember when I went to Cancun over New Years?" I blinked a few times and looked at her.

She frowned. "Yes."

"Well, I never told you, but I hooked up with a guy there and one thing led to another." I cleared my throat. "I'm pregnant." The word squeaked out. I'd never actually said it aloud.

"What? Are you sure?" She stood and paced. "Who's the guy? Are you still seeing him? Do you love him? Why haven't I heard about him before? Why didn't you—"

"Stop," I said quietly, but loud enough for her to hear. "I'll tell you, but you need to stop grilling me and just listen. Sit."

Mouth still open, she perched on the bed. "Go on."

My story tumbled out. How Lori and Janet and I were drinking in the hotel bar and we each met a guy. How the six of us drank margarita after margarita until we closed the place, and then we went with our new partners to their respective hotel rooms and didn't see each other again until the next morning, headachy and hung-over. While my friends and I were lying on the beach recovering, Dan found me, and we spent the next two days almost exclusively together.

"Lori and Janet didn't care," I told Tilly. "They were busy with their own romances. It really was a glorious few days." I exhaled, recalling that happy, sun-filled time.

"Are you in love with this guy? Have you seen him since?" Tilly gaped at me as if she didn't recognize me.

I shook my head. "No." I swiped at my eyes. "We

talked about whether to stay in touch, but decided that while we'd had a fun couple of days, that's all it was. A couple of days. I didn't care. I'd had a good vacation" I attempted a feeble smile. "It wouldn't have worked out anyway. He's way older than me; in fact, you're closer to his age than me. And I've just started university." The tears streamed. "But now...."

"Oh, honey." Her arms wrapped around my shoulders, and I sobbed into her chest. For a brief time I just wanted to melt into Tilly's kind-hearted softness. Somehow she must have sensed that and didn't speak, but I knew her brain was churning, trying to solve my problem.

I pulled away and ran my hands over my face. "Anyway, I can't have this baby. I'm going to get rid of it. Will you come with me to the clinic?"

She glared at me. "Lydia. You can't abort it. That's a life inside of you. You're what, two months and a bit?"

I nodded.

"That baby already has a face, and tiny hands and feet. A brain."

"Don't do that. It's barely the size of a walnut." I moved to the opposite end of the bed. "I'm not ready to have a baby. You should know that."

"But I'll help you. I'd love to help raise a baby." She clasped her hands together. "Have you contacted this Dan to tell him? He needs to know. It's his child too."

My jaw dropped in astonishment. "That didn't even cross my mind. Did you not hear what I said? He probably hasn't even thought of me since Cancun. He won't want anything to do with this." I folded my arms across my chest. "I'm having an abortion whether you help me or not."

However, Tilly had a way of persuading me back then. Over the next few days, she wore me down, induced me to look up Dan's address, even took me in her car to stake out his apartment building. There we sat like a couple of cops on surveillance duty, with Tim Horton's coffee cups in hand, parked on the curb across from the building. I'd brought along my calculus text to study but never opened it. Nauseous and edgy, I sat beside Tilly and stared out the window, half hoping we'd never see Dan.

Then he suddenly emerged from the subway entrance. I gasped as he crossed the street just in front of our car. "That's him," I croaked. My heart beat like the wings of a hummingbird. The attraction I'd felt for him in Cancun rushed through me in waves. Then I remembered why we were there and I felt sick.

Tilly clenched the steering wheel. "He's pretty handsome. You have good taste, at least."

"I can't do this, Tilly. He won't want to see me. What if he has a girlfriend? What if she's waiting for him in his apartment? I can't just spring this on him. Let's go." I reached across her to turn the ignition.

She gripped my fingers. "No. You have to do this. If someone is with him, he can step out in the hall to talk. But you need to tell him." She glared at me. In the faint light of dusk, her eyes blazed. "This is the father of your child."

I pulled my hand back and swallowed. I couldn't fight her. Wishing I'd never told her and just gone into the darn clinic like I'd wanted to, I yanked open the car door and stepped out, slamming it hard. Then I stood, staring at the apartment building, feet frozen to the ground and unable to move. I shoved my cold, ungloved hands into my coat pockets.

Tilly opened the window and called out, "Well, go on. Do you want me to come with you?"

That was enough to propel me forward, toward the creation of the family that I have now ripped asunder.

I should mention that Dan reacted beyond expectations. He was thrilled to reconnect, claiming he'd been unable to stop thinking about me. And while not exactly delighted about the pregnancy, he was happy enough. We married quickly and quietly, dropping the bomb on my father after the fact.

Now, staring at the store and thinking how all those years ago Tilly railroaded me into this whole mess, I realize that on some level it was something I wanted too. Tilly couldn't have talked me into any of it if I'd been determined to do otherwise, could she?

I sigh. This time, standing in the road unable to move, I don't have Tilly in the car cajoling me to go talk to Dan. This time, I need to spur myself into action.

I push away from the vehicle and cross the street. In the store window, someone who isn't Dan takes a hockey stick from a mannequin's hands and rearranges the display. It's a woman, slightly overweight. Dan must have hired somebody new. There is something familiar about this person, though, something in the way she moves.

Oh my God. It's Tilly. I stop where I am and shrink against the wall.

"Excuse me, ma'am. Can I go in?" A young man wearing a gray suit stands in front of me. He points at the door of the card store next to Burgess Sport Shop, which I happen to be blocking.

"Oh, I'm sorry. Of course." I move out of the way and step around the sandwich board to the front of Burgess Sport Shop. Tilly is no longer in the window, so I peer in. My gut clenches when I spot Dan crouched in front of a boy who sits in a chair. Dan helps him remove the skate from his foot and places it in a box beside him. The boy gesticulates happily as he pulls on his shoe. A man standing nearby, presumably the boy's father, smiles and nods. Dan touches the boy's shoulder as he picks up the box with the skates and leads the pair in the direction of the register.

My throat tightens as I watch. I've observed this scenario many times. Dan has a way with customers that makes them happy to part with their money. The kids especially love him, eager for his approval in their choice of equipment. In many ways, Dan is a special guy.

I close my eyes. I will not think about that. My choice has been made, because as my husband, Dan is not so special. For many years I've been unhappy in this marriage, and I need to end it. I cannot let the good memories change my mind.

My resolve strengthened, I again glance through the window.

All I can see are the backs of Dan and his customers. A teenage girl holding a hockey stick obscures the person behind the counter. The girl hoists her purse on her shoulder and spins around, almost bumping into Dan as he approaches. Dan does a mock bow, extending his arm to let her pass, and then hands the box to the cashier. That's when I see Tilly behind the register. It seems she has stepped into my place at the store.

A realization washes over me like a cascading fountain. This is what should have been, Tilly and Dan. Not Lydia and Dan, but Tilly and Dan. I married the man Tilly should have married, had the baby Tilly should have had, lived the life Tilly should have lived.

Our roles should have been reversed. I ought to have been the career woman and Tilly the wife and mother. She is a nurturer, unlike me, and Dan thrives on being nurtured. All Tilly ever wanted was to have a family of her own. She often says that ship passed her by, and although she throws that comment out lightly, I sense the sadness behind it. Has Tilly, all these years, watched Dan and me from the sidelines wishing for my life?

No wonder she wouldn't understand what I needed from her on the beach on Hyde Island, wouldn't support my actions in any way. She couldn't. I was discarding everything she wished for herself.

The door opens, interrupting my thoughts, and the girl with the hockey stick walks out. She sends a puzzled glance my way and crosses the street. I must look odd, gawking in the window of the store. I take a deep breath, square my shoulders and head inside.

The bell jangles and both Dan and Tilly glance in the direction of the door. Their eyes widen and they gape at me. Tilly opens her mouth but makes no sound. Dan immediately steps away from the counter, and in doing so nudges against the boy, who almost falls over. The boy cries out and that pulls Dan from his shock. He leans over to help him.

"Lydia," Tilly shrieks and runs over, enveloping me in her arms. "You've come home. I can't believe it. I've missed you. Welcome back." She gives me an extra squeeze before letting go and then glances at her hand. "Oh my God, I still have this credit card." She waves a MasterCard in the air. "Wait, okay?" She rushes back to the counter and speaks to the man. "Sorry. That's my long-lost sister."

I cringe at this characterization. Long-lost indeed. It's not even been a month. The man inclines his head in my direction and smiles. "That's okay."

I stay where I am, watching Dan and Tilly steal glances in my direction as they tend to their customers. I am uncertain about my next step and feel like I've lost my bearings in this familiar yet unknown place.

Eventually Dan, who has calmed the boy by giving him a pack of hockey cards, approaches. "Lydia," he says coolly, as if I were a distasteful stranger recently introduced. "Before I get too excited about your return, can I ask what your intentions are?"

He is wary. I understand that. I'm not sure what I expected or hoped his reaction to be. I guess this stoical calmness is okay. I shift my weight from foot to foot. "We really shouldn't get into it here."

"Decidedly not." He places his hands on his hips. "How could you just show up like this? Why didn't you let us know you were coming?" His brow furrows. "Oh wait, spontaneity is your new modus-opera—"

"Thank you, Mr. Burgess." The boy edges past us. We both jerk our heads in his direction. His arms are wrapped tightly around the box containing his new skates and in one hand he clutches the pack of cards.

"Yes, thanks." The boy's father holds open the door and looks in my direction. "Welcome back, long-lost sister."

That catches me off guard. "Oh. Thank you. Enjoy your skates."

At the same time I say this, Dan cheerfully replies,

"You're welcome. Come again."

Our words blend to create a brief jumble of sound and simultaneously we turn to face each other again. Once more I'm adrift, uncertain of how to be.

Tilly bursts in on this moment, whatever this moment is. "When did you arrive? Does Carly know you're here?" Without waiting for an answer she grabs my arm. "I'm so glad you've come back to us."

"If she's come back to us." Dan locks the door and flips the closed sign. "That's a big if. And we—at least I—am not so sure I want her back."

My cheeks get hot. Unable to respond I cross my arms.

Tilly clears her throat. "I'd better leave you guys alone. Shall I go home, Dan? Will you need me at the store any more tonight?"

Dan scratches his head. "No, I think we're done for the day. But could you stick a sign in the window saying something like 'Closed for an emergency. Will open at nine tomorrow?' And maybe change the phone message too?"

"Sure, I can do that." She glances at me, a zillion questions in her eyes. I know she's dying to talk to me but is respectful of the fact that I've come here to see Dan, not her. "I'll close up here. Why don't you two go over to The Bistro where you can sit quietly and discuss things?"

Good old Tilly. She knows exactly how to handle an extremely awkward situation. I touch her wrist. "That's a good idea. Somewhere neutral. Are you okay with that, Dan?"

He looks at me with an expression that says he didn't expect me to be so civil. He glances from me to Tilly then back to me. "Sure. Thanks, Till."

As we walk out to the street, Tilly calls, "Come to my place when you're done. We have a lot to talk about."

For just a second, in my disoriented state, I'm not sure if she means Dan or me.

Chapter Twenty-Two

It is inconceivable to me that I left Hyde Island little more than three months ago. So much has changed in those hundred-plus days that it seems as if I've traveled into another time dimension to arrive where I am now. I can't believe I'm the same person who boarded the plane to Toronto, afraid of facing my daughter and husband and my sister. Even more, that I am the same person who became Anne Cooper, hotel maid, flirt, and friend-betrayer.

If I reflect too much on the stupid things I did as Anne Cooper, I burn with embarrassment. How could I think it was reasonable to abandon my life and family, adopt a different persona, take a job illegally, and try to hook up with my landlord and with my friend's boyfriend? What possessed me?

However I did need something to shake up my existence and help me break out of the box that was my unhappy life. As long as I was stuck going to work at the store every morning and spending every evening with a detached, dispassionate husband, nothing would change. My *Hyde Island Hiatus*, as Carly has dubbed that brief period in my life, precipitated a transformation for which I will be forever grateful, no matter how foolish and thoughtless it was. My life now makes sense, something it hasn't done for many years. Nevertheless, my self-centered journey hurt the people I love, and for that I am sorry.

Even so, I sense that their hurt is healing. If anything, Carly and I are closer than we ever were. And my relationship with Tilly is as close as it was, only better, more on an equal footing.

I've inflicted scars, though. My first weeks back were challenging for all of us as we attempted to figure out where we stood with each other. It took a while for us to get the hang of our new dynamics. On some level, I'm still working on regaining their trust, although they might deny it.

My first meeting with Dan was especially painful, as I knew it would be. I realize now it was unfair of me to unexpectedly drop in on him at the store and shake up his equilibrium, like a bomb dropping from the sky.

After Tilly closed the shop door behind us, we walked to the bar without speaking, without looking at each other. We moved like automatons, swinging our arms. Once I accidentally brushed against Dan's hand, and he jerked it away and widened the space between us. Nonetheless, when we arrived at The Bistro, he held the door open for me.

"Thanks," I said as I went past him, trying to make eye contact. He directed his gaze inside without acknowledging my appreciation. The place was devoid of customers, probably because it was early. Dan made a beeline for a table in a semi-lit corner away from main area. We sat down and abruptly he stood and approached the bar, returning a few minutes later with two beers.

"Thanks," I said again when I picked up the heavy glass mug he placed in front of me. He grunted in response and then took a sip. I did the same. The beer tasted good, and I drank some more, gauging the tension between us. So far our conversation had consisted of two words, both the same, both expressing gratitude, and both said by me. I set my glass on the table. "Do you want to talk first, or should I?"

"You." He pushed up his glasses. "Tell me why you're here. You've called the shots since you started all this. No reason to change that now." He glared at me.

"We don't have to be antagonistic," I said, louder than I intended. "I'd like it if we could discuss things like two mature adults."

He pursed his lips and raised his eyebrows.

So it would all be up to me. I calmed my voice and began. "Dan, I don't want to hurt you any more than I've done, but I also don't want to give you any false hopes."

He snorted. "Please. Don't sink to platitudes and insult my intelligence. Just tell me why you've come back. Did you finally read my email?" He rested his elbows on the table and held his glass aloft in both hands in front of his face, as if to shield himself from what I might say. "I'm guessing, since you don't want to give me false hopes, that you aren't here to beg for forgiveness or to ask me to take you back. Are you here to finally settle things? To own up to your responsibilities?" Over the rim of his glass, he stared at me. His eyes pierced into mine like knives.

I exhaled and cleared my throat. His words, and even more his body language, made me feel small and guilty. I resented him doing this to me even as I understood he had the right. I straightened my back and squared my shoulders. "You're right. I'm not here to ask you to take me back. Our marriage is over and we both need to face that." I reached across the table and touched his elbow. He didn't move his arm away. "Dan, I am sorry, and in a way I guess I am asking for your forgiveness because I know the way I handled things was selfish and insensitive."

"Hmph." He put his glass down and grasped my hand, which lay on the table next to his arm. His fingers were cold and damp from the condensation on his beer glass. "I've been doing a lot of thinking, Lydia. Your desertion made me examine our life together. Tilly's insights also enlightened me somewhat." The corners of his mouth edged upward. "That sister of yours. She really cares about you, you know. What you did to her is just as unforgivable." The smile disappeared.

"I hope she'll be able to forgive me," I said in a small voice.

"Probably she already has, with her big heart." He squeezed my hand so tight my fingers were crushed together and pain radiated through my finger joints. I pulled out of his grip.

"That hurt." I scowled at him.

"Sorry." He didn't sound sorry at all. "I guess I don't

have Tilly's capacity for forgiveness. I still feel a lot of anger toward you." He leaned back and crossed his arms over his chest. "As I was saying, I've been examining our life together, and honestly? I still don't understand why you reached a point where you couldn't bear to come home. I'm not a monster. I would have listened. Why didn't you talk to me about your—" With his fingers, he made air quotes at the side of his head. "—unhappiness? We could have tried to work things out. Why did you just abandon me? Abandon us?" He emphasized the word abandon, throwing it out at me like an accusation. I opened my mouth to reply, but he held up his hand. "Never mind. I don't want to hear it."

I stared at him. "What do you want to hear, then?"

"I want you to tell me that we can go back to the way we were. I'm ready to forgive you. And I want my wife back, dammit."

I shook my head. "I can't be your wife anymore, Dan. I'm not the same person I was."

"Oh, don't I know it." He exhaled loudly. "Are you not even interested in going to counselling? To try to fix things?"

"Now you're willing to go to counselling? After all the times I asked..." I twined my fingers together. "No. I'm beyond that. I'm sorry, but it truly is over for me. I need my life to move forward without you. I want a divorce." His face paled, and I suddenly felt tenderness toward him. "I'm so sorry."

"Right." He cleared his throat and took his glasses off, pinching the bridge of his nose. "So we're getting legal about it. Then we'll need to come to a financial agreement. We obviously can't work together anymore. I hope we can divvy things up so we won't have to sell store. I can't lose that too." He stared pointedly at me, the pleading in his brown eyes belying the anger of his frown. "A friend gave me the name of a mediator. Would you at least be willing to see her with me?"

I nodded.

"For Carly's sake." He blinked. "We need to be civil with one another. Can you stand me enough to manage that?"

"Of course." I shifted my mug from hand to hand. The beer sloshed around and a small layer of foam surged to the top, not unlike the mix of emotions that rose to become a lump in my throat. I swallowed.

"Well, good." He stood, scraping back his chair. "It might take *me* a while, though, because at the moment I can't stand to be with you." He was out the door before I could respond.

I stared at our half-filled glasses of beer, the sight of which blurred as my eyes swelled with tears, and reflected on the many ways in which I'd hurt my family. How long I sat there I don't know, but eventually the thought of Tilly waiting for me propelled me out of my chair. I trudged out of the bar in a fog, experiencing a numbness I couldn't explain. At the store, the *Closed* sign hung in the door and all was dark. Tilly would be at her condo expecting my visit, but I couldn't go to her right away. I needed to shake off the barb Dan had hurled at me with his parting words.

So I drove to my hotel room and had a shower. I donned the same slacks and sweater I'd had on earlier and as I fussed with the spikes in my hair, I could almost hear Tilly tutting at my new look, but I didn't listen. If I decided to change my hairstyle, it would be because I chose to, not because Tilly thought I should.

Shaking my head at the inner dialogue I seemed to be having with my sister, I grabbed my purse and headed out.

Tilly answered my ring immediately with a squeal, and was standing in the hall when the elevator doors opened. I had barely stepped out when she flung her arms around me. "I knew you'd come back. I knew it was just a matter of time." She linked her hand into the crook of my elbow and led us down the hall. "The month you were away was like a bad dream. I decided you must have had some kind of breakdown or something, but I was sure you'd figure things out and return to us."

It was just like Tilly to claim to know more about me than I knew myself. "I'm glad you managed to keep your faith in me." I slipped out of her grasp as we entered her apartment.

She headed straight for the kitchen. "Want some tea or coffee? No wait, how about wine? I have a Shiraz that I picked up on the weekend."

"Wine is good. Thanks." I stood in the living room and glanced around. The blue couch with the woven cushions, the Persian rug, her paintings on the wall, it all felt so familiar, a comforting familiar, an atmosphere I wanted to sink into. Not unlike what I first experienced when I stepped into my house the day before, but in the house that feeling didn't last. The undercurrents of my unhappiness and memories from my empty marriage pierced at my psyche, the pain intensifying the longer I stayed. Here in Tilly's home I felt a serenity wrought from a sibling relationship that, although competitive and intense, was governed by love and friendship. My tension eased, and I was struck with an overwhelming sense of regret that I had so easily tossed Tilly aside a month ago.

"Does it feel strange to be back?" Tilly spoke from behind me.

I wiped my eyes and turned. She held in each hand a glass containing garnet-red wine. Her eyes glistened with tears. I took both glasses and placed them on the table, then wrapped my arms around her and hugged tightly.

"I'm so sorry I hurt you." I looked straight into her eyes. Using my thumb, I gently wiped a tear that had spilled onto her cheek. "My life needed to change, but I should never have handled things the way I did. I was selfish, and I completely ignored how important you are to me."

She sniffled, then picked up one of the wineglasses and sat on the couch. "It's true. What you did was selfish, and you shouldn't have run away from us like that." She swirled the deep red liquid in her glass. "But I need to apologize too."

"Why? Because you tried to stop me from staying on

Hyde Island?" I lowered myself beside her and had a sip of my Shiraz.

"No." She shook her head. "Because I never listened to you. Or I listened, but didn't hear you. All the times you tried to tell me about how unhappy you were in your marriage and I just shut you down. I was always defending Dan and blabbing on about commitment and family, telling you that you had to do the right thing." She touched my knee. "When you stopped talking about it, I figured you'd worked it out and were happy, that it had just been a phase you went through that had ended. But now…" She exhaled loudly. "I've been doing a lot of thinking while you were gone, and I realize that when you stopped confiding to me about it, it wasn't because your marriage was better. It was because I never listened to what you were really saying. All I did was be the bossy sister who knew better about your marriage than you did." She stared at her hands. "While you were on Hyde Island, and Dan and I were trying to figure out what was going on with you, I began to understand more about what it must have been like to be married to him."

I couldn't help but smile, albeit ruefully. "So you got to know the real Dan."

"Yes." Her eyes widened. "Oh, but I still think he's a good guy, and I love him like a brother, but he's not exactly what I'd want for a husband. I now get why you were so discontented."

I leaned back into the couch. "Tilly, you have no idea what it means to me to hear you say that you finally understand. It validates my decision to end my marriage."

"But you still hurt all of us by deserting us the way you did."

"I know. I'm not defending that. I just mean—"

"Never mind. I know what you mean. I have to tell you something else." She brought her legs up, tucking her feet under her bottom and drank her wine. I waited, wondering what she was going to say. She glanced at me. "While I was thinking about everything, I also started to feel guilty." Her face flushed.

"Guilty? For what?"

She cleared her throat. "Remember all those years ago, when you told me you were pregnant and asked me to go to the clinic with you for an abortion? I started it all then." She fiddled with her earring.

My stomach did a flip-flop, returning to those memories I had so recently revisited. I was afraid to speak, needing to hear Tilly's recollection unbiased by anything I'd say.

"Go on," I ventured when she continued to gaze silently into the dark red of her wine.

She placed her glass on the table and swiped her hand across her eyes. "You were so young, just starting life. You didn't even know what you wanted to do yet. And I was almost twenty-eight, never even had a boyfriend. I figured I'd never get married, never have kids." She bit her lip. "I was right, too."

"Aw, Tilly."

"Never mind. I'm content with my life." She shrugged. "But Lydia, I think I wanted you to have the baby because *I* wanted a baby. Not because it was the right thing to do. I was the one who persuaded you to contact Dan. I was the one who pushed you into having the baby before you were ready, into quitting school, into getting married. I should have listened to what you needed, supported what you wanted to do, and taken you to the clinic."

"Okay, now stop right there." I put my hand on her shoulder. "Yes, you did convince me to change my mind and you pressured me to get in touch with Dan, but honestly? I wouldn't have agreed if on some level I didn't want it all to happen too. It's not completely your fault, okay? I made the choice in the end. It was my life, after all."

"You really believe that?"

"Yes. And it wasn't all bad. I've had a good life, and I—we—got Carly out of it. I can't imagine life without her."

"Me neither. She's pretty awesome." A smile played on

Tilly's lips. "Does Carly know you've returned? Have you seen her?"

"She's the first person I went to. I was so glad to see her." I thought back to my reunion with my daughter, how accepting she'd been. "Everything is good between us. She was very understanding."

"She's been amazing through all of this. She handled your desertion to Hyde Island better than me or Dan"

I nodded. "I think that's because she recognized that I haven't been happy. Kids don't want to see their parents split up, but she knew things weren't right between Dan and me for many years. She's been independent so long. That allowed her to view us more objectively, don't you think?" I recalled the conversation Carly and I had had all those months ago after I bumped into her outside the clinic. Even then I was struck by her maturity.

"Definitely. You know, she even enlightened me as to what you needed for your life to be happier, and that included ending your marriage. Pretty rare for a daughter, I think."

After that, our conversation veered to my experiences on Hyde Island. Tilly had many questions. I told her how I became Anne Cooper, and shared stories about the hotel and my trailer, and Agnes and her boyfriend. I did not offer any details about my involvement with Rhett, of course. There was no need to unsettle the mood by describing foolish choices I'd made that hurt other people.

We chatted until well after midnight, opening a second bottle of wine. I ended up staying the night, having consumed too much alcohol to drive back to the hotel. During my first weeks back, we had more nights like that, and we talked—really talked—more than we'd ever done. She and I have a new understanding of the dynamics our relationship, how the early loss of our mother contributed to establishing the roles we'd adopted. We're closer than we've ever been, less competitive and more accepting of one another.

Things with Dan have gotten better. We are civil with

one another. Our sessions with the mediator, Gillian, really helped and not just for the division of our finances. She guided us to move past our resentments and anger so we've been able to understand one another's points of view and pain. I don't believe Dan will ever forgive me, and probably I don't deserve it, but he's been able to accept our new status as a divorced couple. At least, an almost divorced couple. We filed the motion a few weeks after I returned, and it'll be final in another month.

When I signed the papers to submit to the court, I was unexpectedly struck with extreme sadness. My hand shook as I held the pen. For weeks afterward I grieved the loss of my marriage. Living through those dark days, I also found it difficult to accept it had taken me so long to understand I had the power to change my life. Acting on that power should have validated and exhilarated me, but the finality of truly ending my marriage distressed me in a way I could not comprehend. Especially considering the way I'd set things in motion when I made the decision to stay on Hyde Island.

Yet never once did I doubt myself or contemplate changing my mind.

After Dan and I reached an agreement on how to proceed, my new life evolved quickly. I now live in a charming one-bedroom apartment on the top floor of an old Victorian house near the lake. If I stand on my toes to look out of the bathroom window, I can just see a sparkle from the water. Down the street there's a subway station, and Carly's place is a short subway ride going west, Tilly's going north.

I see Tilly quite often, and Carly and I get together every other week. That is more than I ever hoped from my adult daughter. Sometimes on a Saturday, we shop together at St. Lawrence market, other times we'll have dinner on a Sunday in the company of her new boyfriend, Mark. I don't know if he was the one who got her pregnant—we don't talk about that—but he is a good man, and one that I would be proud to call son-in-law if their relationship develops in that direction. I often wonder, though, if Carly wants to marry. Certainly her parents' marriage was not the best model to incite a desire for going down that path.

I'm still part owner of the store, but as a silent partner now, basically an investor. So Dan can keep his dream, and I don't have to work in it anymore. The house is up for sale too, although Dan is living in it until it's sold. In many ways, I found it harder emotionally to let go of the house than I did of Dan. How twisted is that? The market being what it is, several months may pass before I see my share of it in the bank.

That's okay, though, because I found a job. Ironically, considering where I worked on Hyde Island, I work in a small boutique hotel that is walking distance from my apartment, on the shore of Lake Ontario. I'm not cleaning but am the office manager and keep the books. Certain aspects of the job, especially the place, often bring Hyde Island to mind. One of the cleaners even bears a striking resemblance to Augusta, and she and I have become good friends.

I'm in the process of discovering more about myself and my awareness continues to evolve. I had thought it was Hyde Island that gave me space to breathe, that I needed to be *there* to become happy. But I've learned the open-air feeling of freedom and validation comes from inside myself, not from a place. Overall I have to say I am now content and at peace, living independently, doing what I want.

I am sometimes struck by comparisons between my reinvention on Hyde Island and what I'm doing to redefine myself here. There I tried to become a completely different person by stumbling blindly from one situation to another; here I strive to simply improve myself through honesty and acceptance. I wish I'd known that to become happier, this was all I needed to do.

At the moment I'm getting ready to go to Tilly's house. We'll be bringing in the New Year together. We'll order in pizza and watch chick flicks before counting down to midnight. She had invited Carly and Dan as well, but Carly is going to a party with friends and Dan declined, giving no reason. I guess he knew I'd be there and decided he'd rather not start the New Year in the presence of his past wife. I'm more than okay with that. Tilly and I will have fun with just the two of us.

I have to say Tilly has been the guiding force and our family's solid foundation as we evolved the new normal. Her take-charge approach and mothering attitude has provided all of us with someone we can lean on and to whom we can unburden.

Even Christmas, which should have been an awkward and emotional time for all of us, was saved by Tilly. She had the three of us over to her place for the day, and because of her unvoiced expectations, we truly were a family celebrating the season together. Although Dan and I barely spoke to one another as individuals, we collectively shared stories and laughed, opened gifts, enjoyed food and wine, and went home with warmth in our hearts. All due to Tilly. Thank goodness for Tilly.

I haven't been completely open with her. I never told her about my dalliance with Rhett, or how that resulted in my losing Agnes as a friend, or how I threw myself at Bill. I'll probably never share that with her. Those incidents are part of the embarrassing history of Anne Cooper, and she is dead and buried.

I often think about my friends from Hyde Island, though. Esperanza's keychain with the photo of her two boys hangs on my bulletin board, and I look at it whenever I feel down. It reminds me of Esperanza's strength and positive attitude even after facing the worst tragedy possible. She gives me something to aspire to. I worry about her and hope she has settled all right back in Mexico or perhaps found a way to get back into the United States.

I also hope that Floyd hired new cleaners to replace Esperanza, Gaby, and me, so that Augusta and Pearl don't have to work all kinds of double shifts. I try to imagine the staff dinners as they are now. Sometimes I actually miss the camaraderie of those mealtimes. Memories of Mason and Steffi and Nathan bring a smile to my face. And thoughts of Pearl and her sister Ruby always make me laugh out loud.

I no longer have nightmares about alligators but often wonder if Rhett has recovered from the gator attack and if he's regained the use of his leg. Are he and Agnes still friends? Still lovers? Whenever I recall my ill-advised flirtation with Rhett, I grow warm with mortification, even after all this time.

The person from Hyde Island who is most often in my thoughts, however, is Bill. I've read his turtle book many times and have given it a special spot on my bookshelf. I continue to feel grateful and honored to have been the recipient of his unconditional friendship, offered when he barely knew me and continued even after he discovered the worst about me. At times I think about calling him, to try to rekindle the relationship that might have been. Wisely, I talk myself out of doing so whenever the idea springs to mind.

****

This New Year's Eve has a special significance to me. During the past four months, I've gone through a major change in my identity, shaken up my life, and embarked on a journey toward happiness. Closing the door on this year is like waving good-bye to the old Lydia.

I'm just about ready to leave for Tilly's. I grab the bottle of Veuve Clicquot that's been chilling in the fridge and place it beside my purse. When I put on my coat, I check my reflection in the mirror and finger-comb my hair before putting on my knitted tam. It's still short, but in a softer cut and no longer spikey. The new style suits the new Lydia: office manager, divorced and independent woman, mother and sister. I pull on my boots and head out in the cold to welcome in the New Year.

THE END

Acknowledgments:

Lydia's story was inspired first by a place. A few years ago I visited Jekyll Island, GA for the first time, and like Lydia, I was awed by walking under the giant Live Oak trees, through the dunes by the beach, and along the tidal marshlands. Hyde Island is fictional, but the settings I created for it are based on beautiful Jekyll Island. Thank you, Sara and Tom Rupnik, for inviting me to visit your home on Jekyll time and again.

I wrote this book through several relocations, and in each location I was lucky enough to find other writers willing to read and offer critiques of various sections. I'd like to thank the input and support of Sara Rupnik, Barb Pedrotty, Lenette Howard, Jim Cotter, and Sally Honenberger in Richmond; Patricia Westerhof, Susan Cockerton, and Sarah Parks in Toronto; Deborah Serravalle, Dawn Boshcoff, Danielle Leonard, and Brian Henry in Oakville; Pat Leon-Jones, Tobie Brealey, and Debbie Rigaud in Bermuda.

I'd also like to thank my sister, Judy Garden, for joining me in those early writing sessions when we would each pen stories about wives who wanted more out of life. Lydia was born out of those writing exercises.

I wish to express my gratitude to my publisher, Kim Jacobs, for believing in me, and to Amie Denman for making the editing process so painless.

Most importantly, I thank my husband Richard, who supports and encourages me in my every endeavor, and Eric, Lindsay, Stuart, and Jake, who are my best cheerleaders.

Book Club Discussion Questions:

1. What was it about Hyde Island that propelled Lydia to stay and forsake all of her obligations in Toronto?

2. Do you think Tilly did the right thing by returning to Toronto and leaving Lydia on Hyde Island? Should she have handled the situation differently? Was Tilly instrumental in causing Lydia to be unhappy in her marriage?

3. Why did Lydia take on the persona of Anne Cooper? Was she deluding herself by believing she could stay hidden on Hyde Island?

4. Why do you think it took this drastic action on Lydia's part before she understood her life needed to change?

5. Was Lydia being fair to Dan in her assessment of her marriage? Was Dan a bad husband?

6. Why was Bill Alpaca so supportive of Lydia? Do you think he was attracted to her?

7. What was the purpose of Esperanza's story in Lydia's journey of self-discovery?

8. Why did Lydia fall under Rhett Sandusky's spell, even when she knew what kind of man he was?

9. Did Lydia's homecoming turn out as you expected? What do you think about Carly's reaction? Dan's? Tilly's?

10. Do you ever wish you could have some breathing space in your life? Escape your life and obligations? How do you deal with those feelings when you have them?

ABOUT SYLVIA MAY

Sylvia May writes women's fiction with characters who approach life with pluck, determination, and sometimes foolhardiness. Her first novel, *The Unraveling of Abby Settel*, received an Honorable Mention in the 2011 Reader Views Literary Awards.

Sylvia is also a musician, artist, and photographer. She believes tapping into our creativity fulfils us in a way nothing else can. Dutch by birth, she is a Canadian who currently resides in Bermuda, where some of her favorite activities include scuba diving and riding her scooter. She lives with her most staunch supporter, her husband, and has three grown children and one precious grandchild.

For more information about Sylvia, please visit:

www.sylviamay.com

If you enjoyed Sylvia May's *Breathing Space,*
please consider telling others and writing a review.

You might also enjoy these authors
published by Turquoise Morning Press:

Grace Greene, author of *Beach Winds*
Margaret Ethridge, author of *Contentment*
Karen Stivali, author of *Meant to Be*

Turquoise Morning Press
Romantically Yours!
www.turquoisemorningpress.com

Made in the USA
Charleston, SC
06 December 2014